THE DEAD MAN
VOLUME 2

The Dead Man
Volume 2

THE DEAD WOMAN
by David McAfee

THE BLOOD MESA
by James Reasoner

KILL THEM ALL
by Harry Shannon

47N⬤RTH

Cover Design by Jeroen ten Berge

Published by 47North
P.O. Box 400818
Las Vegas, NV 89140

ISBN13: 9781612182759
ISBN10: 1612182755

TABLE OF CONTENTS

THE DEAD MAN: THE DEAD WOMAN   1

THE DEAD MAN: THE BLOOD MESA   107

THE DEAD MAN: KILL THEM ALL   197

THE DEAD MAN:
THE DEAD WOMAN

By David McAfee

CHAPTER ONE

A bump in the road jolted Matt awake just in time to read the sign welcoming him to Crawford. He checked the road atlas in his duffel. The dim light in the cabin of the Gray Line bus made it difficult to read, and the fact that the driver seemed determined to ride over every pothole in the fucking road didn't help. After flipping through a few pages, he came to Tennessee. Then, just as he'd done back in Nevada when he bought his ticket, he ran his finger along Interstate 30 until he found the tiny speck that represented the town.

Crawford, Tennessee, population 5,421. At the time, it was as far as he could get on the money in his pocket. From here he'd have to walk, at least until he could find a few days' work to put more cash in his hand. Then he'd buy another ticket and go...somewhere. He didn't really know where yet. Mr. Dark didn't exactly leave a forwarding address.

The drive from Nevada had been long, but he was able to get some sleep, even if the seats in the bus weren't very comfortable. At least it was cheaper than a motel, which he couldn't afford anyway. He'd have to find something, though. A town the size of Crawford probably didn't have a Y.

The bus pulled into town just as the sun peeked over the eastern horizon, slowing down in what passed for Crawford's downtown district. A few buildings here and there rose to three or four stories, and an aging brick post office stood next to a silver, fifties-style diner on the left side of the street. On the right, the courthouse sat in the middle of a large, manicured green lawn. The white concrete building was the most modern thing he'd seen in the town so far, and sported an entire floor of tiny barred windows. Like a lot of small towns, Crawford must keep its jail right inside the courthouse.

Convenient.

The bus pulled up to the courthouse and stopped. The hiss of brakes accompanied the metallic squeal of the vehicle's door as the driver opened it to let Matt out.

"Here?" Matt asked.

The driver—a chunky, balding man who looked eighty but was probably much younger—smiled, showing Matt a handful of discolored teeth amid his brown, swollen gums. "Ain't no terminal in Crawford, son," the man said. "Too small. Courthouse is the best I can do." With that, the driver grabbed a clear plastic bottle, brought it to his lips, and spat out a thick brown wad.

Matt stepped off the bus, his duffel bag in hand, and waited for the driver to follow him. The driver rose from his chair amid a volley of creaks, cracks, and grunts and stepped off the bus behind Matt.

Matt followed him to the middle of the bus, where the driver produced a set of keys and unlocked the bottom compartment.

"It should be in the back," the driver said.

Matt poked his head inside. There, nestled against the back of the compartment, was his ax. It lay snug between two pieces of soft red luggage, probably the property of the dirty blonde in the back row. The driver had said he'd make sure it was safe. Matt pulled a five dollar bill from his pocket and handed it over.

"Thanks," he said.

"You're welcome," the driver replied.

Matt pulled the ax from the hold, smiling at the reassuring weight of it in his hands, and waited for the question. *Why you carryin' that thing around, anyway?* He'd been asked the same by dozens of people from Oregon to Nevada, and by the look on the driver's face, he wanted to ask, too. All Matt could ever think to say was that the ax had belonged to his grandfather, and it was sentimental. But the driver didn't ask. Instead, the old man closed the compartment door, then turned around and walked back to the front of the bus, shaking his head and muttering to himself. His chorus of bodily creaks and pops went with him.

As the bus pulled away, Matt put the ax into his duffel bag and looked around. The sleepy foothills town was just starting to wake up. A few cars ran up and down the road, their headlights still ablaze in the early morning light. The small diner he'd seen from the bus was closed, but down the street he saw the bright yellow *M* of a McDonald's. The rumble in his belly reminded him he hadn't eaten much of anything the last couple of days. Bus terminal food consists mainly of whatever can be found in the vending machines.

He checked his wallet and found twelve dollars. That would be enough for breakfast. Hopefully the restaurant would have a newspaper and he could check the want ads. He didn't need much. A few days chopping wood on a farm would pay more than enough to get him to his next stop, wherever that turned out to be.

Matt started walking down the street. Several signs hung out on the sidewalk proclaiming local businesses; a tax specialist here, a law office there, even a tanning salon advertising its location with a picturesque scene showing a bright yellow sun shining down on a bronze woman who had clearly had some work done. A row of young weeping willows lined the road, their wispy branches swaying in the light breeze. A sign on the corner told him he was on Main Street. He could've guessed as much, given the courthouse. Quaint.

Just as he reached the parking lot of the McDonald's he caught the sound of a siren in the distance, which soon turned into several. Long and low, with a slow warble. Police sirens. Matt stopped and waited, listening to the sounds as they drew closer. Soon they were joined by the more rapid, high-pitched scream of an ambulance. In the distance, Matt saw the telltale red and blue glow over the tops of some buildings.

Then a police car burst into view, turning on Main Street and whizzing past the McDonald's. Two other identical cars followed immediately behind. All three cars were white Ford Crown Victorias with the words "Crawford Police" stenciled on the side in big blue letters. Behind them, the ambulance brought up the rear, a big white and orange Ford that read "Blake County Emergency" on the side. It whizzed by the restaurant and, like the police cars, disappeared down the street, the siren fading in the distance.

Matt turned his back on the emergency vehicles and walked into the McDonald's. Above the counter, brightly lit menu options glowed. The images of the food made his stomach growl, and he stepped up to the counter. A slender young woman who looked barely old enough to buy beer stood behind the register. She wore her long brown hair tied in the back—probably due to restaurant policy— and wore a tag on her shirt that read, "Hi. My name is Annie."

Annie paid him no attention. Her face was locked in the direction of the departing emergency vehicles. After a few moments, she shook her head.

"Looks like they found another one," Annie whispered.

"Another what?" Matt replied, but Annie ignored him. Matt turned back toward the cars. Only the red and blue glow was still visible. He could barely see it above the build-ings on Main Street. Then, after a few seconds, even that disappeared.

Once the lights were gone, the girl seemed to come back to life. She turned toward Matt, smiled, and cleared her throat. "Can I help you, sir?"

Matt looked up at the menu again. "The biscuits and gravy, please. And a medium coffee."

"Yes, sir. That'll be $4.38."

Matt handed her five one-dollar bills and waited for his change.

"Will there be anything else?" Annie asked.

"Yes," Matt said. "What did you mean when you said they must have found another one? Another what?"

For the first time, Annie actually looked at Matt. Her eyes took in Matt's clothes, his dusty jeans and wrinkled shirt, then settled on the long duffel bag on the floor by Matt's feet. The girl's gaze lingered on the bag for a few seconds. Then she shrugged and looked up.

"You're new around here, aren't you?" Annie asked.

Matt nodded, thinking it was obvious. "Got here a few minutes ago. Just passing through."

"You picked a bad place to stop, sir," she said, handing over the coffee. "Check the newspapers. Crawford's got a serial killer running around. The Blake County Killer, they call him. Been operating in this county for a couple of years now. Those cops—" Annie inclined her head in the direction the police had gone "—are probably on their way to check out another body."

Something beeped behind the counter, and she turned around to grab Matt's biscuits and gravy. She set them down on a small brown tray and handed it across the counter. "Welcome to Crawford, sir."

CHAPTER TWO

The old single story building was made of dusty red bricks. The windows had a cloudy look, as though they hadn't been washed in a long time. Matt looked at the hanging sign above the peeling green door. "Abbey's Antiques" was written across it in curvy purple letters. Beneath the name of the shop was the address: 3411 Maple Street. Matt checked it against the one from the newspaper ad.

Yup, he thought. *This is the right place.*

A small brass bell mounted above the doorframe jingled as he stepped into the shop. The smell of dust and age waited inside like a low-hanging mist, and pulled him into the store before he realized it. Behind him, the bell tinkled a second time as the door swung closed.

"I'll be right with you," a woman's voice said from the rear of the store.

"No hurry," Matt called out, as he looked around the store.

Cluttered didn't begin to describe the layout of Abbey's. Thousands of items lined the shelves, aisles, and floor. Some even hung from hooks on the ceiling. Dust-covered pots, saws, picture frames, tea sets, figurines, and a host of assorted bric-a-brac sat in every available space, leaving just enough room for him to walk through.

Light reflected off hundreds of colored-glass pitchers, glasses, and decanters. A crystal serving tray with a wolf's head etched into the surface sat on a stand on the counter, complete with a set of wolf's-head utensils. Antique signs advertising everything from Coke to Hoover vacuum cleaners covered the walls like posters of Justin Bieber in a tween girl's bedroom. And everywhere he looked, every item was covered with a layer of dust.

He looked at the ad again. *Wanted: Someone to help clear out excess inventory for storage. Short term. Pay negotiable. Apply at Abbey's Antiques, 3411 Maple St. Crawford.*

"Excess inventory," Matt whispered. "No shit."

A few seconds later an attractive woman rounded the corner of an aisle and stepped into view. She looked to be in her late twenties, probably five and a half feet, with a slender, athletic build. She wore her blue and pink striped blouse—lightly covered in dust—tucked into a pair of Levis so tight they looked painted on. Her strawberry blonde hair was tied back with a spotted blue bandana, and a pair of dirty white New Balance tennis shoes finished off the look. Despite the dust, Matt caught the scent of rose perfume. She raised her hand to tuck a wayward lock of hair back into place and offered him a smile that was anything but dusty.

Matt's first thought was to wonder what a woman like this was doing in an antique shop. His second was to wonder how his hair looked. He made a mental note to thank Annie for pointing him toward the newspaper ad the next time he saw her.

"I'm Abbey," the woman said, extending her hand. "Can I help you?"

"Abbey?" Matt took her hand. The long, slender fingers curled softly against his skin. "From the sign?"

"That's me. I own the place." She took her hand back and shoved it in her pocket. Matt noticed she wasn't wearing a ring. "What can I get you?"

Matt held up the newspaper ad. "I'm here for the work."

Abbey smiled again, even wider, if that was possible. "Thank God," she said. "I thought I was going to have to move all this shit by myself."

"Where are you moving it to? The back room?"

"Storage."

"All of it?" Matt looked around at the various piles of trinkets from decades past.

"Yeah," she replied. "Closing up shop. This place has been sucking money out of my bank account for too damn long."

"Oh. Sorry to hear it."

"It's okay. This store was my mother's dream, not mine. She named it after me." Abbey swung her arms out in a wide arc, encompassing the entire place. "She was never very organized."

"Was?"

Abbey looked back at Matt. "Yeah. She died a little over three years ago."

"I'm so sorry," Matt replied.

For the first time since he stepped into the room, Abbey's face grew hard. "She was one of the first victims of The Blake County Killer. Bastard got her on her way home from the store in December 2008. The cops found her car with a bunch of Christmas gifts in the trunk. They didn't find the body for weeks, and when they did, they had to identify her with dental X-rays because..." Abbey stopped, then shook her head. "I'm sorry. Sometimes my mouth just goes and goes without permission. You didn't come here to hear all that."

"It's okay. I—"

"The job is to help me load all this stuff up into a box truck and haul it to storage, where we'll unload it and come back for more until the place is cleaned out. Pay is ten dollars an hour. Cash. You interested?"

"I thought the ad said the pay was negotiable."

"Well, mister...what was your name again?"

"Matt."

Abbey nodded. "Matt, then. That was just to get you in the door. It's an old trick." She winked at him. "It's ten an hour. You want it or not?"

"I'll take it, but only if you pay me daily."

"You thinking about getting drunk tonight?"

"I'm new in town. No friends or family. Just passing through, really. Gonna need a place to sleep. Even the cheap hotels won't let me pay for lodging with my good looks."

Abbey laughed. "Tell you what, Matt," she said. "There's a back office with a cot and a bathroom on the far wall. It's even got a shower. Save your motel money. You can sleep there."

"Sounds good," Matt replied.

"Great. Now, get to work."

Matt chuckled, but went to the back wall of the store. He had to turn sideways to get through the clutter, but he managed to get by. Once there he set down his duffel and took off his jacket. His gray T-shirt was thin, and would be ideal for a day of heavy lifting. When he turned around, he noticed Abbey staring at his arms.

"Looks like I made a good choice," she said. "Can you rip a phone book with those things?"

"I chopped a lot of wood back home," Matt said.

"Farm boy, eh?"

"Sawyer."

Abbey nodded. She was about to open her mouth to speak when the bell above the door jingled again. Both of them turned to see a man in a khaki-colored police uniform step through the doorway. The newcomer was tall and thick, with dark beetle eyes and brown hair. The hard creases on his shirt and pants spoke to the care he gave his appearance, at least in uniform. His expression looked like he'd just tasted something sour, and the scowl lines on his face seemed permanent. He took off his wide-brimmed hat and stepped farther into the building.

"Sorry to bother you, Abbey."

Abbey sighed. "It's all right, Dale. What do you need?"

Dale looked at Matt. His eyes traveled the length of Matt's body, then settled on his face. "Who's this?" By the tone of his voice, Matt guessed the officer was not pleased by his presence.

He stuck out his hand, anyway. "Name's Matt. I'm just here to help Abbey move all this sh—stuff."

Dale didn't take Matt's hand. "Where you from, Matt?"

Matt held his hand out for another moment, then took it back and stuck it in his pocket. "North," he replied. Fuck the guy if he didn't like it.

Dale seemed about to say something else, but Abbey stepped in front of him. "Did you need something, Dale?"

Dale gave Matt one last hard look, then turned back to Abbey. "Just wanted to let you know they found another one. Over at Black Creek. Same as the others."

Abbey gasped. Apparently, she hadn't seen the police cars or heard the sirens this morning. Matt had, but then again, Matt didn't sleep much these days.

"Who?" she asked.

Dale's eyes fell to his boots, and right away Matt knew that whoever the victim was, Abbey wasn't going to like it.

"It was Eloise," Dale said finally.

"Stinnet?" Abbey asked. "Jim's wife?"

Dale nodded.

"Well, ain't that a fucking trick!" Abbey yelled. "She accuses me of sleeping with him, and then she turns up dead. Is that why you're here, Dale? To arrest me? You know I never laid a finger on either one of them. I'd rather fuck a porcupine with no lubricant."

"Damn it, Abbey. Don't you know me better than that by now?" Dale's eyes were earnest, even a bit moist, as though the big fellow might start leaking any minute.

Matt took a step back, wanting to fade into the background. He shouldn't be part of this discussion. It felt like he was intruding, somehow.

Dale noticed him and straightened his expression, clearing his throat as he did. "I just wanted to let you know, Abbey. Folks're liable to start talkin' again. I wanted you to be prepared."

Abbey took a long, deep breath, and then her lips split into a wan smile. "Of course. Thanks, Dale. I appreciate it."

"You're welcome." Just then, Dale's radio crackled, and a woman's voice called him back to the station. She sounded like an older lady who'd spent most of her life a smoker. Dale thumbed the volume down and gave Abbey one more look, then turned to go. He paused when his eyes settled on Matt again. "You know, Abbey, if you need to talk to someone...about anything...you can call me."

"I know," she replied. "Thanks, Dale. I've got work to do, though."

"Of course," Dale said. "Be careful." Even though he spoke to Abbey, his eyes never left Matt's face. "See you later."

With that, the tall country policeman turned his back on the two and strode out the door. The tinny ring of the bell followed him out.

"Nice guy," Matt said. "Friend of yours?" Matt couldn't help but notice the looks that Dale kept giving Abbey, but she hadn't returned them. For some reason, Matt very much wanted to know what the cop's position in her life was.

"Ex-husband," she replied.

"Sorry to hear it."

Abbey sighed. "Not as sorry as he was." She let out a deep breath and shook her head. Then she turned to face Matt. "Well Matt, you've already seen more in this town than you bargained for, I'll bet."

Matt just shrugged. How could he explain the things he'd seen? How could he tell her about his death? Or Mr. Dark? Maybe he should tell her how he'd been forced to shoot his best friend to keep him from murdering that asshole Silbert. Or about how, ever since he died, he had been able to actually *see* evil in people, which manifested as a rotting, festering sore that spread across the person's skin like leprosy. *Ha! Fat chance!* If he tried to tell her about himself, about how he was chasing across the country after a mysterious evil "man" that no one else could see, he'd lose the job and probably get locked up in a mental ward. Hell, a run-of-the-mill serial killer seemed more normal than anything in his life. At least since his wife died.

The thought struck him as a pretty sad indictment.

"So when do we start?" he asked.

CHAPTER THREE

Matt loaded the last box into the storage shed, setting it on top of another box with an audible grunt. The fucking thing was heavy! He wiped the sweat from his forehead with a damp towel, then stuck the tip of the towel into his back pocket.

"That's the last one," he said. "Should we do another load?" They'd been at it for seven hours, stopping only for a quick lunch at McDonald's, which seemed to be the only fast food restaurant in town, but so far they had managed to move about two-thirds of the inventory from the store to the storage unit.

"No," Abbey replied. "It's almost six o'clock. We'll pick up again tomorrow. Right now I just want to eat something, then go to bed." She groaned as she bent sideways, stretching her abdominal muscles. Matt had been expecting to shoulder most of the work himself, but she surprised him. Abbey stayed with him the entire day, lifting, moving, and hauling just as much as Matt. If the soreness in his back—and Matt had spent a lifetime chopping wood—was any indication, she must be beat, too.

"Dinner sounds great," he said, wiping his hands on his jeans. "Any good places to eat around here?"

"A few," she replied, a hint of a smile on her lips.

"What? What are you smiling about?"

"You're about to ask me out, aren't you?"

Matt stared, his mouth slightly open. "I...uh..."

"Don't worry, Matt. I don't bite." She stepped down from a box of antique clocks and winked. "But if you're going to buy me dinner, you might want to ask me for a raise. I know how much you make, remember?"

"Oh?"

"At ten dollars an hour, I doubt you can afford me."

Abbey turned and walked out of the storage room, jingling the keys to the box truck in her hands. "And wash up first. Use the shower at the back of the store. I hope you have your own shampoo in that duffel, or else you're going to spend the evening smelling like Cucumber-Melon Suave."

Matt smiled. "I do. I even have some deodorant."

"Great," Abbey said through the window of the truck. "I'll pick you up at eight."

"It's a date," Matt replied.

It wasn't until she started the engine that he remembered she was his ride back to the store.

The truck started to pull out of the parking lot. "Oh, shit," he said, and took off at a run, trying to reach the door before she drove away. "Abbey, wait!"

—

At a tiny restaurant called Malloy's in downtown Crawford, Matt and Abbey sat outside in patio-style plastic chairs, enjoying the cool evening air after a sweaty day. She had picked him up at eight, as promised, in a white Ford van with the "Abbey's Antiques" logo painted on the sides. Matt had asked if she was going to repaint the van now that she was closing the store, and she'd laughed and asked if he did auto-body work as well as moving and sawing. Her laughter reminded him again of Janey, and he'd had to force her out of his mind for the rest of the drive.

The waitress brought over a fresh pitcher of Miller Draft and a pair of frosty mugs, just the thing to wash down a very dry burger and some greasy fries. He poured a mug for Abbey, then one for himself, and set the pitcher in the middle of the table.

"Thanks," Abbey said, smiling. She must have taken a moment to freshen up before she left her house, because she once again smelled of her rosy perfume. She wore a thin white blouse and tight jeans again, much the same look as she had all day long. The only difference was this time, her hair wasn't shoved under a bandana and she'd gone to the trouble of putting on her makeup. The sandals on her feet bore three-inch heels that emphasized the shapely curve of her calves, which Matt couldn't help but notice. Abbey certainly had all the right curves in all the right places. He could see why Dale didn't want to let her go.

"You're welcome." He took a swig of his beer. The cold liquid flowed into his throat, but didn't do much to cool him off. "So you were married, huh? To a cop, no less."

"Do you always bring up failed relationships on a first date?" Abbey asked.

He leaned back in his chair, a hint of a smile on his lips. "I'm a bit out of practice," he conceded.

"Oh? Are you divorced, too?"

A mental snapshot popped into Matt's mind. A resort in Cozumel, not long after his wedding. Palm trees swayed gently in the breeze as Janey lay on a towel at the pool. The only thing separating her skin from the air was a thin red bikini she'd picked up the week before, and even then her nipples poked through the fabric, drawing his eyes right to them. She held a frozen drink in her hand. On the side of the glass that touched her lips, the salt had worn away, but he could still taste it if he licked his lips. Her kiss had tasted like margaritas that day.

Divorced? Never. Not in a million years.

"My wife died," he replied. "About a year and a half ago."

"I'm sorry."

"Not as sorry as I was," he said, echoing her comment from earlier that day.

"If you don't want to talk about it..."

"No," he said. "No, it's okay. I've gotten past it. It's just...I never know what to say to that." Matt realized he was wringing his hands and grabbed the mug to stop himself. "You know what I mean?"

Abbey nodded, then took a sip from her own mug. Her eyes never left Matt's.

"So what have you been doing since then?" she asked.

Nothing much. Just dying and living again, Matt thought. *And killing my best friend. Oh, and I've been chasing the Devil. Have you seen him?*

"Not much, really," he replied. "Just kinda wandering around. Seeing as much of the country as I can."

"That sounds great."

"Well, I'm not exactly building up my 401K."

"At least you're living," she said. "I've been stuck in that damn store for years."

"Not anymore," he said.

"True enough. I just wish I knew what to do next."

"I feel that way every day." Matt smiled.

"I bet you do." Abbey laughed. The sound was throaty but soft, almost sensual. Like silk against bare skin. She raised her glass. "To the great unknown," she said.

Matt clinked his mug against hers and took a long, hard drink. For a moment, all he could see was the bottom of his mug. The night was looking up. He finished his beer and set the mug down on the table.

And that's when he saw him.

The man on the sidewalk wore a wrinkled blue suit and scuffed loafers. The tail of a white shirt hung below the back of his sport coat, and his hands were shoved into his pockets. His dark hair was slightly messy, and his face showed a bad case of five o'clock shadow. He looked like a perfectly ordinary businessman on his way home from work.

Except for the moldy green blotch covering half his cheek.

Matt watched him walk by. The man had an angry look on his face, and muttered to himself as he passed. The decay on his cheek grew larger right in front of Matt's eyes, and when Blue Suit got to within a few feet, the smell of decay came with him. Matt had a hard time not gagging on the stench, but managed to keep the reflex in check.

Blue Suit walked right by his table and kept going. Matt tried to keep his eyes on him without being too obvious, but he wasn't doing a very good job of it.

"What is it, Matt?" Abbey asked.

"Who is that guy? The one in the suit?"

Abbey looked over Matt's shoulder. "That's Brad Linderholm. He's a local stockbroker. Why?"

Matt turned back to look at her, and almost choked.

There, about twenty feet behind Abbey and looking far too happy for Matt's liking, was Mr. Dark.

CHAPTER FOUR

He didn't look quite the same as he had before. The smile was still there, but the outfit had changed. Still, Matt knew Mr. Dark when he saw him, and right now, the asshole was laughing at him. "Hello, Mr. Cahill? Having a nice dinner?"

Matt shot from his chair. Finally! He'd caught up to Mr. Dark. This time he would get the answers he needed.

"Matt?" Abbey asked. "What is it?"

Matt ignored her, focusing on Mr. Dark. He stepped around the table and moved toward the man who'd been haunting his dreams. The muscles in Matt's arms twitched as he imagined himself choking the life out of him.

Mr. Dark laughed. "Did you happen to see my friend Mr. Linderholm? I wonder where he's going. Don't you want to find out? Of course, you can stay here with me, instead."

Shit! Brad! Matt turned to see which way the man in the blue suit had gone. He caught a glimpse of Linderholm walking around a corner. The sores on the side of his face had gotten bigger, nearly engulfing his whole head. Whatever Linderholm was doing, it wouldn't be long before someone got hurt. Maybe a lot of people. Matt recalled the way his lifelong friend, Andy, had gone off the deep end and murdered half a dozen people after being afflicted by Mr. Dark's touch. Could the same thing be happening with Brad Linderholm? Could he take that chance?

Damn!

"Matt?" Abbey asked again. "What are you staring at?"

Mr. Dark laughed again, his glittering black eyes daring Matt to make a choice: save someone or confront the evil son of a bitch who'd brought so much pain into his life.

Matt made his choice. "I have to go, Abbey," he said, and turned to run after Linderholm.

Mr. Dark's laughter followed him down the street.

———

Matt ran around the corner, chasing after the blue suit. He pushed and shoved his way through a small crowd of people, trying to keep Linderholm in sight. Fortunately, in a small town like Crawford, there were never any big crowds, and although Matt couldn't quite catch up, he was able to keep the back of the man's blue sport coat in sight. After a few minutes, Brad walked out of the busy district and onto the side streets. There the crowd thinned, and Matt was able to keep a safe distance without fear of losing sight of the man.

He followed him for several blocks, past a carpet store, a diner, and a small house with a sign on the front lawn that said "Madame Carla's Tarot Reading. Know what tomorrow has in store for you today!" Matt shook his head. Fuck tomorrow. Today was hard enough.

A few blocks later, Brad turned right into the driveway of a white two-story house. It was nicely trimmed, with a white fence, a neat, tidy lawn and a blue BMW in the driveway. Brad spat on the BMW as he walked by, leaving a sticky wad of greenish goo on the car's hood. He reached the front door and shoved his hand into his pocket. From where Matt stood, he heard the jangle of keys. He could also smell the odor of decay, and see the moldy green of Brad's hands. The rot had spread that far in just the short time it took him to walk from the restaurant to the house. Not good.

Here we go, Matt thought.

Brad stepped into the house, not bothering to shut the door behind him. Matt stalked up the driveway, waiting to hear shouting or screaming. He noticed the license plate on the BMW. JOHNSON1.

Johnson? I thought Brad's last name was Linderholm. Unless his wife…

Then it clicked.

Matt stood up and sprinted into the house, hoping to catch Brad before he could kill his wife and her lover. He didn't know who Johnson was, but he was willing to bet that Brad did.

Just inside the door was a foyer with three openings. The one on the right led into a large living room. The one on the left led down a long, windowed hallway with several doors. The one directly in front of him led to a stairway. He spent a few precious seconds trying to decide which way to go, then theorized that the master bedroom would probably be on the second floor. Halfway up the stairs his reasoning was justified as a trio of voices began yelling.

Two men, one woman, he noted. He couldn't understand the words, as they were muffled by doors and walls, but he was able to make out the tone, and it wasn't good. He ran up the rest of the stairs and stood on the landing. A hallway branched off in either direction. Matt paused, listening.

"Bitch! You fucking, whore-ass bitch!" That had to be Brad, and it came from the left. Matt ran. At the end of the hall, a set of double doors stood open, revealing a shadow on the floor.

"Put the gun down, Brad," a woman's voice cried. "Please! You don't want to do this!"

"The hell I don't!" Brad replied. The shadow on the floor moved. Matt noted the raised shape, which looked like an arm pointing deeper into the room. "Say good-bye, Laura."

He wasn't going to make it. He did the only thing he could think of.

"Stop!" Matt shouted. "This is the police!"

"Fuck!" Brad's voice again.

"Help me! He's crazy!" That would be Laura. A third voice, a man's voice, joined in the chorus but Matt couldn't make out his words.

"Put the gun down, Mr. Linderholm!" Matt ordered, trying his best to sound like a cop.

The shadow arm lowered, and Matt breathed a sigh of relief. He stood just outside the door now, not wanting to go into the room until he knew the gun was on the floor. "That's good. Now, drop the gun. Nice and slow."

"Oh thank God." Laura's voice. "Thank you, Officer."

The other man in the room, Johnson, whimpered, but Matt couldn't tell if he was talking or just blubbering.

"Hell with this," Brad said. The shadow arm snapped up again, but this time it pointed the other way, back toward the hallway. Matt couldn't figure out what it meant. At least, not until the shot went off and a piece of the door exploded two inches in front of his face.

"Fuck!" Matt screamed. He dove for the floor just as another round tore through the door right where his head had been and thudded into the wall opposite.

"You don't sound like a cop," Brad jeered. "Where's your authority now, fucker?"

Two more shots split the door in half. One of the rounds embedded itself into the floor by Matt's feet. The other tore a line of fire across his shoulder. Matt yelped. *That fucking hurt!* He looked at the wound and was relieved and horrified to see it was just a graze. Relieved because he knew he'd be fine, and scared because now that he knew how much a grazing bullet hurt, he was in no hurry to find out what a solid hit felt like.

Brad Linderholm, his blue suit wrinkled and his shoes scuffed, stepped around the splintered door and out into the hall, his gun leading the way. It was a big bastard, too. It looked like a hand-held cannon. But that wasn't what drew Matt's attention.

When he had seen Brad near the restaurant, his face had just begun to fester. Now it looked as though Brad had been dead for a month or more. His face was half rotted away, allowing Matt to see the bone of his lower jaw. What flesh remained on the skull was limp and gray, and a host of insect larvae had set to devouring it. The stench of rot flowed into the hall like a thick, noxious cloud, making Matt gag despite the severity of his situation.

He scrambled backward, but soon found his back against the far wall. Brad smiled, his face dripping bits of flesh on the floor as the tattered muscles forced his lips into a grin.

"You're no cop," he said, and leveled the gun at Matt's head. Matt closed his eyes, waiting for the inevitable.

"I am," came a voice from down the hall. It was followed by a gunshot. The loud crack of the shot sounded like Armageddon in the confines of the hall, and Matt would have sworn his ears split open. At first, he thought Brad had done it. He'd pulled the trigger and blown Matt's brain all over the wall behind him. But he hadn't felt any pain. Then again, maybe he wouldn't. He couldn't remember the last time he died. Had he felt pain then?

"Son of...a...bitch..." Brad's voice. But it sounded strained, almost a wheeze.

Matt opened his eyes. Brad still stood in front of him, but the big gun was now pointed at the floor. Brad held his left hand clamped over his heart, where a large red stain grew bigger by the second. His face was turned down toward his chest, probably watching as his blood drained away. "Fucking...bitch..."

Brad slumped to the floor, his torso leaned sideways against the wall. The gun fell to the hardwood with a clatter. As he died, the rotting sores vanished, leaving his face clean and smooth, an ordinary man after a day at the office. *Just like Andy,* Matt thought.

The sound of a woman weeping came from the bedroom, as well as a man's voice saying, "Oh shit oh shit oh shit," over and over again. Matt could sympathize. If he had his voice, he'd probably be saying the same thing.

"Well, look who's here," said a voice behind him. "We meet again."

Matt turned to see the cop from Abbey's, Dale, standing ten feet away, his gun raised and pointed at Matt. He didn't look happy.

"You mind telling me just what the fuck you're doing here, Matt?"

CHAPTER FIVE

"Well?" Dale asked. Matt couldn't help but notice that the lawman had yet to holster his pistol. A thin trickle of smoke rose from the barrel. It wasn't as big as Brad's gun, but it could still put a big hole in something. Or someone.

Matt found his voice. Finally. "I was just trying to help."

Dale nodded. "Uh huh. And how did you know what Brad was doing?"

Good question, Matt thought. *I wish I knew.*

"I...Just a hunch, I guess."

"A *hunch?* You expect me to believe that?"

"How did *you* know to come here, Officer?" Matt shot back.

"Don't take that tone with me, fella. I'll haul your ass in for the sheer fun of it if I want to. I can make up a charge if I wanna."

"Leave him alone, Dale," a new voice said.

Both men turned to look at the end of the hall. There was Abbey, standing at the top of the stairs. "Matt's a hero. He saved Laura and David. You should be thanking him that you aren't having to clean bits of them up off the floor right now."

A woman wrapped in a blanket emerged from the bedroom, nodding her head. "That's right, Dale," she said. "Brad was gonna kill us. Said he was gonna paint the walls with our blood." Tears streaked down her face, leaving thin mascara smudges down her cheeks. With her makeup in ruins, she looked a bit like Alice Cooper. "If that man there"—she pointed at Matt—"hadn't gotten here when he did, David and I would be dead."

Dale looked from Laura to Abbey, then back. Finally he grunted and shoved his pistol back into its holster. Matt breathed a sigh of relief and looked up at Abbey, silently thanking her for her help.

"I don't like this," Dale said to Abbey. "That guy's hiding something. You can tell just by looking at him."

"Like what, Dale?" Abbey asked. "He's got his own tarot deck or something?"

"I don't know," Dale replied. Then he turned toward Matt and glared from under his wide-brimmed hat. "But I'm gonna find out. Don't go anywhere. You either, Laura. You're all going to have to answer some questions." With that, Dale walked to the far end of the hall and grabbed his radio off his belt.

While Dale called in the incident, Laura slipped back into the bedroom, where David had finally stopped his litany of never ending *oh shits*.

Abbey squatted down next to Matt and put her hand on his cheek.

"You all right?" she asked.

Matt nodded. "Just a scratch. I've had worse."

"Big tough guy, aren't you?"

"Depends. Did I piss myself?" Matt asked.

Abbey's eyes flicked to his crotch, then back to his face. "Nope."

"Then yes. I am a big tough man." Matt smiled.

Abbey smiled back and proceeded to tear off a piece of Matt's shirt. "I wouldn't feel right rummaging through their bathroom, you know what I mean?"

Matt nodded. Suddenly he was very tired. He closed his eyes and let Abbey bind his shoulder without interruption.

"Tell me something, Matt."

"What?"

"How *did* you know to come here?"

"Just a hunch. Like I told Dale."

"Bullshit."

Matt opened his eyes to find Abbey staring at his face. Her gray eyes bored into his. She knew he was lying, but what could he tell her? He could *see* evil? That would go over well.

He sighed. "You wouldn't believe me if I told you."

Abbey turned to look at Dale, who stood about twenty feet away chattering into the radio. Then she turned back to Matt and leaned in close, putting her lips right next to his ear. "I know better, Matt," she whispered. "You see them, too, don't you?"

"See what?" Matt asked, so low even he had trouble hearing the words.

"Them," Abbey said, pointing at Brad's corpse. "When they start to rot and fester. Just before something bad happens."

Matt couldn't breathe. He couldn't speak. Could she? Could she really?

"You *can* see it. Can't you?" she asked. "The evil. I thought I was the only one."

CHAPTER SIX

Matt and Abbey sat at a folding table in the back room of Abbey's Antiques, a half-empty bottle of Jack Daniels between them. Matt's glass was empty, but Abbey's still had an inch of booze in it. She reached across the table and refilled his drink. Her hand shook a little, but whether it was from the alcohol or the events of the day, Matt didn't know.

"I still don't know how you convinced Dale to let me go," Matt said.

"And I don't plan on telling you," Abbey said. "So stop trying to get it out of me."

The officer had seemed determined to keep Matt in custody after he'd given his statement. Admittedly, Matt's statement was pretty weak, but he couldn't very well tell the truth. Then Abbey had intervened, taking Dale into a separate room. When they emerged, Dale said Matt was free to go, but warned him not to leave town in the next few days in case he was needed for more questioning. Matt assured him he would stay put, and then he and Abbey had left the place together, pushing through the throng of police, EMTs, and lookie-loos. On the way out, Matt could feel Dale's eyes boring into his back.

"Hang on," Abbey said. "I'm kind of a sugar junkie, especially when I drink." She reached into a drawer behind her and pulled out a plastic bag of candy. She reached into the bag and pulled out two lollipops, both red, and offered one to Matt. Seeing them brought Mr. Dark to Matt's mind, and he grimaced. Just the thought of sticking one of those things in his mouth almost made him gag.

"No thanks," he said. "Not big on sugar." Did she know about Mr. Dark? He'd have to find out.

"Suit yourself," she replied, and popped one into her mouth. She put the other back into the bag and shoved it back into the drawer. "So what's your story, Matt?" Abbey asked. "How is it that you can see what I see?"

Matt leaned back in his chair, trying to figure out the best way to answer. In the end, he settled on the truth. "In November of 2010, I was skiing with my girlfriend. The last thing I remember is being crushed by a mountain of snow. Next thing I knew, I was in a morgue and some guy was cutting into me with a scalpel."

"That must have been terrifying," Abbey said.

Matt nodded. "I'd been dead for months. They only found my body because of the spring thaw. Some little girl was building a snowman and—"

"Holy shit!" Abbey slammed her glass on the table, sloshing bourbon onto the tabletop. "You're *that* Matt Cahill?"

"You heard about it, huh?"

"It was all over the news. They called you a modern miracle."

"I guess." Matt finished his glass. "Never felt much like a miracle to me, though."

"No, I don't suppose it did." Abbey crunched into the lollipop and chewed the candy off the stick, which she tossed into the wastebasket. Then she lit a cigarette. The smoke curled lazily up toward the ceiling. Matt caught himself before he could make a comment about her obvious oral fixation and poured himself another glass of Jack, instead.

"So how about you?" he asked. "Did you die, too?"

"Not big on tact, are you?"

"Does it matter?" Matt replied.

"It might. Later." Abbey winked.

"Tell me."

For a moment she looked like she might, but then she shook her head. "Not right now," she said. "Story for another time."

The two lapsed into silence, Matt nursing another drink and Abbey staring at her glass. He wanted to ask her about Mr. Dark but wasn't sure how. Despite the fact that he'd found someone else who could see evil in people, he wasn't entirely convinced he had complete control of his mind. Even though the whole day had been crazy, he didn't want to make it worse.

Somewhere out in the shop, a bell chimed twice. Abbey looked at her watch.

"Two in the morning," she said, stretching. "I think it's time I went home."

Matt looked around, remembering he'd be sleeping on a cot in the back room. The thought didn't sit well with his back, but after the uncomfortable bus ride that morning— had it really only been that morning?—and almost getting killed, even a cot in a rundown shop would be a luxury. He stood and stretched, reaching over his head and wincing as the bullet wound on his shoulder reminded him of its existence. His shirt rose up just a bit, but he barely noticed.

When he finished his yawn, he found Abbey staring at him. Her expression was hard to read. A mixture of amusement and mischief. And something else. He couldn't help but notice how her chest rose and fell with each breath, perhaps a little more than normal. The fabric of her blouse strained to keep everything covered. She answered his quizzical look by putting her arm on his shoulder and rubbing her thumb along his bicep.

"You wanna drive me home, cowboy?" she asked, her voice deep and throaty. It left no doubt in Matt's mind that he would not, in fact, be sleeping on the cot in the back of the store.

"I thought you'd never ask," he replied.

—

Matt had never considered himself a slouch in bed. Whenever the opportunity arose he always did his best to give as good as he got, and so far, he hadn't had any complaints.

But Abbey kicked his ass eight different ways.

They hadn't been in her house five seconds before she pushed and shoved him into her bedroom, kissing him and slipping out of her clothing the whole way. He didn't even get a good look inside the place. By the time the back of his legs hit the bed, she was already naked, and working her hands through his belt.

Her body was solid and toned, a woman used to working out, and it showed in the strength of her arms and legs as she held his hands to the bed and straddled him. She rocked back and forth on top of him for several minutes, breathing heavily, until her eyes closed and she dug her nails into the skin of his back. He felt the pinch in his flesh and knew if he checked he would find blood. The thought excited him more than he thought it would.

From there, she rolled over, pulling him on top of her. By now she was gyrating her hips and grinding into him like a piston, and Matt was just trying to keep up. She wrapped her legs around his back and used them to force him deep into her.

"Push!" she breathed. "Push that fucker right through me!"

Matt pushed for all he was worth.

Abbey moaned and ground her hips into his groin. She wrapped her hands in his hair and pulled as her body tensed. She moaned again, louder, and told him not to stop. So he didn't.

When he finally came, it was rough and hard, but felt wonderful. His muscles relaxed as the tension left his body. He rolled away from her, surprised at how much he was sweating, and thought about how much he'd needed that.

But Abbey had other ideas. She grabbed his shoulder, sending a twinge of pain down his arm as she brushed the bullet wound with her fingers, and pulled him back toward her. Then she maneuvered him on his back, climbed on top of him, and grinned. "That was just round one," she said. Then she kissed his abs, rubbing her lips into the muscle. She ran her tongue along the ridges, licking the salt from his belly.

Then she slid her tongue further down his body, teasing the base of his cock. To his surprise, he felt himself stiffening again. By the time her lips slipped over the head and down his shaft, he was as hard as a fucking rock.

Time for round two, he thought.

CHAPTER SEVEN

Matt raised his ax. He'd brought it with him from the store. Abbey had given him a strange look, but hadn't said anything. He just couldn't bear the thought of leaving it behind. It was his only connection to the past. To the person he used to be. On the bus ride, he'd been forced to stow it in a compartment, and even that had bothered him.

He brought the heavy blade down on the wood, smiling as it split in two. His shoulder barely hurt at all anymore. He'd checked the wound in the mirror after waking up and was surprised to find it had all but healed. One of the benefits of his condition, he supposed.

Good thing Abbey had a mountain of logs to split. Matt loved to work the wood. The labor cleared his head and kept him trim, plus it gave him time to think. He settled into the rhythm of the task: placing a log on the stump, hefting the ax, and splitting it. Repeat as desired. The steady thud of the blade into wood was as comforting to him as the sound of his own heartbeat.

Place.

Heft.

Chop.

Repeat.

DAVID MCAFEE

It felt good to be outdoors. The day was starting off warmer than normal for this time of year, and the birds serenaded him as he worked. Abbey's place, it turned out, was set far back into the country. The house sat in the middle of the only cleared patch of land on sixteen acres. Her father, she said, had built the house with his own two hands. The man apparently liked his privacy.

He placed another log on the stump.

Last night with Abbey wasn't love. Matt knew that. He attributed it to a combination of alcohol consumption and the shock of finding a kindred spirit.

But were they kindred spirits? Really? Sure, Abbey could see evil, but what did that tell him about her? Nothing. Other than her ability to see the festering decay of evil and the fact that she was a demon in the sack, he really didn't know much about her at all.

Matt raised the ax over his head.

Obviously, she had been the one to call Dale the day before. Matt realized that now. Once he'd left, she must have figured where he was going, since she could see the sores on Brad's face, too. But why hadn't she come along? Was she afraid? Or just apathetic? Did she use her "gift" to help people, as Matt did? Or did she let it go to waste? Was she a potential ally? The thought had its appeal, and it was more than just the mind-blowing sex.

Matt brought the ax down, splitting the log with a sharp crack.

Matt hated to admit it, but he was tired of being alone all the time. Until now, he'd just figured it was his lot in life. His destiny. But if he could share his mission with someone else, a like-minded person who could help him hunt Mr. Dark...

Hell, did she even know about Mr. Dark? Matt needed to know, and he could think of only one way to find out. It was time to finish the discussion they'd started the night before.

He leaned the ax against the stump and turned toward the house. He entered through the same door in the side of the garage that he'd used to go out into the yard. Inside, Abbey's van sat cold and silent, waiting for them to make their trip back to town. He passed through the garage and into the house.

"That's none of your business, Dale." Abbey was on the phone when Matt walked into the house. She looked fantastic in a faded red T-shirt that was barely long enough to cover her ass. The smoke from her cigarette danced through the house. Matt could have lived without the smoke, but somehow he didn't think she would look the same without it. He felt his crotch stir again as he watched her pace through the living room.

"You don't get to ask me questions like that anymore," Abbey snapped into the phone. "That's what divorce means. It means you have to stay out of my goddamn business." She placed her palm over the mouthpiece and smiled at Matt. "Sorry, cowboy," she whispered. "I'll be off in a minute. I made breakfast, though. Help yourself."

The smell of bacon and eggs wafted through the living room, reminding him that he hadn't eaten yet. According to the clock on the wall, he'd been chopping for an hour and a half. It didn't seem like it, but time often moved at a strange pace when he was working the wood. Since she was on the phone, and since his stomach had started gurgling loud enough to be heard in the other room, Matt decided their conversation about Mr. Dark could wait.

He followed his nose into a small kitchen with a checkered floor and burled wooden cabinets. The gleaming white and chrome oven looked ancient, as did the fridge. He couldn't see a dishwasher anywhere, but the sink was full of soapy water and a couple of cooking pans. The walls were covered with a daisy-patterned wallpaper that looked spotless, even in the bright light of the morning that filtered through the window above the sink. The whole place had a very fifties feel to it, and Matt liked it immediately.

A platter of bacon, eggs, and fried potatoes sat on the linoleum table. Abbey had already set two places and poured a couple of glasses of orange juice. She must have been just about to get him when her ex-husband called. He sat in the seat closest to the window and tried not to eavesdrop on their conversation while he shoved food into his mouth.

Unfortunately, that was harder than he thought. Abbey's voice carried through the house like a bell, and he had a hard time distracting himself from it. To help him focus on something else, he began to look through the kitchen.

The fifties vibe really struck him the more he looked at it. Even the pictures on the wall looked antique. *That's probably her mother's doing,* he thought. After all, she did run an antique store. She probably had a fondness for them.

One picture in particular caught his attention: an old black and white shot of a woman who looked a lot like Abbey (*probably her mom,* he reflected) standing in front of a car lot. The woman stood next to a smiling man in a tweed suit as they posed in front of an old Buick. There were other older cars in the background, their windows decorated with words like "On Sale! Today Only!" and "Bring one home to the Missus!" written in white shoe polish. The man held a set of keys toward the camera, beaming like a child with a gold star on his report card.

Matt smiled. He could see where Abbey got her looks. He got up and stepped over to the wall to get a better look at the photo. Abbey's mother smiled prettily back at him. They had the exact same smile: big and bright and full of life.

"Wait a minute," he whispered. He reached up and plucked the picture from the wall, bringing it closer to his face. *No fucking way...*

"Nice picture, isn't it?" Abbey's voice came from behind him.

Matt turned to see her leaning against the doorframe.

"That's not your mother, is it?"

Abbey shook her head. "Nope. That's me with my first husband, Clark, on the day we bought our very first car."

Matt looked back at the picture and took it in. The cars, the clothes, the way Abbey's hair was styled. Like Rita Hayworth's but not as dark. "When was this taken?"

Abbey sighed. "Nineteen forty-seven." She walked over and grabbed the picture from Matt's hand and placed it back on the wall, tracing the outline of Clark's face with her index finger. Her lips bent up into a rueful smile. "The same year we got married."

Matt stared back at her, his mouth agape. Nineteen forty-seven? Sixty-four years ago? But she looked exactly the same. "How...?"

"What do you say we go have a drink, cowboy?" Abbey asked.

Matt looked at his watch. "It's only ten a.m."

Abbey folded her arms over her chest. "Do you honestly give a fuck what time it is?"

"No," Matt replied, looking at the picture on the wall. A picture that told him he'd just slept with a woman who had to be in her eighties. "Not really."

———

"I was pretty wild back then," Abbey said. "Clark loved that about me. We would party all night long and sleep through the day."

They were seated at a small corner table at a restaurant called the Candlewood. The place was open and airy, with a shitload of miscellaneous movie memorabilia plastered all over the walls. One such wall was devoted to Marilyn Monroe, while another was covered with movie posters featuring Clark Gable. Their wall, Matt noted, housed the restaurant's Alfred Hitchcock collection. It seemed fitting.

The place had opened at ten o'clock, and so did the bar, but for the moment they were the only two people in the bar section. No one else in town, it seemed, had cause to drink before noon. Abbey held a glass of Grand Marnier in her hand, while Matt nursed a beer.

"Must have been hard to make a living that way," Matt noted.

"You don't know the half of it," Abbey replied. "Neither one of us could hold down a job, but Clark's father was wealthy. When he died, he left everything to Clark, and that's when we got married and bought the Buick."

"Clark looked pretty happy in that picture," Matt said.

"We were," Abbey said. "Both of us."

"What happened?"

"I died."

"That seems to be going around," Matt said. "How?"

Abbey turned her glass up and downed the remaining liquor in a single gulp. Her face tensed, and she set the glass back on the table. "Drug overdose. Heroin. I wasn't dead for three months, though. More like three hours. Clark came home from work and found me. He took my pulse, realized I was dead, and called the medics."

"The medics?"

"We didn't call them EMTs or paramedics back then, but they were essentially the same thing. You have to realize, there was no 911 emergency system. Every branch of emergency services—police, fire, medical—had its own number and location. We called the people who responded to medical emergencies medics."

Matt nodded and took a drink of his beer. "And?"

"I woke up before the medics arrived. It really freaked Clark out."

"What did the medics have to say about it?"

"I managed to convince Clark he was mistaken, and that I'd only fainted. Once he believed, the medics accepted it. After all, he didn't know a damn thing about medicine. They told him not to panic next time and that they'd be sending us a bill. But I know the truth. I died. Just like you. And the next day, I started seeing these weird blotches on people. Some had it worse than others, and some people looked like they'd been dead for years. Those people were usually the mean ones. The things I saw them do..." Abbey shuddered. "Anyway, it didn't take long to figure out what the sores and rot represented."

"Did you tell anyone?" Matt asked.

"Are you crazy?" she replied. "I'd just overdosed on drugs. I figured it was a side effect or something. My husband was already looking at me like something out of a horror movie. I didn't want to make things worse. I figured it would pass. Of course, it didn't."

"No," Matt agreed. "It didn't."

The waitress came over and refilled Abbey's glass. She offered Matt another beer but he declined. Abbey raised her eyebrow but said nothing. After the waitress left, the two stayed silent for several long minutes. Matt was trying to figure out how to ask his next question, and couldn't quite get it out.

Abbey must have noticed. "You have something else, don't you?"

Matt nodded and finished the remainder of his beer. He wiped his lips with a napkin and leaned forward. "That picture, you said it was taken in 1947?"

Abbey nodded. She took a drink from her fresh glass. "Shit, I need a smoke. Or even a lollipop. Goddamn anti tobacco lobby. Who goes to a bar and doesn't smoke? Fascist bastards."

"How old were you?"

"Twenty-six."

"How is that possible?"

Abbey smiled again. "I have no idea. But it must have something to do with my—with *our*—unique condition."

Matt had never given much thought to that. He had always assumed that his life would run a normal course. As normal as a dead man running after a ghost could get, anyway. He figured he would someday grow old and eventually die. But if Abbey was right, then how many years did he have left? Would he be sitting in a bar in another sixty years looking exactly the same as he did now?

"So," he said, "the antique shop..."

"Was never my mother's," she finished. "Sorry about the lie, but I didn't know you then. Telling someone your mother was killed by a serial killer right before Christmas is a convenient way of getting people to change the subject."

"No problem," he said.

"I move around every few years," Abbey continued. "As you can imagine, it would get pretty complicated if I stayed in one town more than five or ten years."

"I bet."

"So what about you?" Abbey asked. "What do you plan to do with eternity?"

This is it, Matt thought. *You're never going to have a better chance to bring it up.*

"I'm going to catch Mr. Dark," he said, and waved the waitress over. Maybe another drink wouldn't be such a bad idea, after all.

"Who the hell is Mr. Dark?" Abbey asked. "He a friend of yours?"

Damn, Matt thought. He was just about to tell her how Mr. Dark had ruined his life when the door to the restaurant slammed open and a very angry Dale stormed in.

"I knew it!" he said, pointing at Matt. "I knew you were with him!" Dale started walking toward them, his eyes blazing and his hand reaching for his baton.

CHAPTER EIGHT

Dale's face was red. His eyes looked like twin slits. As he approached, his lip curled into a sneer. "You should have never come to Crawford, mister," he said, his speech just a bit slurred.

Matt got to his feet and stepped away from the table, wanting more room just in case the worst happened. He didn't want any trouble with the police, but if Dale came at him with the baton, he wouldn't have a choice. Matt, no slouch at self-defense, readied himself for a brawl.

Abbey stepped between them, putting her hand on Dale's chest. "Cut it out, Dale!" she shouted. "You're gonna get written up again, maybe even suspended."

"This is between me and him," Dale said, and tried to move past Abbey. "You gonna just let her stand there and protect you, Cahill?"

Abbey would have none of it. She stepped up to Dale, putting her face only inches from the enraged policeman's. "Dale, get out of here. Now!"

"I ain't leavin'," Dale said. He pointed a shaking finger at Matt. "Not until he and I have a talk." A glint on his finger caught Matt's attention. Dale was still wearing his wedding ring.

"You're drunk. Again!" Abbey said. "You're such an asshole. You're gonna lose your job if this gets back to the mayor."

Dale stopped, then looked around the club. Dozens of eyes stared at the confrontation. By the looks on everyone's faces, Matt guessed this was not a new scene for any of them. Just how volatile had Abbey's marriage to Dale been? Maybe he was better off not knowing.

Dale's shoulders slumped. "I ain't drunk," he said. His voice had lost quite a bit of volume but none of its anger. "I haven't had a single drink."

Abbey snorted.

"Oh, you don't believe me, huh?" Dale asked. "Well who *do* you believe? Him?" Dale pointed at Matt again. "What kinda shit has he told you? Whatever it is, I'm willing to bet he hasn't told you *everything.*"

Fuck! Matt tensed. For the first time, it sunk in that Dale was a cop, with access to all sorts of information. Police records, fingerprints, and God knows what else. If he'd been checking up on Matt using police resources, there was no telling what he'd have been able to dig up. *Here we go.*

Dale must have caught Matt's expression. "That's right, Matt. I know all about you. And I know all about Happy Burger, the sawmill, and Andy Goodis, too. Did you tell her about *that?*"

Matt's fists clenched. He couldn't help it. Dale's words, along with his twisted face, brought back too many memories.

—

Andy lay on the ground in a growing pool of blood. The two blasts from the shotgun had obliterated his once massive chest. Jagged ribs poked out from the red, oozing mass where his best friend's heart had once been. Bits of bone and gore covered the floor directly behind the body. In the background, Silbert continued to whimper, perhaps thinking Matt would follow his friend's lead, after all.

But all Matt could see as he lowered the smoking barrel was Andy's face. The rot and decay that had covered him were gone, leaving the skin smooth and undamaged. In that whole, unblemished expression, Matt saw the sadness his friend had borne his whole life. If only Matt had seen it sooner, maybe he could have done more to help. Then again, maybe not. Andy had always been a bit of an asshole, even when they were kids.

Now it was too late.

Matt's eyes fell to something else lying in the sawdust. A sticky wet lollipop. The calling card of Mr. Dark. And then Matt had his answer.

Andy had always been a prick, but he'd never been a murderer. Not until he met Mr. Dark. From the rafters came the sound of Mr. Dark's gleeful laughter, and Matt realized what he had to do. He took one long last look at the body of the man who'd been his best friend his whole life, then turned to leave the mill.

Laugh it up, you motherfucker, he thought. *I'm coming for you.*

—

"You don't know anything, Dale," Matt said sadly. "I loved Andy like a brother. No one misses him more than I do."

"Then why did you kill him?" Dale didn't even try to hide the sneer in his voice.

"Because," Matt whispered, "I had to."

"Matt?" Abbey asked. "What's going on?"

Matt looked at her, unable to speak. He could only shake his head.

Dale beamed, his face triumphant. "Yeah, Matt. Tell her what's going on. Tell her all about how you shot Andy Goodis twice in the chest and then split town. Tell her how you killed the guy who'd been your best friend since you were kids. Go ahead, I bet she'd love to hear it."

Abbey took a step back. Her hand went to her mouth as several people nearby gasped. "What?" she asked, looking at Matt. "What's he talking about?"

The fear in her voice took the last bit of fight out of him. He tried to look at her, but all he could see was Andy's face. His sad, lifeless face as he slid to the floor in a wet, bloody heap. Matt's fault. Matt's finger on the trigger. Matt's failure to notice his friend's pain. His shoulders fell, and he shrugged his arms free of the people holding him back.

"Yeah, that's what I thought," Dale said.

"He's a murderer? Why isn't he in jail?" someone behind him asked.

"Shit, Dale. Arrest that fucker!" someone added.

"Can't," Dale said. "They never charged him with anything, but damned if I know why." He turned his sneer back toward Matt. "What happened, man? Your buddy go soft on you? Wanted to stop? That why you shot him?"

Matt felt his anger rising. Bad enough he had to relive that same day in his mind over and over again, but to have some hick lawman accuse him of murder? It was almost more than he could take. *Time to go*, he thought, *before I do something I'll regret.*

He stepped around Dale and Abbey. The other patrons in the restaurant gave him a wide berth. He heard their whispers as he walked by, but he couldn't understand them past the roaring in his ears. In his mind, all he could see was Andy. Dead.

Someone grabbed him by the shoulder and yanked him around. Matt found himself face to face with Dale. Despite the officer's earlier words, he did, in fact, smell like booze.

"Oh, no you don't," Dale said. "We still have a few things to talk about." He grabbed Matt by his shirt with his left hand and reared back with his right fist. "Here comes one."

Matt whipped his hand around and knocked Dale's arm aside. Dale tried to recover but managed only to grab Matt's sleeve. Matt then grabbed the lawman by the collar of his shirt and jerked him forward, driving his forehead into the stunned police officer's face. Dale's eyes lost all focus, and his grip on Matt's sleeve lessened.

"You don't know anything," Matt repeated, then shoved Dale backward. Dale flipped over a table, snapping it in two and sending a plate of food and a soda into the air with a crash. He landed hard on the other side amid a tangled mass of splintered wood and someone's lunch. Matt didn't stick around long enough to see if he was all right. He headed for the door in a rush. The crowd of people in front of him parted to let him pass.

As he reached the door, he heard Dale's voice behind him. "Just keep on walkin', mister. When you get out the door, just keep on walkin'. You ain't welcome in Crawford no more."

Yeah, Matt thought. *Like I ever was.*

—

Matt spent the rest of the day walking around the town. He kept his distance from the people he saw, not wanting to find out if Dale had told anyone else about his past. It turned out that he didn't need to worry about that. Crawford, Tennessee, was a small town, and Matt, who grew up in a small town himself, knew that news traveled fast in a place where the best entertainment around was the local gossip. It didn't take long before people were pointing at him in the street and whispering. Most of the town's residents avoided his eyes and crossed to the other side of the street when he approached. He heard a few of them mutter insults, but none of them did so loud enough for him to make out their words.

Matt liked those people. They left him alone, giving him time to think.

Every once in a while, Matt would come across someone who didn't avoid him. He liked those people a lot less than the others. This second group of people usually stood their ground and frowned or sneered at him as he walked by, almost daring him to try something. Matt didn't want any more trouble. He'd already had enough to last a lifetime.

Just keep on walkin', Dale had said. *You ain't welcome in Crawford no more.*

Matt intended to take that advice. The last thing he needed was a feud with the local police. No good could come of it, and it might slow him down too much to ever catch up with Mr. Dark again. It would be far better for everyone involved if he just left Crawford and everyone in it far behind and never set foot in the town again. But he couldn't go yet.

His grandfather's ax was still at Abbey's.

CHAPTER NINE

Matt didn't know the way to Abbey's house, and he didn't want to ask for directions. *With my luck, they'll arrest me just for asking,* he thought. So he spent the day wandering around the area near Abbey's Antiques, hoping she would make an appearance. Then maybe he could explain away Dale's accusations.

Yeah, right. What the hell am I gonna say? Abbey didn't know him and had no reason to believe anything he said. He should just cut his losses and go. But something kept him circling the area of the store. It took him a while to figure it out, but the walking helped to clear his head, and eventually he put his finger on it.

She could see the sores, too.

Of all the people Matt had met, she was the only one who could ever understand what he was going through. Even Rachel—the girl he left behind back in Deerpark—didn't get it, and *she* was in love with him. But Abbey knew what it was like. If anyone outside of his hometown would believe him about Andy's death, it would be her.

Or so he hoped.

Granted, it was a small hope, but it kept him hanging around Crawford when his better judgment told him to get lost.

As another group of strangers moved to the far side of the street to avoid him, Matt walked past a newspaper machine. He'd passed it several times already but hadn't really noticed it. This time, the headline caught his eye.

"KILLER STRIKES AGAIN," it read. Then below that, in smaller text: "Blake County Killer Claims Another Victim." Below the headline the article talked about the latest in a string of bodies. The photo showed none other than officer Dale Everett at the scene. In the background Matt could make out the black outline of a body bag lying on the bank of a creek. Other officers milled around in the photo, performing their various duties.

Matt checked his pocket to see if he had the correct change, and came up with two quarters, a dime, and three pennies. He put the quarters into the machine, opened the door, and grabbed a copy of the newspaper. There was a wooden bench about a hundred feet down the street from the newspaper machine that offered a good view of Abbey's Antiques, so Matt sat down to read.

According to the article, the latest body was that of a twenty-seven-year-old woman named Eloise Stinnet, and victim number seventeen for the Blake County Killer. Like the previous sixteen, she'd been young and attractive, with a gym-toned body and a head of long brown hair. Also like the previous victims, she'd been stabbed multiple times in the legs, arms, and chest with a large knife. All the bodies had exhibited ligature marks on their ankles and wrists, and each one had traces of ketamine in their system. The victims all had needle punctures in their arms, which explained how the killer administered the drug.

Curiously, none of them had shown any signs of sexual assault, leading the police to believe the killer was impotent. Since the killer was meticulous about cleaning the bodies after he killed them, the police had very few other real clues. Still, the paper was full of theories the police were happy to share. Most of them read like your standard Hollywood profile. The killer was probably a white male aged twenty-five to forty-five, most likely quiet and unassuming, the type of person the neighbors would never suspect. He probably drove a nondescript van or SUV, which he could use to dispose of the bodies. And he probably had a garage, so he could clean up in private.

Matt shuddered to think what the killer would look like to him. A walking skeleton, maybe? A mummified corpse? Most likely, Matt would see him as a half-decayed zombie. Either way, he didn't want to meet the guy.

The article went on to say that Eloise Stinnet had been reported missing from nearby Cranston, Tennessee, over a month ago. The body, which had likely been dumped into the creek shortly after her disappearance, showed signs of having been in the water for weeks. That meant that the killer hadn't struck in almost a month, the writer warned, noting that the killer had been escalating his attacks. At first he'd killed only once every few months, but lately the bodies had rolled in every other week. It ended with a warning from Officer Everett for people to use utmost caution when traveling at night. Walk with a friend, try to be home before dark, don't answer the door for strangers, et cetera.

Matt was just about to fold up the paper when another photo caught his eye. In this one, the county medical examiner stood next to a uniformed officer. Both of them were looking at something on a clipboard. But they weren't what caught Matt's attention. To the right of the ME another officer was putting something into an evidence bag. The image was small, and the resolution none too sharp, but Matt thought he could make out what it was.

A lollipop.

"Fuck me," Matt said aloud.

Just then a rumble alerted him to the approach of a large truck. He looked over the top of the paper and saw Abbey driving the rented box truck up to the store. It looked like she was alone, and he breathed a sigh of relief. He'd half expected Dale to be riding shotgun, but the cop was nowhere in sight. Good. This was going to be hard enough without that asshole around.

Matt waited until Abbey got out of the truck and walked up to the door. Her black jeans and matching tank top left very little to the imagination, and Matt had a sudden image of her straddling him the night before. He shook his head and ordered himself to snap out of it. The last thing he needed right now was to picture her naked.

Focus!

After she walked into the store, Matt stood from the bench. She probably wouldn't listen to him, but he wanted to catch her inside so she couldn't run away before he had a chance to explain himself. Most likely, she'd just yell at him to leave or call the police, but he meant to at least *try* to talk to her. If nothing else, he wanted his ax back.

He made it halfway to the door before he heard a noise behind him. Matt whirled around just in time to catch a flash of something shiny as it cracked him on the side of the head.

The sudden flare of pain tore into him like a wild animal, and Matt stumbled backward on wobbly legs. A warm, wet sensation spread down the side of his face, covering his right eye in a sheen of red. Blood, Matt realized, as his legs gave out.

His eyes focused just enough to see a figure advancing on him, aluminum baseball bat in hand. One of the townspeople, perhaps? Come to get rid of the murderer in their midst? Matt tried to get his hands up to ward off the next blow, but the circuits from his brain to his nerves hadn't had time to reset, and all he could to was twitch as he sat on the ground.

"You should have listened to me," the figure said.

That voice! Matt thought. It sounded familiar, but he couldn't quite place it through the fog in his mind. Was it Mr. Dark?

Then the image solidified enough for Matt to recognize his attacker.

"I told you to keep walkin'," Dale said as he raised the bat for another blow. A small green sore began to sprout from the side of the officer's face.

Matt felt another round of pain. Then there was nothing at all.

CHAPTER TEN

Pain brought Matt back to his senses. His head hurt like a bastard, pulsing and throbbing with every agonizing heartbeat. He tried to touch his head, but his arm wouldn't move. His fingers tingled, sending hundreds of needle like pains running up and down his arm.

What the fuck? He tried to move his head and a wave of nausea hit him, almost strong enough to send him back to dreamland.

"Wake up, asshole." The voice stabbed into his ears like a blade, multiplying the pain in his head by a factor of ten. "Open your eyes."

Matt tried to reply, but all he could manage was a gurgle that might have been "fuck you," but he couldn't be sure.

A sudden, sharp pressure on the side of his head, right where it hurt the most, caused a white-hot burst of pain to bloom in Matt's head. He couldn't keep the scream inside, and his attacker laughed. The pressure held for a few seconds, then faded. The laughter didn't.

"You better open your eyes, mister," the voice said. "Next time I won't be so gentle."

Matt tried to comply, but a gummy, sticky substance covered his eyes, gluing the lids shut. Blood. It had to be. There must have been a lot of it.

"I can't," Matt mumbled. "They're stuck."

More laughter. "Shit. I shoulda known that'd happen. Hang on." Rough fingers pried his eyelids apart, none too gently, and cleared away some of the gunk with a wet towel.

Finally, Matt opened his eyes. He found himself sitting in a small, dim room. His arms and legs were strapped to a wooden chair with duct tape. The concrete floor had a drain in the middle, which Matt took as a bad sign. On the floor next to his chair lay a blood-crusted aluminum base-ball bat. Matt couldn't see the logo, but underneath the blood the bat was blue and silver.

He raised his head to see Dale leaning over him. The officer's face sported a decaying green sore on his right cheek. It wasn't big, but it was there. A thin dribble of pus poured from it and ran down his chin. Whatever was going through Dale's mind, Matt had a feeling he wouldn't like it much.

"What are you doing, Dale?" Matt asked, hoping to stall. "I'm pretty sure this isn't procedure."

"Fuck you," Dale replied. "You think I don't know about you and Abbey? I know everything. I know you spent the night there last night. Was it worth it?"

Dale's eyes looked wet. Matt tried to think of something to say that would slow him down, but he couldn't. Nothing the officer would believe anyway, so he settled on the truth.

"You're right, Dale," he said. "I did spend the night at her place. But you two are divorced. Don't you think it's time you moved on? It's obvious she has."

"Oh, that's a good one," a new voice said. Matt looked around the room, his vision still a bit hazy, and finally spotted the source. In the far corner, standing in a shadow, was Mr. Dark. "Now tell him how there are still plenty of fish in the sea," the asshole said, giggling. "I'm sure he'll get a kick out of it."

"I might have known," Matt said. Suddenly it made sense. Dale, the attack, the green sore. Everything. "Of course this is your work."

Dale turned to the corner, then back to Matt. "Who are you talking to, Cahill?"

Matt ignored him. "You're going to ruin his life."

Mr. Dark laughed. Matt understood. Mr. Dark's existence was about pain and suffering, what did he care about ruining the life of one small-town cop? Not a damn thing.

Fuck!

"Goddamn it, Cahill, what the hell are you trying to pull?" Dale snarled.

Matt turned back to the officer, trying his best to ignore Mr. Dark, who was still laughing in the corner. "This isn't right, Dale. And you know it."

"Fuck you, Cahill. What do you know about right? You're the one sleeping with another man's wife."

"You're *divorced*, Dale."

"The hell we are!" Dale shoved his left hand in Matt's face. The dim light of the room glinted off the gold band on Dale's ring finger. "We've been married almost three years now. Abbey..." Dale's breath caught in his throat, and the tears that had been building finally spilled over onto his cheeks. "She just tells people we are. She never wears her ring. She keeps that little house of hers so she can take guys like you there and...and..."

Matt winced. He couldn't help it. If what Dale said was true, then Abbey had lied to them both, but Dale was the one paying for it.

"I'm sorry," he said. "I didn't know."

Mr. Dark came out of the corner then, walking slowly toward Dale. "He doesn't care. You fucked his wife. Why should he care?" Mr. Dark said, his black eyes mocking Matt's predicament. "Ignorance of the law is no excuse. Isn't that what cops say?" He winked.

Dale's face blazed and he raised the bat, ready for another swing.

"Dale, you don't want to do this," Matt said. "You're pissed. I get it, but this is murder, man."

"Oh, damn, you're smart," Mr. Dark said. "This *is* murder. You'll get your prize in a minute." He leaned over to Dale, his gnarled finger inching closer to the small sore on Dale's cheek.

"I...I...I love her, Cahill," Dale said. The bat trembled in his hands. "I've loved her for years. You should have seen her on our wedding day. She was so beautiful."

"You really need to watch where you put your pecker," Mr. Dark said, smiling. "It does seem to get you in trouble."

"Go to hell, Mr. Dark," Matt said.

"Damn it," Dale shouted. "Stop doing that! This is about me and you. Who the fuck is Mr. Dark?"

"That would be me," Mr. Dark said, and touched the sore on Dale's cheek.

"No!" Matt tried again to free his hands, but it was no use.

Mr. Dark laughed even harder.

The sore on Dale's face expanded, doubling in size in a matter of seconds. The trickle of pus became a steady stream, and a small beetle appeared and began chewing on the rotting skin. The officer's breathing came faster and faster, and his eyes burned. The smell of decay grew strong as the sore spread across half of Dale's face.

"Was she worth it?" Dale asked again. "Answer the question, asshole. I wanna know if fucking my wife was worth it."

"Don't do this, Dale," Matt said. "You're a cop. You *know* this is wrong."

"I don't think he cares," Mr. Dark said.

"Answer me!" Dale shouted. "Was she worth it?"

"Tell him, Matt," Mr. Dark said. "Tell him what a wild fuck Abbey is. I bet he'd love to hear it."

"This won't make her stop," Matt whispered. "She's just gonna keep doing it, Dale."

"Fuck you!" Dale's hands shook, but he hadn't swung the bat yet. Matt noted the tension in the man's arms and the way he gritted his jaw tight. He looked like a man on the edge, but had he gone completely over? Matt was starting to doubt it.

Mr. Dark was having his doubts, too, it seemed. He stared at Dale like a viper watching a rodent. Waiting for the moment when his poison would do its job.

The green sore had spread all across Dale's left cheek, but it hadn't gone farther than that. It looked...contained. Matt had never seen anything like it before, but he knew what it meant.

Dale was fighting it.

"Dale, look at my face," Matt said. "Look at the blood on it. Is this you? Really?"

Dale did look, and he quickly looked away. The bat dropped a few inches.

"I don't think this is you at all, man," Matt said. "I think you're just hurt right now. But if you do this, you can't take it back. You know that."

Dale looked up, and the bat slipped a few more inches toward the floor. "I don't know what it is. I...she just makes me so crazy. Why does she do shit like this?"

"I don't know," Matt replied.

"Well, that's enough of that." Mr. Dark's face blazed. He stepped forward again and placed his entire hand on Dale's cheek. The sore bloomed outward like an explosion, and Dale's eyes and jaw clenched shut so hard Matt could see the veins in his head throbbing. When Dale's eyes opened, Matt felt a chill in his spine. There was no humanity left in them.

"No, Dale, think about this for a second!" Matt said.

Dale shook his head. Matt could almost hear the man's jaw muscles straining as he wrestled with Mr. Dark's insidious disease, but it didn't look like it was doing any good. The green rot continued to spread across the man's face.

"Fuck this!" Dale shouted. Then he swung the bat. Matt closed his eyes and braced for the blow.

But it never came.

Matt jumped in his chair as a loud clang sounded through the room. With his eyes closed, Matt couldn't see what was going on, but he heard Dale sobbing well enough. *He couldn't do it,* Matt realized. *When it came right down to it, Dale couldn't kill me.*

There was another sound, too. Mr. Dark's laughter. "You think you've won?" he chortled. "It's only halftime. The game isn't over yet, Matt."

He opened his eyes to see Dale sitting on the floor, his face in his hands. The bat was on the floor by the far wall, rolling along the concrete with a metallic whisper.

Matt almost shouted with relief. The sores on Dale's face were gone, replaced by healthy pink skin. The smell of decay that had clung to him had also vanished. Did that mean Dale was out of danger? Matt looked to the corner, but Mr. Dark was gone.

"Good for you, Dale," Matt whispered. "You beat him."

In his mind, he heard Mr. Dark's parting comment: *It's only halftime. The game isn't over yet, Matt.*

Great, Matt thought. *Just fucking great.*

CHAPTER ELEVEN

"You sure you don't want to go to the emergency room?" Dale asked. "That's quite a bump."

"I've had worse," Matt replied, eyeing the lump in the passenger mirror of Dale's cruiser. It was true. After all, he'd *died*, hadn't he? What's a lump on the head after freezing to death under a thousand tons of snow and ice? "I'll be fine." In truth, it didn't hurt as much as it should. Probably another benefit of his situation. He seemed to heal a lot faster than normal these days.

"You sure?"

"Yeah, I just need to get something. Then I can go."

They drove on for a few minutes in silence. Several times, Dale looked over at Matt, but he never said anything. Finally, they pulled into the parking lot of Abbey's Antiques. The lights inside were off. Abbey was probably out again. Dale swung the car around to the side of the building and shut off the engine.

"Look, Cahill," Dale said, "for what it's worth, I'm real sorry about everything."

"It's all right, Officer."

"No, it ain't. This ain't like me. I don't know what came over me."

"It's okay." Matt knew what had come over him, but he wasn't about to tell Dale he'd been attacked by a shadow man. The guy'd been through enough already. All Matt wanted to do now was get his ax and get the hell out of Crawford.

"Probably stress," Dale mused. "I've been tracking that damn serial killer for months. It's one of the reasons I'm never home. That's probably why Abbey..." He didn't finish the thought, but Matt understood well enough. Dale blamed himself and his job for Abbey's infidelity. Matt would have offered him something comforting but wasn't sure what to say. Hell, for all he knew, Dale's assessment was right on target.

"Stress can fuck a person up pretty good," Matt said. *So can a baseball bat,* he added mentally.

"You sure you don't need a ride anywhere else?"

"No," Matt replied. "I'll just grab my ax from the shop and walk to the next bus terminal."

"But that's in Cranston. It's ten miles away."

"I'm used to walking," Matt replied. In truth, he'd have loved a ride to Cranston, but not from Dale. Who knew what would happen if the green sore came back?

It's only halftime.

Matt didn't want to find out. With any luck, he'd catch Abbey, and she could give him a ride. That is, if she would talk to him. He had his doubts, but he meant to try. He needed to talk to her about her husband and Mr. Dark. She claimed to have never seen him, which was probably a good thing, but he needed to warn her about him just in case. Besides, his ax was back at her place anyway, but he didn't think it would be a good idea to mention that to Dale.

"All right, then," Dale said. "Have a good life, Matt Cahill. Sorry about your head."

Matt got out of the car. "Sorry about your wife."

Dale held up his left hand. Matt noted the man was no longer wearing his wedding ring. "Soon to be ex-wife. You're right. She's just gonna keep doing it. But I don't have to live with it. Or her addiction."

"Addiction?"

"Yeah, Xanax or Keflex or something. I can't remember what it's called, but those damn little bottles are all over the place. Abbey says it's a sedative. She uses it to fight off panic attacks and shit like that. If you ask me, she's messed up enough without it."

Matt nodded. He had to agree. He opened the passenger-side door and stepped out, careful not to bump his head.

"By the way," Dale said. "That back door is probably locked. Here." He tossed something to Matt. It jingled in his fist when he caught it. A key ring. "The big one is the key you're looking for. Just leave them in the shop when you go."

"Any message for Abbey if I see her?"

"Give her the keys. She'll know what it means." Dale put the car in drive and wheeled slowly out of the parking lot. A quick left and the lawman was gone, leaving Matt alone in the back of *Abbey's Antiques* with the keys to the store.

He let himself in the back, shaking his head. Dale trusted him with the keys to his wife's business, even after everything that happened. Not that there was much left in the place to steal. Matt and Abbey had pretty much cleaned the whole place out. There were still a few things that needed to be moved, but Abbey should be able to take care of them herself. She could probably even return the box truck. Most of the remaining pieces should fit in the back of her van.

Matt stepped into the back room and walked toward the cot. His bag with all his things was still at Abbey's house, along with his ax. He'd have to wait for Abbey to show up. Sooner or later she would stop by to check on the shop, and he would try to talk to her then.

Matt settled down to wait.

It didn't take very long. About twenty minutes after he arrived, a pair of headlights shone in the front window of the store. They were high off the ground and far apart, just like they should be for a truck or van. Matt stood up and moved into the hallway. When the lights outside cut off, he heard the slam of the van's door. He was just about to say something when he heard another door slam, and then voices came to him from the front of the store.

Matt ducked back into the office. Abbey had someone with her? Who? It couldn't be Dale.

The tiny bell at the front door rang, and Abbey's voice followed it.

"...coming. I feel safer having someone with me," she said.

"I understand," came a second voice. A female voice. Matt thought it sounded familiar, but he couldn't quite place it. "I'm glad to help."

"He seemed like such a nice guy," Abbey said.

"He sure did," came the reply. "It must have been terrifying to learn you had a murderer at your very own house."

They were talking about him, Matt realized. His heart sank. Abbey wouldn't be giving him a ride tonight, or any other. Damn. He needed that ax. He couldn't bring himself to leave it behind.

"I should have known," Abbey said. "The way he stared at me when I asked him to chop some firewood. Gave me the creeps. I thought I was imagining things, but now I wonder."

"No use second-guessing yourself now," her guest said. She sounded younger, like a woman in her late teens or early twenties. "You're safe, and he's gone."

"Yes," Abbey said. "But I'd still appreciate it if you came home with me. You know, safety in numbers..."

The soft, sultry tone of her voice sent a shiver up Matt's spine. So Abbey played for both teams...interesting. He supposed it shouldn't come as such a surprise, but he hadn't really expected that. There would be more going on at Abbey's tonight than making sure it was safe. Poor Dale. He was right. Abbey was quite a vixen.

"Of course I will," the voice said.

"I just need to grab a few things first," Abbey said. "Will you wait here for a second?"

"Sure."

Footsteps approached from the front of the store. Matt looked around for a hiding place, not sure how she would react if she found him in her store waiting for her. He ducked behind a shelf full of old clocks and waited.

Abbey walked by, wearing her tight jeans and thin T-shirt. Her tennis shoes made almost no sound as she walked by Matt's hiding spot and into her office. She passed close enough so that Matt could almost have touched her, but she wasn't paying attention. Her eyes were focused ahead, not to the side, and Matt got a good look at her face as she passed.

Damn, she was gorgeous.

The memory of her face between his legs the night before came unbidden to his mind, and he found himself getting aroused. He shut his eyes and forced the image away. This would definitely be a bad time.

While she rattled around in her office, Matt poked his head around the back of the shelf and caught sight of the person with her. It was the young woman from McDonald's. Annie. She couldn't be more than twenty years old. Abbey was really robbing the cradle tonight.

Matt couldn't help but smile. Young Annie was in for quite a workout.

The sound of footsteps brought his mind back to the present. Abbey was leaving her office. The light clicked off, casting the whole building in darkness again, and Matt ducked back down behind the shelf.

Wait, he thought. *It's just Annie.* Matt knew he could handle the skinny girl from McDonald's. He was more worried about Abbey. She was solid and strong and could no doubt pack a good punch. With him already weak and reeling from his stint as a piñata, he didn't think he could fight off both of them. Still, he needed to get his ax. Maybe he would try to talk to her, after all.

He was just about to stand up when she walked by him again, and Matt's breath caught in his throat. He'd seen her right side as she walked into her office. Now, as she was walking out, he caught sight of the left side of her face.

And the large green sore on her left cheek.

CHAPTER TWELVE

Matt dialed the Crawford Police Department from a pay phone. It had taken him twenty minutes to find one, but he didn't have a cell phone and doubted anyone would let him in to use theirs. Word had spread around town that Matt might be a killer, and every person he passed shied away from him. As it was, he had to look up the number in the phone book. He'd almost called 911, but didn't know what he would tell them. He didn't even know Abbey's address. How could he inform them of what was going on?

No, he needed Dale.

The operator came on the line. "Crawford Police Department. Can I help you?"

"I need to speak to Dale Everett, please. It's an emergency."

"If this is an emergency, sir, you should call 9-1-1."

"No. I need Dale. Could you just get him on the line, please?"

There was a long pause. Then she said, "I'll see if I can get him on the line. I believe he's out patrolling."

"Thank you," Matt replied. He could have kicked himself for not seeing it sooner. Abbey's van, her big garage, the house way out in the country, and her addiction. Dale hadn't known what the drug was called, but Matt would have bet anything those bottles Dale talked about were labeled ketamine. What was it all the Blake County Killer's victims had in common? They were all young, attractive brunettes.

Just like Annie.

There was a crackle on the other end of the line, and then Dale's voice came though.

"This is Dale, can I help you?"

"Dale, it's Matt."

Another long pause. Then, "I thought you were leaving town. It says here you're at the pay phone by Walton and Fitch."

"I was going to leave. I still am, but something's come up. Something important. I need to meet with you. Now."

"What's this about, Matt?"

In the background, Matt heard the receptionist ask if Dale was talking to "that Cahill fella."

"I can't tell you everything because there isn't time, but it's about Abbey."

"I told you I'm done with her."

You might be done with her, but she *isn't done with the people of Crawford,* Matt thought. "It's not Abbey I'm worried about. It's Annie."

"Annie? Jordan? The kid from McDonald's? What's she got to—"

"Can you just come here and get me? Please? It's an emergency, Dale. We don't have much time."

It's only halftime. The game isn't over yet, Matt.

"It might already be too late," Matt said.

"All right, I'm coming. But if this is some sort of—"

"Thanks, Dale. See you soon." Matt hung up the phone.

Abbey was the Blake County Killer. It all added up. He should have seen it. But she didn't have any sores on her face when he met her, and she seemed so nice. Plus he'd been taken in by her similar ability to see evil, and her story was almost as sad as his own. No wonder he couldn't put the pieces together until now.

Plus, she was one hell of a wild fuck, he admitted.

Matt shook his head. *Focus!* He needed to figure out how to get Dale to believe him.

One thing at a time, Matt, he thought. *One thing at a time. Let him get here, first. Then worry about how to get him to believe you.*

The street was dark and eerie but not entirely silent. A faint wisp of laughter rolled up the sidewalk. If he didn't know better, Matt would have sworn it was Mr. Dark. He looked behind him but saw no one. To his right was an empty building that looked like it had once housed a Burger King but now just stood silent sentinel on the sidewalk. To his left the empty street yawned, lifeless and black, with not a car in sight.

Must be my imagination. He tried to convince himself that was the case as he looked up and down the street. All the streetlights in this section of town seemed to be out, and Matt waited in near darkness for Dale to come. He stepped away from the phone booth and walked toward a wood and metal bench set back from the road, barely visible in the shadows of Fitch Street. Might as well have a seat while he waited.

Matt reached the bench and stopped cold. It was a coincidence. It had to be. There was no way the bastard could have known where he would be.

On the bench, stuck to the wooden planks, was a half-finished lollipop.

This time, it was not so easy to dismiss the mad laughter. Matt turned to see the asshole standing right behind him.

"You!" Matt snarled, and clenched his fists. He took a step toward Mr. Dark, who shimmered in the low light. "What did you do to Abbey?"

Mr. Dark licked his lips and flashed Matt a lascivious wink. "A better question would be: What *haven't* I done?"

"You sorry piece of shit." Matt swung his fist but connected only with empty air.

Laughter at his back. Matt swung around and launched another blow, a powerful roundhouse that would clean the clock of any normal man.

Mr. Dark wasn't there.

Overbalanced, Matt fell to the ground. He managed to get his right arm up in time to shield his face from the concrete, but he hit hard, scraping his palm and sending a sharp stab of pain through his left wrist.

"Son of a bitch!" Matt said, holding his hand close to his chest.

"I've been called much worse," Mr. Dark said. "Your lack of imagination is showing."

"Fuck you."

"No. Thanks for the offer, though. I've got to get going. Wouldn't want to miss the show."

"I know all about Abbey," Matt said. "And I'm going to stop her before she kills anyone else."

"You really are simple, aren't you?" Mr. Dark shook his head. "It makes me wonder why they chose you."

"Who? Chose me for what?"

"No matter," Mr. Dark continued. "You'll be in prison soon enough."

"What?"

Just then headlights pierced the night, and Matt had to blink at the sudden brightness. When they faded, he was left staring at a black-and-white hood with the words "Crawford P.D." painted in reverse.

The driver's door opened, and Dale stepped out, holding a flashlight. "Matt? What are you doin' on the ground? You okay?"

"I'm fine." Matt rose to his feet, looking left and right but seeing no sign of Mr. Dark. "But we need to get to Abbey's right away."

Dale balked. "Why?"

"I'll tell you in the car," Matt said as he stepped around to the passenger side. His wrist felt sprained, but he couldn't stop to see a doctor just yet. He crawled into the car and sat in the passenger seat, closing the door with a grunt of pain.

"I don't like this," Dale muttered as he got back into the car and closed his own door.

"Neither do I," Matt said. "Just hurry."

Prison, Mr. Dark had said. It took Matt a minute to figure out what he meant.

Abbey had taken Annie back to her cabin in the woods. The same place she'd taken Matt. The same place where he chopped several cords of wood for her.

The same place he'd left his ax.

CHAPTER THIRTEEN

"Bullshit." The vein in Dale's forehead throbbed so hard Matt could actually see it. "There's no way Abbey is the killer."

How could he convince Dale without telling him about their ability to see evil? He'd never get Dale to swallow the idea that Abbey was almost eighty years old. Hell, Matt wasn't sure he believed it. If it wasn't for the picture that he'd mistaken for Abbey's mom...

Abbey's mom! That's it!

"Dale," he said, "who was the killer's first victim?"

"Abbey's mom," Dale replied. "Her name was Abbey, too. But she was an older lady. She'd lived here almost her whole life."

"Did she have any children?"

"Just the one. Abbey," Dale said. "But she didn't live in Crawford. She lived with her father up in Pocatah, Kentucky. Abbey moved here right before her mom died. Then she decided to take over the store since there was no one else. You should have seen her. She was a wreck."

"Did Abbey, the older Abbey, ever mention that she had a daughter in Kentucky?" Matt asked.

Dale grunted. "I can't recall if she ever did. But now that you mention it, I don't think so."

"So Abbey moves here, then her mom dies, and she takes over the store. Just like that?"

Dale didn't say anything. He just stared at the road ahead.

"You didn't find that suspicious at all?"

Dale shook his head. "She seemed so scared. So afraid. I never thought she could have..."

Matt understood. Dale had never considered that Abbey could be a suspect because he'd never *wanted* to. "The stuff Abbey has in little vials at her house," Matt said, "the stuff she has a ton of—it's ketamine, isn't it?"

Dale's mouth dropped open. "Yeah, that's the stuff. How did you know?"

"Isn't that the same drug the coroner found in every single one of the Blake County Killer's victims?"

Dale looked at Matt, and understanding lit his face.

"Son of a bitch," he said. "All this time. Could the answer have been right under my goddamn *nose*?"

"I bet if you call the Pocatah Police Department," Matt said, "you'll find out they have a string of unsolved murders. Murders that stopped three years ago. Right about the time that Abbey moved here."

"No," Dale said. "I still don't believe it. Not Abbey. There's an explanation. I'm sure of it. I'll drive you out to her place, but just to prove you wrong."

"I hope I am wrong," Matt said. Deep down, he knew he wasn't.

CHAPTER FOURTEEN

They pulled up to the house just after midnight. Matt had asked Dale to kill the car's headlights, but the officer had refused, insisting that there was nothing to worry about. Matt disagreed, but knew he couldn't win the argument, so he let it go. With any luck the two were in the bedroom, which was at the back of the house. If so, the house was wide enough to block the headlights and they could surprise her.

If not, then Abbey would know they were here.

Luck was not with them that night.

Abbey opened the front door and stood silhouetted by the light of her living room. She raised her left arm to her face, probably trying to block the car's headlights. Maybe they weren't such a bad idea, after all. "Who's there?" she asked.

Dale got out of the car. "Abbey, it's me."

"Dale? What are you doing here?"

"I just want to talk to you, hon," Dale said.

"Damn it, Dale! I thought I told you this was *my* place. Go home. I'll be there tomorrow."

Matt stepped out of the car. "I don't think that's going to happen, Abbey."

Abbey turned her head toward him. "Matt?"

"Yeah, it's me. And we both know you aren't going home tomorrow."

"I don't know what you are talking about," she said. She turned back to Dale. "You didn't tell me you brought company."

"We just want to talk to you," Dale said.

"Fine. But turn those goddamn headlights off. I can't see a thing."

Dale reached into the car. Matt caught a glimpse of something behind her back. It was long and straight and glinted dully in the light.

"No!" Matt shouted, but it was too late. The headlights snapped off, and Abbey brought the shotgun up faster than he or Dale could follow.

The shot sounded like a cannon.

Dale grunted in pain as his body flew backward in a spray of blood and gore. He landed in a heap a few feet away from the cruiser, blood flowing freely from a large hole in his thigh.

"Fuck!" Matt yelled, and dove behind the car just as another shot peppered the dirt where he'd been standing.

"I told him not to come here," Abbey said. "This is my place. My *private* place."

Matt poked his head around the back of the car just in time to see Abbey step off the porch. Now that the light wasn't directly behind her, he saw the huge gaping sore on the side of her face. The edges were rotted away, leaving nothing but dead skin and insect larvae. As he watched, the area of rot spread across her whole face, covering her nose and mouth. Even from ten feet away, the stench of decay was almost a physical presence.

But as horrifying as her face had become, it still didn't scare him as much as the shotgun in her hands. And she was coming toward the car.

Fuck.

Matt scrambled around to the driver's side, where Dale lay on his back in a growing pool of blood. The lawman's left thigh was a mess. Blood poured out of it like water from a pitcher. His breath came in rapid gasps that sounded like wet slaps. Dale's eyes stared up at the sky but didn't seem to settle on anything for more than a few seconds. His whole body shook, making him look like he was having a seizure.

Matt grabbed Dale's belt and slid it off, then jerked it tight around the injured man's upper thigh and cinched it into a makeshift tourniquet. The blood slowed, but didn't stop. It would have to do until he could get medical attention.

This was his fault. He had insisted Dale come to Abbey's. If he'd just left Crawford like he was supposed to, Dale would be fine and probably filing divorce papers right now. Just another person Matt had managed to hurt with his very presence. Maybe he'd be better off if Abbey took that shotgun to his head.

"You still here, Matt?" Abbey asked from the other side of the car. "Where'd you go? You can't hide from me, you know."

Matt would have to worry about Dale later. Right now he needed something from the fallen cop's waist. He reached down, trying not to look at the ruin of Dale's leg, and unclipped the holster for Dale's service revolver. He wiggled it free and brought it to his face. A .38-caliber Smith & Wesson, minus the safety and, thank God, sporting a full cylinder.

He brought it up just as Abbey rounded the back of the car, leading with her shotgun.

Matt was faster. He fired off two rounds as fast as the revolver would shoot, and one of them hit Abbey in her left arm.

She yelped in pain as the bullet spun her in a circle, sending her shotgun to the dirt. "You cocksucking asshole! I'll kill you for that!"

You were gonna kill me, anyway, Matt thought. He jumped to his feet and ran around the car, hoping to catch her on the ground, but all he saw of her was her backside as she ran back into the house, presumably for another weapon.

Matt sprinted up the yard to the doorway, not wanting to give her time to find another gun. With luck, he could catch her unarmed and force her to surrender, and then he could call the police. He didn't want to kill her any more than he'd wanted to kill Andy, but he couldn't let her hurt any more people, and Annie was probably still in the house. If she was even still alive.

He stepped into the house, looking left and right, but there was no sign of Abbey. A dull green telephone on the end table gave him an idea, and he pulled it off the hook and dialed 9-1-1.

"Nine-one-one. What's your emergency?" a voice said.

"Officer Everett has been shot. He needs medical attention. Send a car to—" *Shit!* Matt didn't know the address.

A muffled cry from somewhere in the house caught his attention. He set the phone's receiver on the table and walked deeper into the house. He might not know the address, but the operator at 911 would. Her voice came through the line asking more questions, sounding tinny and small. When she couldn't get an answer, she'd have to send a car.

Or so he hoped.

Directly in front of him was a large living area, which opened onto a deck on the rear of the place. He knew from his previous visit that the kitchen and dining room stood to his left, while Abbey's bedroom was to his right. He'd spent most of his time here either in the bedroom or in the backyard, and while he hadn't seen any weapons in the bedroom, that didn't mean there weren't any there. Besides, that's probably where Abbey had Annie. He set off down the hallway, keeping his back to the wall and listening for any sound of her presence.

Along the way he noticed more pictures on the wall. Lots more. They had been there the other night, of course, but he hadn't paid any attention to them. Now that he looked, they were all of Abbey and various men. There was one of her and Dale, obviously only a few years old, and one of her and another man that, by their clothes, looked like it was taken in the seventies. Beyond that was another picture of her in front of the old car lot with the man she claimed was her husband, Clark. And beyond that were many more. All of them showed Abbey as one half of a smiling couple through the decades. There was even one done in the very old style, with the man sitting in a chair while Abbey stood behind him with her hand on his shoulder. The clothing looked to be from around the early 1900s.

Jesus. How old *was* she?

Matt stopped in the middle of the hallway, looking back at the line of pictures. Was that what was in store for him? Would he someday have a hallway full of old photos, too? *Not if I let her kill me tonight*, he thought, forcing his mind back to the present. The implications of Abbey's pictures would have to wait. First he had to stop her from killing Annie. He walked the rest of the hallway's length. It ended at the bedroom door.

Matt put his hand on the doorknob, then took a deep breath, and turned it. He pushed open the bedroom door a half inch at a time, waiting for the gunshot that would end his life. When it didn't come, he opened the door the whole way.

There was Annie, gagged and tied to the bed but very much alive, despite a few cuts across her chest that oozed blood onto her shredded T-shirt. Matt breathed a sigh of relief. "Thank God you're all right."

Annie's eyes grew wide when she saw Matt, and she tried to mumble something under the gag, but Matt couldn't make it out. He crossed the room and leaned over the bed, putting his finger to his lips.

"She's still here somewhere," Matt whispered. "I'm gonna undo your gag, but you have to keep quiet, okay? Nod if you understand me."

She nodded.

"Good," Matt said, and he reached over and pulled the gag down over her chin. "That better?"

"Yeah," she said. "That bitch is fucking crazy. Get me the hell outta here."

"I will. Just give me a second." Matt tried to undo the knots on the ropes. His wrist flared with pain. He gritted his teeth and tried again but soon realized he couldn't maneuver his fingers while holding the gun, so he set it on the nightstand. "You let me know if you see her, okay?"

"You got it, man."

Matt went to work on the knots, but he couldn't loosen them. Abbey had tied them very tight. He could probably get them if he had an hour to spare, but he didn't. "Shit."

"There's a knife in the top drawer of her nightstand," Annie said. "It's the one she used to cut me."

Matt opened the drawer and grabbed the knife. The smell of decay hung in the room like an invisible fog. *Abbey must really be rotting,* he thought. *I can still smell her in here.* He knelt beside the bed and sawed through the rope on Annie's right wrist. Then he went to cut the one at her feet. As he moved, he caught another whiff of the decay. It smelled strong. Too strong.

Annie shifted in the bed and Matt caught a glimpse of the girl's skin beneath her torn pants. He stopped sawing through the rope and stared at the greenish, oozing skin hidden under Annie's clothes. No wonder the smell had been so strong.

"I should have known," he said, just before the gun barrel poked him in the side of the head.

"Finish cutting," Annie instructed, punctuating her words by jabbing the barrel into Matt's temple. Matt resumed sawing the knife through the rope, trying to think of a way to dodge a bullet from point-blank range.

"I got him, Abbey!" Annie yelled.

From somewhere deep in the house, Abbey's voice floated into the bedroom. "I'm coming."

"How long?" Matt asked, still sawing through the rope. "How long have you and Abbey been working together?"

"Since the beginning," she said. "Right after she came down from Kentucky."

"Abbey's not even her real name, is it?"

"Fuck if I know. Fuck if I care. That pussy's so good, she could call herself Fred Flintstone if she wanted. You just get back to cuttin' that rope before I spray your brains all over the wall behind you."

Matt cut through the rope on her right leg and moved to the one tied to her left. "Bitch sure can tie a knot," he muttered.

Annie smiled and ran her tongue across her upper lip. "That ain't all she can do."

Too true, Matt thought.

Abbey stepped into the room carrying Matt's ax. Her face was half eaten away with rot, and Matt could see her lower teeth and part of her jawbone though the dead tissue on her cheek. The smell was overpowering, and he swallowed the urge to vomit. He didn't want to look at her. How had she hidden the decay from him while they were...He couldn't even finish the thought.

"I knew you'd come to save her," Abbey said, pointing at Annie.

"What do you mean?" Matt asked.

"We watched that spineless husband of mine drop you off at the store," she said. "I knew you were there. But I needed you here, out in the country, where no one would hear anything."

So the whole conversation back at Abbey's Antiques was for his benefit. Another trap. "And I fell right into it," he said.

"You sure did," Annie giggled. "She told me you would."

Abbey smiled. "Toss the knife aside, Matt," she said.

"Tell her not to shoot me." Matt glanced at Annie, who was still pointing the gun at Matt's head.

Abbey set the ax in the corner of the room, then walked around the bed, giving Matt a wide berth. She stopped on the other side of the bed and held out her hand to Annie. "Give it to me," she said.

Annie looked disappointed. "But I wanted to do this one."

"He's mine," Abbey said, her face stern. "You can finish off my sorry-ass excuse for a husband. Give me the gun."

Annie handed the pistol over. Abbey took it and pointed it at Matt's chest. "Don't worry, hon," she said to Annie. "You'll get to decide head or gut. I'm just gonna be the one to pull the trigger."

That made Annie smile, and she was about to open her mouth, but Abbey cut her off. "Not yet," she said. "Think about it for a minute."

She nodded and smiled at Matt. Head or gut. If Matt had to choose, he'd rather get shot in the head. It would take less time to die. But one look at Annie's subtle smirk told him the girl from McDonald's had already made up her mind, and it didn't jibe with Matt's preference.

Abbey walked back around to the front of the room, keeping the gun pointed at Matt the whole way. "The knife?" she asked.

Matt tossed the knife to the side of the room, thus relinquishing his only weapon. He eyed the blade as it lay on the carpet, glinting red in the light of Abbey's bedroom.

She stepped in front of him and squatted down, bringing her face level to his, and poked the pistol into his chest. Her shoulder where he'd shot her was wrapped with a bandage that had started to bleed through already. She wouldn't be using that arm for a while. From this vantage point, he could see that the rotten green patch had spread all the way to her chest. It disappeared under her shirt, leaving Matt to wonder how far it went. If she took off her shirt, would he see her ribs? He decided he didn't want to know, but it did bring up an interesting question.

"How did you hide them?" he asked.

"The sores?" Abbey replied. "It's easy. Live long enough and you'll figure it out," she finished with a mischievous wink. Matt knew what it meant. He wouldn't live long enough to figure out what to have for breakfast tomorrow, let alone how a person could hide sores.

Abbey reached up and grabbed his chin, forcing him to look her in the face. "So, did you miss me, baby?" she asked.

"Doesn't look like it," Matt replied, nodding toward her shoulder.

Abbey smiled, revealing a mouth full of blackened gums and rotting teeth. "Clever," she said. Then she leaned in close so she could whisper in his ear. "But you shouldn't have done that. I was going to let you live."

"Bullshit."

Abbey pulled away, a wounded expression on her face. "It's true. I thought we were kindred spirits. Soul mates, even. Even though you went running after Brad like some goddamn knight in shining armor. Why? To save that whore wife of his? She deserved it. She's been fucking everything that moves for years. But even then I thought I could change your outlook, given enough time. Then you shot me. I could have dealt with you being a white hat, but I draw the line at letting you get away with shooting me."

"I don't believe you."

"Who gives a fuck what you believe?" she said. Then she turned to Annie. "Okay, sweetheart, did you choose? Head or gut?"

"Gut," Annie said without a moment's hesitation.

Matt groaned.

"Gut it is," Abbey said. She lifted the revolver and pointed it at Annie, who stared back in shock and fear.

"What are you—"

The sound of two shots fired in rapid succession cut her off, and her question turned into a howl of pain as two slugs tore into her abdomen. Her left arm and leg were still tied to the bedposts, preventing her from curling into a fetal position, but she slapped her right hand onto her belly in a vain attempt to hold her life's blood inside her ruptured gut. She stared at Abbey, her face a mixture of pain and confusion, and started to babble incoherently. The words were too garbled for Matt to make them out, but the meaning was clear.

"Hey, don't blame me." Abbey shrugged. "You're the one who picked gut." Then she pointed the gun back at Matt. "I've got two bullets left," she said. "Before I kill you, I think I owe you one."

She pointed the gun at Matt's shoulder and fired. The sound rang through the small room like thunder, and Matt screamed as fire punched him in the shoulder and stayed there to burn. He brought his hand up to stem the flow of blood and gasped in pain.

Being shot fucking hurt!

"Smarts a bit, doesn't it?" Abbey said, chuckling.

"Fuck off."

"You deserve it. You shot me first."

Matt wanted to point out that she'd almost blasted him to bloody bits outside long before he'd shot her but didn't figure it would do any good.

Abbey squatted down in front of him again and shook her head. "Such a waste," she said. "We've been waiting for you, you know."

"Why me?"

"Not you specifically. A drifter. Someone who doesn't belong. Someone no one would trust. Why do you think Annie worked that shitty-ass job? She's been keeping her eyes peeled for someone like you to come along. We were beginning to give up hope. When you stepped into the restaurant, with your line about 'just passing through,' she almost jumped for joy. She couldn't wait to tell me about you."

"I don't understand," Matt replied.

"Yes, you do."

"He probably doesn't," came a familiar voice from out in the hall. Mr. Dark stepped into the bedroom, a red lollipop in his mouth and a hideous grin on his face. "He's really quite simple, you know."

CHAPTER FIFTEEN

Matt stared at Mr. Dark for a few heartbeats, then looked back to Abbey and shook his head. "Is anything you've told me true?"

"Oh, don't look so surprised," Abbey said. "You should listen to him sometime. He's brilliant. Hell, he's been around forever and knows just about everything there is to know. He even knows a lot about you, Matt. In fact, he told me you'd never go for this."

"I sure did," Mr. Dark said. "Did I call that one, or what?"

"Yes, you did," she said, then looked back at Matt. "Like I said. It's a shame."

"Go for what?" Then Matt understood. The van, the escalation of the attacks, the fake divorce, even killing Annie. "You're leaving," he said. "And you wanted me to come with you."

Mr. Dark smiled again, and Abbey leaned over and kissed Matt on the forehead. A loud, wet smack that made him want to wipe his brow. Her lips felt like a pair of rotting leeches. The last thing he wanted was to die with any of her goop on him.

"If you hadn't shot me, I'd be fucking your brains out right now," Abbey said, much to Mr. Dark's amusement. "I hope you remember that."

Matt stared at the gun in her hand. The gun with only one bullet left. It had his fingerprints all over it. When forensics pulled the bullets out of Annie's gut and Matt's skull, they would be a match. He doubted there would even be much of an investigation. Here he was, a drifter, who just happened to come through town and fuck a local cop's wife. All Abbey had to do now was finish off Dale. Then, with the cop dead and the wife missing, they would look at Matt as the prime suspect.

He thought about his call to the police. He'd asked for Dale and refused to talk to the receptionist. That would look bad. The local police would think he and Annie set the whole thing up to kill Dale, but something had gone wrong. Still, it didn't quite add up, and Matt knew why.

"But you shot Dale with the shotgun," Matt said. "My prints aren't on that."

"Nope," Abbey agreed, "but soon hers will be." She nodded to Annie, who grunted a weak reply. "Sorry, sweetheart. It would have been gut no matter what you picked. I needed you to stay alive long enough to grip the shotgun." Abbey winked.

"Fuuuuuuh yooooo," Annie wheezed.

"Not likely," Abbey replied, then turned her attention back to Matt. "Your prints are all over that knife," she said. "That'll be interesting. Especially when the police match it to eight of the Blake County Killer's victims. You'll be famous all over again."

"But what about you? When they don't find you here, they'll know you were part of this."

"Oh, they'll find my body in a few weeks. It'll be floating down Black Creek. One last victim of the Blake County

Killer. They might be surprised to find it with a full set of ID, but at least that should make it easier for them, since they won't be able to identify the face."

By then no one would even be looking for it. Matt knew how small towns worked. He grew up in one. He was just a drifter. No one knew him, but by tomorrow morning half the town would swear they'd seen him around the last few years but never thought anything about it. He'd be found guilty post mortem, and that would be it. Then Abbey would find another partner in another city and start all over again, this time with help from Mr. Dark.

Like she needed it.

"So, Matt," Abbey said, raising the gun to his forehead. "Mr. Dark here is pretty anxious to get this over with. Is there anything else you'd like to say before I kill you? Make it good, now."

"Just one last question," Matt said.

"What is it?"

The sound of sirens came to them, warbling and loud. Above, the steady chop of a helicopter could be heard, its rotors getting louder and louder by the second. Matt smiled.

"Did you check your phone?" he asked.

CHAPTER SIXTEEN

Abbey cocked her head to the side, a frown on her rotting features. The sirens grew louder by the second.

"Your hall phone is off the hook, Abbey," Matt said. "I wonder why."

Understanding lit Abbey's face. "You asshole."

Matt nodded. "I'm not that dumb. They'll be here soon, too. You wanna get out of here? Better do it quick."

"My, my." Mr. Dark grinned at Matt and winked. "That was quite clever."

Abbey turned to face Mr. Dark, probably intending to tell him to shut the fuck up. Matt would never know what she was about to say, because he seized her momentary distraction and grabbed the gun. Abbey jerked her hand back, but Matt held his grip, and the two of them wrestled with the pistol while the sirens approached. Matt's finger inadvertently closed on the cylinder release and for a moment it came free, but Abbey put her hand on it and forced it back into the body of the gun with a click, pinching Matt's palm in the process.

Matt was stronger than Abbey, his body hardened by years of heavy manual labor, but Abbey was faster. She twisted to the side and launched a straight kick to Matt's face. Matt was able to jump aside, but the blow hit him in his wounded shoulder. The flash of pain that rolled over him made the initial gunshot feel like a paper cut. He lost his grip on the gun and fell to the floor, trying to clear the stars from his vision.

When his vision cleared, Abbey was standing over him, the gun pointed right at his temple. Mr. Dark was nowhere to be seen.

"See you in hell," Abbey said. Her voice sounded muffled, probably because of the maggots chewing on her tongue. She pulled the trigger.

Click!

Abbey stared at the gun in her hands, the question forming on her rotting lips. "What the fuck?" She pulled the trigger again.

Click!

Matt held up his clenched hand and slowly opened it, allowing Abbey to see the bullet he'd managed to palm during the struggle. He smiled as he let it drop on the floor.

Just then, two police officers burst into the bedroom, pistols drawn and pointed right at Abbey's chest.

"Drop the gun," one of them yelled.

Abbey turned to face them and dropped the pistol to the floor. "Thank God you're here, officers," she said. "I caught this asshole breaking in. He shot Annie Jordan, but I was able to—"

"Save it," the officer said. "Turn around and put your hands behind your back."

"But I—"

"Now!"

Abbey turned around to face Matt, who watched as the officer walked up behind her and pulled what looked like a thick plastic zip tie from his belt. *Better than handcuffs*, he thought.

"We found Dale," the officer said to Abbey. "Alive. He told us everything. Next time you shoot a cop, make sure you kill him. Otherwise he's just gonna put the finger on you."

"I'll take that under advisement," Abbey said. The look on her face could have cracked granite.

Just as the cop was about to bind her wrists, Abbey spun into a low kick that sent him to the floor. The other cop fired his weapon, but the shot went wide and thudded into the wall behind Matt. Faster than Matt could follow, Abbey grabbed the gun from the downed officer and fired a round at the cop who was still on his feet, hitting him square in the chest. He flew backward into the hall as Abbey readjusted her aim and pointed the gun at the prone officer's head.

"What was that advice you gave me about shooting cops?" she asked, winking. Then she pulled the trigger.

Outside, new voices shouted in alarm at the gunshots, and the sound of a dozen booted feet pounded through the house. Abbey didn't seem to notice. She turned to face Matt.

Matt had grabbed the only thing he could find to use as a weapon, his grandfather's ax, which Abbey had leaned against the wall. The familiar weight and heft felt like an old friend, and a comfortable warmth spread through him as he swung.

Abbey pulled the trigger.

The ax bit into her shoulder.

Both of them went to the floor. Matt heard the bullet whizz by his head, missing him by a hair's breadth. He landed hard on his injured shoulder, sending fresh waves of pain through his whole body. The room blurred and spun, leaving him in a state of vertigo. The blood loss didn't help. He tried to stand, but somehow his feet wouldn't listen, and the last thing he heard was one of the cops yell, "She's alive!" just before he slid into darkness.

CHAPTER SEVENTEEN

"You should stay a few more days, just to be safe," Dr. Mayhew said. "The bullet missed your humerus and rotator cuff, but you still have some soft-tissue damage."

Matt looked up from zipping his pants. "I'll be fine," he said. "I'm a fast healer." His left arm hung from the sling the doctor had given him, but he still had full use of his right. He extended his arm and shook the doctor's hand. "Thank you," he said.

Mayhew snorted and left the room, muttering about stubborn patients. Matt watched him go, a smile on his stubbled face. The good doctor had sewn him back together after the paramedics brought him in two nights ago. He'd had a slug in his shoulder that had to be removed, and he'd lost a good deal of blood. Mayhew had removed the slug, and several pints of blood later Matt awoke feeling much better. Mayhew had then spent the entire next day telling Matt how lucky he was, that he could have lost the use of his arm, but Matt wasn't so sure.

His mind kept flashing back to all the photos of Abbey in her house. Some of them were more than a hundred years old, yet she looked no older than thirty. Would that be his future, as well? He hoped not, but given the rapid state of his body's healing and the way Abbey hadn't aged at all in more than a century, he had to wonder if that last bullet would have killed him if he hadn't moved in time.

He didn't know.

And he didn't intend to find out.

He slipped into his shoes, which were very hard to tie with one hand, and stood up. The hospital room reminded him of the one he'd had back at the university. Cold, white, barren, and far too expensive for his tastes. In the case of the university, they'd claimed he owed them millions but were willing to wipe the slate clean for a few more days of tests and tissue samples. Then, as now, he was sick of the room and just wanted to go.

While Dr. Mayhew certainly wasn't trying to get Matt to stay for his own personal gain, the end result would be the same: Matt would sit in this damn white and bare room with several beeping machines until he went out of his mind.

Further out of it, he corrected.

"No, thanks," Matt said to himself. He grabbed the bag with his things. The only item missing was his ax, which the police had taken as evidence. He supposed he wouldn't be getting that back for a long time, if ever.

He walked out into the hallway, already feeling better than he had when he'd woken up in the ER two days ago. Matt hadn't been lying when he told Dr. Mayhew he was a fast healer. He just chose to leave out *how* fast. Ever since he'd come back from the dead, his body had seemed stronger and more able to heal, and this time seemed no different. His left shoulder was sore, but that was about it, and his sprained wrist didn't hurt at all. Tomorrow morning there would likely just be an angry red scar on his shoulder. Next week there probably wouldn't even be that much.

A blessing or a curse? Matt had no idea.

Mr. Dark's jibe came back to him. *You really are simple, aren't you? It makes me wonder why they chose you.*

So who the hell were "they?" And what did they want with Matt?

One thing at a time, Matt, he thought. *Get out of this damn hospital first.*

"Good fucking advice," he said, and left the room.

—

A familiar face was waiting to greet him when he reached the lobby. Officer Dale Everett hobbled up to him on a pair of shiny aluminum crutches. His left leg was heavily bandaged, but Dale was smiling for the first time Matt could recall. He extended his right hand to Matt. "Thanks for saving my life, Cahill," he said. "I was wrong about you. You're a good guy."

"Glad to help, Officer," Matt replied. "I see you're feeling better."

Dale snorted. "It's just one leg. I have another."

Matt chuckled. "How is Abbey enjoying jail?"

Dale said nothing, but his expression darkened. He looked at the floor and sighed.

"What happened?" Matt asked.

"Abbey escaped."

"How?"

"Somehow she got out of the wrist restraints. She killed both of the officers in the car and took off with the cruiser. We found it the next day about forty miles west, headed toward Nashville, but that's where the trail went cold."

Matt looked at the front entrance of the hospital. The sun shone through the glass and hit the polished white floor, making the room a little too bright. Tiny motes of dust floated in and out of the sunbeam, whisked away by the wind of people walking by.

"So she's out there. Right now. And no one knows where," Matt said.

Dale nodded. Somehow, the room upstairs no longer seemed like such a bad place to be.

"Damn," Matt said.

"Yeah, that's about how I feel about it, too," Dale replied.

The two stood in the lobby for several minutes, Matt lost in his thoughts of Abbey. Dale's thoughts were probably similar, but Matt wasn't about to ask. Matt had lost his wife to cancer several years ago. Dale had just lost his to another type of cancer, only in his case she wasn't dead, just gone. Probably planning her next killing spree. Knowing Abbey, it would eventually bring her back here to Crawford for revenge. Matt didn't think it would be a good idea to bring that up. Besides, Dale probably knew it, anyway.

"So you've come to see me off?" Matt asked.

"Sort of," Dale replied. "I came to offer you a ride. Want a lift to Cranston?"

"You bet."

—

Twenty minutes later, Matt and Dale were headed east on Interstate 90 toward Cranston in a Crawford P.D. cruiser. Dale had been making small talk the whole way. How was Matt feeling? Did the doctor treat him well? Where was he headed next? Matt answered every question as precisely as he could, but he got the impression Dale was working up to something.

Dale finally spilled it when they reached the Cranston city limits.

"You know, Matt," he said, "there was a reward for information leading to the arrest of the Blake County Killer. Fifty thousand dollars."

"That's a lot of money, Dale. But she escaped. She won't be convicted."

"Eventually we'll catch her," Dale replied. "When we do, we'll make sure she doesn't escape again. The reward will still be valid. If you leave me a way to contact you, I'll make sure you get it."

Matt thought about it for a moment. Fifty grand was a lot of money. He could probably do a lot of good with it. Hell, maybe he could even buy a reliable car to get from place to place. And gas, and insurance, and maybe even a decent hotel every now and then. And then...

Matt smiled and shrugged. And then what? Where would it stop?

"When that day comes," he said, "give the money to the families of the officers Abbey killed the night she shot me."

"You sure?"

Matt nodded. "I don't need it. Hell, I couldn't really use it. Those guys died saving my life. Maybe it'll do their families some good."

"I thought you'd say that." Dale pulled into the Gray Line terminal and parked the cruiser. Matt grabbed his bag and reached out to shake the cop's hand a final time.

"Hang on," Dale said. "I have something for you." Dale got out of the car and walked around back. Matt shrugged and did likewise.

Dale opened his trunk and pulled out Matt's ax. "Here you go, Cahill. You should probably take this with you."

Matt, too stunned to speak, reached out and grasped the handle. The familiar warmth spread through his arm, and he couldn't help but smile as he held his grandfather's ax once again. He brought it close to his chest and looked up at Dale, who smiled a big, toothy grin.

"Thank you," Matt said. "This means a lot to me."

Dale nodded.

"I thought it was evidence..."

"You thought *what* was evidence?" Dale asked with a grin.

"Thank you," Matt said again.

"You saved my life. It was the least I could do."

Matt shook Dale's hand one last time, then shoved the ax into his duffel bag and turned to walk into the terminal.

—

Matt sat on the bus, drinking a Coke he'd bought from the vending machine. He was the only passenger to depart from the Cranston terminal. The driver had inspected his duffel before letting him board and insisted he leave the ax in the compartment under the bus.

"You can't bring that on board," the driver said, pointing at it.

Matt knew the drill. He had placed the ax in the storage compartment and climbed into the bus.

Now, half an hour later, he wanted a snack. He'd bought a bag of chips back at the terminal and stuffed them into his duffel for later. He unzipped the bag and rummaged through his belongings, searching for the blue and silver foil pack. It didn't take long to find it, but as he pulled it out, a small yellow envelope fell out of the bag and plopped onto the floor.

Matt picked it up and examined it. The smell of rose perfume reached his nose.

"Abbey," he breathed.

The envelope contained an old photograph. He pulled it out and was not surprised to see it was the one of her and Clark at the car dealership.

He couldn't imagine when she'd stuck it in his bag. The police had arrested her and taken her to the hospital while the paramedics revived him. The only possibility he could think of was that Abbey had paid him a visit in the hospital.

He turned the photo over and read the back. Near the top right, in ink that had dried long before Matt was even born, someone had written the words *Mina and Clark, October 14, 1947.*

Below that, in much fresher ink, she had written him a note.

Matt,
This was fun. We'll have to do it again sometime. The sooner the better.
Abbey
P.S. Mr. Dark says hello.

So she had been Mina back in 1947. How many names had she taken over the years? What was her real name? Had she always been evil? Or had she once been like Matt? Just a poor soul who tried to fight the evil around her any way she could? Would Matt become like her if he couldn't stop Mr. Dark? He recalled Abbey's gleeful expression as she pumped two bullets into Annie's belly. Was that his destiny, as well?

He stared at the picture for a few moments, then put it back into the envelope and shoved it into his bag. *One thing at a time, Matt,* he thought. *One thing at a time.*

EPILOGUE

Dale sat in the station watching the bulletins, looking for any sign of Abbey. So far there hadn't been any sightings, but that didn't mean anything. The United States is a big country, and Abbey could be anywhere in it. Hell, for that matter, she could have left the country altogether. He sighed, then leaned back into his chair, rubbing his temples with his thumbs. All the letters were starting to blur together. He'd been at this for days. Maybe he needed a break.

He stood up and walked into the front entrance of the Crawford Police Department. The building was small and compact, but fairly modern. The town had built it in 2003 at a large cost to the taxpayers, but it had been necessary. The old P.D. was so outdated and ancient that one of the cell walls had collapsed in 2001, allowing several inmates to escape and putting another in the hospital. The large open lobby afforded him a view of the front doors, which were made from big sheets of bulletproof Plexiglas.

Outside, a large black SUV pulled up to the station and parked in front of the doors. A big man in black sunglasses stepped out. He wore an impeccable black suit and black shoes that shone like glass. His head was clean shaven and free of any hint of stubble. *Meticulous* was the word that came to Dale's mind when he thought of the man's appearance.

The stranger entered the station—he had to duck to fit his head under doorway —and took off his sunglasses. After several seconds spent looking around the lobby, his eyes settled on Dale, who was in full uniform. His face turned to concrete, and he approached. His walk was cool, measured, and confident. His demeanor exuded quiet control. *Ex-military,* Dale guessed.

Dale stepped forward and extended his hand. "Officer Everett. Can I help you?"

The stranger pulled a card from his pocket and placed it in Dale's outstretched hand. It bore the logo of some university hospital up north—Washington, he thought—as well as a name: Dr. Franklin H. Simpson, PhD. What the hell was a doctor from a Washington hospital doing in Crawford, Tennessee?

"What can I do for you, Dr. Simpson?"

Simpson frowned. His hard, chiseled features and solid, muscular body—only partially hidden by the suit—didn't remind Dale of any doctor he'd ever met. More like a linebacker or Special Ops team member. Dale knew some of the local SWAT guys from Cranston and they all had a similar bearing.

If he's a doctor, Dale thought, *then I'm Martha Fucking Stewart.*

"You might be able to help me, yes," Simpson said. He reached into another pocket and pulled out a photograph, which he handed over to Dale. "I'm looking for this man. I understand he passed through here recently. He's stolen some very valuable hospital property, and we would like it back."

Dale checked the picture and barely kept from gasping out loud.

Matt's face stared back at him.

He handed the picture back. "Never saw him before."

———

Simpson opened the door to the SUV. Inside, Watts was waiting, passing the time by sharpening his Ka-Bar.

"Well?" Watts asked, scraping the blade slowly along a piece of ceramic.

"The officer inside says Cahill hasn't been here," Simpson said.

"He telling the truth?"

"No," Simpson replied, putting the SUV in drive and turning out of the parking lot. "He's been here, all right."

"How long ago?"

"A few days, maybe."

"We're catching up," Watts said, pulling the blade along for another pass of the ceramic.

"That we are," Simpson replied, smiling.

"So where to now?"

"There's only one town within a hundred miles that has a bus terminal."

Watts looked at his knife, testing the blade with the tip of his thumb. He winced, then pulled his thumb back. A thin line of blood welled from the fresh cut. Good enough. "Cranston it is, then," he said.

THE END

THE DEAD MAN:
THE BLOOD MESA

By James Reasoner

CHAPTER ONE

With fear shooting through his veins and his pulse hammering in his head, Matt Cahill twisted the key and tromped the gas, hoping he wouldn't flood the engine of the two-and-a-half-ton truck. It cranked a couple of times with a maddening lack of results, then caught with a rumbling growl.

Horrific, decaying figures that had been normal people only a short time earlier swarmed around the vehicle, howling with rage and bloodlust. Several of them lunged in front of it, trying to cut off Matt's escape route.

Matt didn't hesitate. He slammed the truck into gear and sent it lurching forward. The woman on the seat beside him screamed as the rotting creatures caught in front of the truck scrambled to get out of its way.

Some of them made it, but one man wasn't fast enough. He threw up his arms and shrieked as the truck ran him down. Matt felt the bump as the heavy wheels passed over the body. Nothing could survive that.

And just like that, Matt was a killer again, through no fault of his own, and he had to ask himself if it would ever stop.

But it wouldn't, he knew, as long as he was a player in this game with no rules, this endless bloody chess match against the nightmarish figure that haunted him.

Mr. Dark.

—

One day earlier

Matt remembered a time, not so long ago, really, when it seemed like he would never be warm again.

Spending three months buried under an avalanche, tons and tons of snow and ice, probably accounted for that. Once you'd survived something like that—somehow—you had to expect to be pretty chilled.

But now all it had taken to convince him that, yes indeed, he could be warm again, was a summer day in New Mexico, in the high, dry desert country of the Four Corners region.

More than warm. As hot as blazes, actually.

The heat came up from the asphalt of the highway's narrow shoulder through the soles of his boots and seemed to bake his toes. *Pigs in a blanket,* he thought.

The trucker had dropped him off a couple of miles south of here, where the two-lane state blacktop crossed the interstate. Matt had intended to ride all the way to Gallup with the man, but when he had seen the red sandstone mesa rising from the desert to the north, something had told him that was the direction he needed to head.

"Not much up that way," the trucker had warned him, "and not much traffic on that road."

"I can walk," Matt had said, feeling confident that he could. Ever since he had returned to life after being frozen for three months under the avalanche, he had felt stronger and more vital than ever. "I want to take a closer look at that mesa."

The trucker had given him a sideways look but hadn't asked for an explanation, which was good because Matt couldn't have given him one.

What Matt hadn't reckoned on was how fast the blazing sun would leech all the juices and all the energy from a man. A dozen times while he was trudging along the blacktop, he had asked himself if he was crazy to be doing this.

And the answer, of course, was yes. He was crazy. But not just because he was walking up a New Mexico highway in the hot sun with a duffel bag slung over his shoulder that seemed to increase in weight with every step he took.

But because he'd been wandering the country for months, following only his instincts, dreading the evil he knew that they would lead him to.

So when he felt the pull to check out a majestic mesa in the distance, he didn't try to talk himself out of it.

He just started walking.

And scorching in the pitiless sun.

He was used to nearly unending rain and cool, piney woods, not this...this oven that called itself a state.

He slowed as he spotted something on the side of the highway up ahead and realized it was a truck of some kind. The heat-distorted scene seemed to swim in front of Matt's eyes for a second. Distances expanded crazily, stretching out so that it was a mile to the truck, a mile he could never cover, the shape he was in.

He had been out in the sun too long. That was all there was to it.

The truck offered some shade, anyway, and maybe the driver had some water he'd be willing to share. Matt forced his feet to keep going, telling himself that it wasn't as far as it looked.

When he came closer, he saw that the truck's hood was open. Somebody else was having some bad luck today.

As Matt approached, somebody stepped away from the front of the truck. The sun's glare made it hard to distinguish details, but the figure's shape told Matt it was a woman. When he finally stepped into the blessed shade cast by the tall canvas cover over the truck's bed, Matt paused to let his half-blinded eyes adjust.

The woman was in her thirties, good-looking, with honey blonde hair pulled back into a ponytail. She wore jeans and a T-shirt with a university logo on it.

And she was watching Matt with the wary look that any woman would display if a stranger came walking up to her in the middle of nowhere, miles from any help.

Matt stopped beside the rear of the truck, not wanting to crowd her and make her any more suspicious than she already was. He lowered his duffel bag to the ground and asked, "Having trouble?"

"Something's wrong with the truck," she replied, "although I suppose that goes without saying. Do you know anything about engines?"

"A little," Matt said. "I'd be glad to take a look at it for you."

She hesitated, clearly still unsure whether to trust him completely, but the idea of being stuck out here must have overcome her nervousness. She turned her head and said, "Andrew, why don't you let this man take a look at it?"

So she wasn't alone after all. The man she called Andrew muttered something and stepped around the front of the truck, where Matt could see him.

The man was about forty, broad shouldered and sandy haired, wearing a khaki shirt and blue jeans. Rotting skin peeled away from his broad forehead, and where his nose should have been there was only a festering, oozing hole in his face.

CHAPTER TWO

Matt didn't show any reaction to the grotesque sight that met his eyes. He had gotten used to hiding his feelings. And the woman didn't react to the terrible sores on her companion's face, of course, because she couldn't see them.

Matt was the only one who could.

"It didn't overheat," the man said, drawing Matt's attention back to the truck. "It just stopped."

That seemed like a pretty mundane concern for a guy who was slowly being consumed by evil. Matt's pulse hammered faster as he moved forward and said, "I'll take a look at it."

He watched the man from the corner of his eye as he circled around to the front of the truck. If either of them noticed his caution, they gave no sign of it.

The truck was built high off the ground, on big tires. Matt stepped up onto the front bumper so he could get a better look into the engine. He came from a family where the men were expected to be able to work on just about anything mechanical and often did. He checked the wiring first and saw the problem right away.

"You've got a loose wire on your alternator," he said. "You've been running on your battery. Didn't you notice that on the gauge?"

The man scoffed. "I'm not a mechanic. The man who should be taking care of such things quit on us; otherwise, I wouldn't be driving this behemoth back out to the mesa."

They were on their way to the mesa? The same mesa that had drawn him to hike up this desolate road?

Considering the rot that he saw on the man's face, Matt wasn't surprised there was a connection.

"Your battery finally went dead," he said. "I can hook up the alternator again, but without any juice to start the engine, you're still stuck."

The woman said, "I think there's another battery in the back. Our driver...our former driver...said it was a good idea to bring along a spare, since we'd be so far from anywhere at the mesa. Come on, let's take a look."

She seemed to have decided that he wasn't a psycho killer. He followed her to the back of the truck, where she pulled the canvas cover aside and held it for him while he climbed in. The truck bed held a number of bags and boxes that appeared to be full of supplies, and sure enough, in the front corner, a spare battery.

"You're in luck," Matt told her. "I'll need some wrenches."

"There's a tool kit behind the seat."

In a matter of minutes, he had taken off the dead battery and replaced it with the spare, as well as hooking up the wire that had come loose on the alternator. The work was hard enough in this heat that it caused beads of sweat to break out on his face.

Better than what was breaking out on Andrew's face, Matt thought as he sleeved away some of the sweat.

"All right, try it now," he said.

Andrew climbed into the truck and turned the key. The engine turned over for a moment, then caught. Matt jumped down from the bumper and went to the open door. In other circumstances he might have stepped up onto the running board and leaned in past Andrew to check the gauges, but he didn't want to get that close to the rotting man.

Instead he said, "Leave it running and let me take a look."

He stepped back to give Andrew plenty of room as the man climbed out.

"Looks good," Matt said after he'd peered in at the gauges. "You ought to get where you're going now."

The woman said, "Obviously you have experience with trucks like this."

Matt shrugged. "I used to work at a sawmill. I drove a few trucks back there."

"Would you be interested in a job?"

Andrew said, "Wait a minute. We don't know anything about this man, even his name."

"It's Matt Cahill," Matt said.

"I'm Dr. Veronica Dupre," the woman said. "This is Dr. Andrew Hammond."

So they weren't married. Matt had figured as much from the lack of wedding rings.

"As I mentioned, the man we hired to be our driver and mechanic decided to quit without any warning. We dropped him off in Gallup when we were picking up supplies. We could use a replacement."

Matt was hoping she would say that. They were going to the mesa, and ever since he'd seen it from the interstate, something about it had reached out to him with an undeniable compulsion.

Not only that, but the festering sores on Dr. Andrew Hammond's face told him that something bad was probably going to happen on top of that mesa.

Unless he could stop it somehow.

Matt cleared his throat and said, "And I could use a job. I accept."

Hammond frowned, which made more pus ooze from the sores on his face, and said, "Ronnie, I'm still not sure about this."

"Do *you* want to drive the truck and keep all the equipment working?" she asked him.

For a moment, Hammond didn't say anything. Then he snapped, "Fine. Consider yourself hired, Cahill. The job doesn't pay that much, though."

"I'm not worried about that," Matt said, which was true.

His real reward would be the opportunity to cross swords with the evil that he stalked.

And that stalked him.

CHAPTER THREE

Matt put his duffel bag in the back of the truck and climbed behind the wheel. Dr. Dupre slid in beside him, and Hammond sat beside the window. In the close confines of the truck's cab, the stench coming from Hammond made Matt want to gag. If he'd been sitting as close to the man as Dr. Dupre was, he probably would have thrown up.

She couldn't smell the stink, though, and for that she ought to count herself lucky.

Matt put the truck in gear and started it rolling along the blacktop. "Are you folks medical doctors?" he asked.

"PhDs," Hammond said. "Doctors of archeology, in fact."

"We're working on a dig on top of Blood Mesa," Veronica Dupre said. "There's an Anasazi settlement up there, or rather there used to be until it was abandoned about twelve hundred years ago."

"Blood Mesa?"

"That's what it's called. Because of the red sandstone, you know. When the sun hits it just right early in the morning or late in the afternoon, it's the color of blood."

That was a nice, cheery thought. He couldn't very well explain to her that he was here because he had felt the mesa calling to him in some way. She would think he had lost his mind.

"Are you familiar with the Anasazi?"

"I've heard of them," Matt said. "Disappeared mysteriously, didn't they?"

"For a long time that's what people thought. The name means *ancient ones* or *people who came before*, which certainly has a mysterious connotation to it." Like any teacher, she was warming to her subject. "Recent theories lean more toward the possibility that the Anasazi were simply absorbed into other tribes like the Navajo and the Hopi, but some of their cities do seem to have been abandoned rather abruptly, including the one on top of Blood Mesa. That's why we're here, to see if we can uncover any evidence of why they deserted this particular settlement."

"Sounds fascinating," Matt said.

Dr. Dupre laughed. "No, it doesn't. It sounds dry as dust to most people, and I know it. And I'm sorry I started lecturing."

"Don't worry. I like to learn new things."

He had learned more about certain things in the past few months than he ever wanted to. Things like evil and tragedy and degradation. The thought made him glance over at Dr. Andrew Hammond, who had his head turned away to look out the window on that side of the truck cab. Because of that, Matt couldn't get a good look at the rot on the man's face, but he knew it was there.

He drove along the two-lane blacktop for about a mile before he came to a dirt road that turned right off the highway and led toward the mesa. Dr. Dupre pointed to it and said, "That's where we turn."

Dust billowed up behind the truck as Matt slowed and wheeled it onto the dirt road. As he turned, he glanced at the big side mirror just outside his window.

Matt caught his breath as he saw the tall, skinny figure standing at the edge of the blacktop. The figure lifted an almost skeletal hand holding something—a lollipop, Matt knew from previous encounters—and waved it slowly in a mocking farewell.

Then the cloud of dust rolled over the asphalt, and Mr. Dark was gone.

—

The mesa was about a mile from the state highway. The dirt road leading to it was rough, forcing Matt to grip the steering wheel tighter as the truck bounced through the ruts toward the base of the mesa. The red sandstone cliffs rose a couple of hundred feet and loomed over the truck. From the top, it probably looked like a toy.

The dirt road circled part of the way around the mesa and then angled straight toward it. "That's where you want to go," Dr. Dupre said, pointing to a trail that was little more than a broad ledge rising and curving out of sight around the mesa. Matt figured the ledge must spiral all the way to the top.

"Still think you can handle it?" Hammond asked. "There's no place to turn around. Once you start up, you have to go all the way to the top or else back all the way down." He shook his head, causing the strips of rotten skin hanging from his face to sway. "I wouldn't advise that."

"We'll make it," Matt said.

The road up the side of the mesa, if you could call it that, was even rougher, making Matt grateful for the big tires, and steep enough in places that the truck's engine growled and labored as it climbed. Matt kept a close eye on the temperature and oil-pressure gauges. The truck seemed to be handling the effort all right.

The ledge was narrow enough that when Matt looked out, he couldn't see anything except empty air on that side of the truck. And on the other side loomed the red cliffs, bulging out in places so they overhung the ledge. It was a little nerve-wracking, all right. As a rule, though, his nerves were pretty steady.

"What's up there on top?" he asked. It was a natural question for someone in his position, even somebody who couldn't see the festering sores on Hammond's face.

"There's not much left of the pueblo itself," Dr. Dupre explained, "just a few walls still standing, and the kivas, of course, although some of them have collapsed in on themselves. But there are enough ruins so that when the wind blows through them, it makes a sort of wailing noise, like there's someone up there crying...I know, that probably sounds crazy."

Matt shook his head. "Not at all."

"Of course I know that no one lives up there and hasn't for hundreds of years, but there are times I catch myself looking over my shoulder, like there's somebody behind me. But nobody's there. You know what I mean?"

"I do," Matt said. *All too well.*

As they approached the top, Dr. Dupre pointed through the dust-covered windshield and said, "There's the Indian's Head. We're not supposed to call it that, even though that's what the few people who live around here have called it for years and years. The university doesn't want anybody to be offended."

Matt saw right away what she was talking about. A huge chunk of rock poised at the edge of the mesa, above the ledge. Centuries of erosion had carved it into a shape that roughly resembled a stereotypical Native American profile.

"It's a hard landmark to miss," she went on. "When you see it, you know you're almost at the top."

Sure enough, a couple of minutes later the trail emerged onto the mesa's top, which was approximately half a mile wide and three quarters of a mile long, Matt judged, and laid out in a roughly rectangular shape, although there were no sharp corners anywhere.

After climbing all the way up the trail, it felt good to be back on relatively level ground again. Stretches of grass grew here and there, along with an occasional stunted bush, but mostly the ground was a mixture of sand and rock. Jagged crevices sliced in from the rim and would have to be avoided. A fall into one of them could be fatal.

As Matt drove across the mesa, he spotted in the distance the ruins Veronica Dupre had mentioned. Some of the eroded walls that were still standing had windows in them, and that probably accounted for the wailing wind she had talked about.

It struck Matt that those openings also looked a little like eyes, watching them approach.

"People actually lived up here?" he asked.

"Oh yeah, several hundred of them. Maybe as many as a thousand."

"How did they get water? What did they live on?"

"They dug cisterns underground and rigged sluices to carry the water down to them when it rained. It doesn't rain much here, as you might imagine, but when it does it's usually a downpour. There are also some springs within walking distance, and they could carry water back from them if they had to. They were able to grow some corn, and hunting parties went out and brought in fresh meat. Getting enough to eat had to be a problem, though. That may be one reason why they finally abandoned this city. They made it work in other places, though. Acoma, southeast of here, is the oldest continually occupied settlement in North America. People still live there." Dr. Dupre laughed. "And I'm lecturing again. Occupational hazard."

Lecture or not, none of what she said explained why the crawling sensation along Matt's spine had gotten even worse since they reached the top of the mesa. He looked around for Mr. Dark but didn't see the scrawny son of a bitch.

Several pickups and jeeps were parked near the ruins. Matt saw a few people moving around, scattered here and there on the mesa. They all appeared to be young, which was no surprise since graduate students did most of the grunt work on archeological digs like this, while the professors just supervised.

A pudgy young man with curly brown hair came toward the truck as Matt brought it to a halt near the other vehicles. Matt opened his door and slid down from the high bench seat.

The young man stopped short and looked at him in surprise.

"Who're you?" he asked.

Drs. Dupre and Hammond had gotten out of the truck on the other side. As they came around the front, Dr. Dupre said, "This is Matt Cahill, Jerry. He's taking Alberto's place."

"What happened to Alberto?"

THE DEAD MAN: THE BLOOD MESA

"He quit," Hammond said with scorn in his voice. "Claimed he was too frightened to come back out here. You know how these uneducated Indians are. Afraid of evil spirits and hogwash like that."

Dr. Dupre frowned at her colleague's comment but didn't say anything.

"Oh. Okay," the young man said. He extended a hand to Matt and grinned as he introduced himself. "Jerry Schultz. I'm glad to meet you, Mr. Cahill."

"Call me Matt," he said as he shook hands.

"Jerry, can you help Matt unload the supplies?" Dr. Dupre asked. "We're going to talk to Dr. Varley."

"Sure, I'd be glad to."

"Jerry can fill you in on anything you need to know about what we're doing up here," Dr. Dupre went on.

"And welcome to Blood Mesa," Hammond added, although the look on his rotting face didn't appear welcoming at all. "I hope you enjoy your stay with us."

Matt doubted the sincerity of that sentiment.

And he had a very strong hunch that he wouldn't enjoy his time on Blood Mesa at all.

CHAPTER FOUR

A number of tents were set up near the parked pickups and jeeps. Matt and Jerry began carrying the supplies into a large one that Jerry identified as the mess tent.

Matt had to move his duffel bag to reach one of the crates, and as he set it down, something in the bag made a slight clunking sound as it landed on the truck bed.

"What was that?" Jerry asked.

"Just some of my gear," Matt said.

He didn't explain that it was the ax he had brought with him from his storage shed at home when he started on his personal odyssey.

The ax that he ought to take out of the duffel bag, carry over to the tent where Dr. Andrew Hammond was talking to an older man with white hair, and bury the keen edge of the blade deep in the evil motherfucker's rotting face.

That would put an end to the trouble before it even began.

But it would leave unanswered the question of why he felt such a compulsion to journey to the top of that mesa. Was there something even worse waiting for him up there, something only he could stop?

Matt didn't know, but he had to find out.

"So you're a graduate student," Matt said to Jerry, just making conversation while they worked.

"Yeah. I'm doing my doctoral thesis on the linguistics of the Anasazi, so I'm hoping we'll find something that'll tell us more about their language, which seems to have been primarily Uto-Aztecan in nature."

"Uh-huh," Matt said.

"Plus it was supposed to be a chance for me and April to spend some, you know, quality time together."

"April?"

"My girlfriend. We came out here together, but we...uh... sort of had a fight."

"Oh." Matt hoped that Jerry wouldn't feel compelled to share all the details of that disagreement. He didn't really have any interest in grad student soap opera.

"But then that damned Scott Conroy had to come along, too," Jerry continued. "I hate guys named Scott."

"Let me guess," Matt said. "He's...April's ex?"

"Yeah. They broke up four months ago. I *finally* get a chance with her, after all this time, and it looks like things are gonna go my way at last, and then...then Scott comes along and starts makin' noises about getting back together with her, you know, and I thought maybe April would tell him to take a hike, but she said she couldn't be rude to him after all they'd been through together, so she had to listen to him, and that just made me, well, you know, that's not something a guy like me wants to hear, since Scott, he's this good-lookin' guy and I'm, well, you can see for yourself what I am, and his name is *Scott*, for God's sake—"

"So you've known April for a long time?" Matt asked, figuring that if he didn't stop the flood of words somehow, Jerry might pass out from lack of oxygen, especially at this altitude.

"Since a seminar on ancient civilizations in our sopho-more year. I looked at her across the room, and suddenly I didn't give a shit about the Hittites anymore."

"Yeah, I know what you mean," Matt said. "So are they going to get back together?"

"April says no...but I don't really believe her."

"And she figured out that you feel that way."

"Oh yeah. Pissed her off, too. She said if I didn't trust her, then maybe we shouldn't be together after all."

"Well, there's something to that, I suppose," Matt said.

"Yeah, probably. Anyway, we're sort of stuck up here now, so I guess we'll have to make the best of it. You'd think we'd be more, you know, mature about everything. I mean, we're *graduate students*. We should be past all this stuff."

Matt just grunted and didn't say anything. He didn't know much about grad school or the whole world of academia, but he had knocked around enough in his life to know that anytime you put a bunch of males and females together, it was junior high all over again.

To distract Jerry from the subject of romance, he said, "This Dr. Varley...I take it he's some sort of hotshot in the archeology field?"

"You've never heard of him?"

Matt shook his head. "I don't travel much in academic circles."

"Yeah, he's one of the top men," Jerry said. "He's writ-ten a bunch of books and been running the department for years and years. This is gonna be his last dig, though. He's retiring pretty soon."

"Dr. Hammond's going to replace him?"

Jerry laughed, then shook his head. "Don't tell anybody I said this, but Dr. Hammond just wishes he was going to replace him. Dr. Varley's picked Dr. Dupre to take over."

"Does Hammond know that?"

"Yeah, and he's not happy about it, either. This is between you and me, right?"

Matt nodded. "Sure. My word on it."

"Hammond figured when he was running things, he'd be able to hook up with Dr. Dupre. He's been tryin' to get in her pants for a long time, and let's face it, who can blame him? But now she's gonna be the boss, not him, so he's not gonna have any leverage, you know what I mean?"

"Yeah. Tough break for him."

And maybe the anger and resentment that had grown in Hammond's heart because of it was what had drawn Mr. Dark to him.

At first Matt had wondered if the evil he saw on Hammond's face was caused by that skeletal, lollipop-sucking bastard, or if the man had started to rot, inside and out, without being touched by Mr. Dark.

The momentary glimpse Matt had gotten of Mr. Dark as they left the state highway, though, convinced him that *something* on this mesa had drawn the creature here, just as Matt himself had been drawn. There had to be a reason they kept winding up in the same places. Mr. Dark had a history of manipulating humans to get what he wanted, and Matt had a hunch that Hammond was one of those tools.

The more information he had, the better he might be able to fight whatever was lurking up here. He said, "Tell me about the other members of the expedition. Is that the right word for it, expedition?"

"Sure, whatever. We're all graduate students in archeology..."

For the next few minutes, Jerry rattled off names and random facts about his fellow would-be archeologists, mostly concerned with the relative hotness of the female members of the group. All of them met with Jerry's approval to some degree. Matt knew he wouldn't be able to remember all the names, at least not until he got to know them better, so he didn't really try.

By the time he and Jerry finished unloading the supplies, Matt was tired. The heat made a man sweat, and the dry air sucked up all the moisture almost immediately. It would be easy to get dehydrated out here.

He turned to look around. The mesa had a stark beauty, and from this height he could see for twenty miles or more in every direction. Miles and miles of nothing but miles and miles, as the old saying went. But the red and brown and tan landscape was dotted with other mesas, too, as well as slender, towering rock spires and other formations in odd, twisted shapes.

"What do you think of it, Mr. Cahill?"

The voice belonged to Dr. Veronica Dupre. She had come up behind him without him hearing her.

"It's something," Matt said noncommittally as he turned to look at her. "And you might as well call me Matt, too. Mr. Cahill still makes me look around for my dad."

She laughed. "All right, Matt. And you can call me Ronnie. I know I should stand on ceremony, like Dr. Varley and Dr. Hammond, but I've never quite been able to do that. I suppose that comes from years of working to put myself through school."

"What did you do?" Matt asked, curious about this woman. She was attractive, but that wasn't it. There wasn't really anything flirtatious about her attitude.

"Waitressed, bartended, you name it. I even worked in a lumberyard for a while."

That was it, Matt thought. She might have transformed herself over the years, but she had started out in the same blue-collar world he came from. In fact, some of the boards in that lumberyard where she worked could have come from the sawmill where he had worked for so many years.

"That's why I was interested when you said you'd worked in a sawmill," she went on. "We're a lot alike in some ways."

"I suppose so," he said.

But they really weren't, not anymore. She had become a professor, and he had become...something. He wasn't sure what. But he wasn't an average joe anymore, no matter how he might wish that were the case.

Ronnie laughed. "Come on. If you're through unloading, I'll show you around. There's a little daylight left, but when night falls out here, it falls hard and fast."

CHAPTER FIVE

The supply tent and mess tent were full of bottled water, crates of food, cases of toilet paper, tents, and supplies that would be used in the dig, such as stakes and rolls of twine for marking off grids, mallets for hammering the stakes into the hard ground, framed screens for sifting dirt, boxes and bags for storing artifacts, and portable lights that ran off the generator that also was in the back of the truck. Matt had already seen all of that, but Ronnie Dupre pointed it out to him anyway.

Then they roamed around the ruins and Ronnie showed him the three dig sites, which were separated from one another by several hundred yards. To Matt they just looked like holes in the ground, but as he stood looking down into one of them, he suddenly tensed.

The surrounding area was just a stretch of hard-packed ground with a few rocks littered around it.

But as Matt looked down into the excavation, he seemed to feel a *pulsing* under the soles of his boots, almost like the ground was alive, with a heart buried somewhere down there underneath its surface.

Whatever was down there didn't need to be dug up.

He couldn't explain that to these rational scientists, though, not in any terms they would understand or accept.

"Is Dr. Hammond in charge of this part of the dig?" he asked. Surely there was a connection between what he felt here and the sores he saw on Hammond's face.

"No, Dr. Varley is supervising this excavation," Ronnie replied.

"Oh." Matt was surprised by that answer.

"I'm sure he'd be glad to tell you more about it, if you're interested. I'll introduce you to him at supper, along with the others."

"Thanks," Matt said. He cast an uneasy glance over his shoulder at the excavation as they walked away.

Ronnie was right about night falling quickly. The members of the expedition gathered in the mess tent, which was lit by oil lamps, and she introduced him to everyone as she had promised.

The grad students all seemed like good kids, and even though he wasn't really *that* much older than them, Matt couldn't help but think of them that way. April Milligan, Jerry's former girlfriend, was the sort of sweet, wholesomely pretty young woman who reminded people of somebody's little sister. Scott Conroy was the handsome, athletic guy who had been the quarterback in high school *and* on the honor roll. Ginger Li was the smart, pretty Asian woman. Brad Kern was another former high school athlete, although with his lanky height he'd probably been a forward on the basketball team. With one exception, the rest still blended together in Matt's mind.

That exception was Chuck Pham, who looked Vietnamese. But when he opened his mouth, what came out was the good-ol'-boy drawl of a West Texas redneck. Matt figured that Chuck had been born and raised a long way from his parents' homeland.

Dr. Howard Varley was a soft-spoken man in his seventies, lacking in the arrogance that made Andrew Hammond such a prick, but he had an air of casual superiority about him. He gave Matt a limp handshake and said, "Glad to have you with us, Mr. Cahill. Andrew has told me how you helped out with that mechanical crisis this afternoon. You seem to be something of a godsend."

"I'm always happy to lend a hand," Matt said. He didn't bother telling Dr. Varley to call him Matt. He knew the man would never be that informal.

Supper was simple fare: biscuits and spam cooked on a propane grill, along with canned vegetables heated in a microwave powered by the generator. The members of the expedition ate by the light of the oil lamps, which gave the meal an old-fashioned feel.

Ronnie came over and sat down beside Matt, who was using a large flat rock as a seat. "You've worked really hard since we got here, Matt," she said. "Maybe Alberto's attack of nerves was actually a stroke of luck for us."

Matt shrugged. "The way I was brought up, when I see something that needs doing, I usually try to do it."

He was aware that Andrew Hammond was watching the two of them from the other side of the circle formed by the expedition members. Hammond didn't look happy that Ronnie was talking to Matt. Of course, to Matt's eyes it would have been difficult for Hammond to look happy with all that rotting flesh and those oozing sores.

Matt wondered what was in Hammond's mind to cause that ugliness. Sometimes when he came across the people

Mr. Dark had touched, it took a while for the creature's plans to become clear to Matt. All he was sure of was that *something* bad was going to happen, and it was up to him to stop it if he could, or try to minimize the damage if he couldn't.

After supper the members of the expedition split up and headed for their tents. Technically, the two students in each tent were supposed to be the same gender, but Matt had a hunch there had been some mixing and matching since they'd been here. The three professors had individual tents of their own because they needed room to work. As Matt looked around, he realized that *he* didn't have a tent. When he asked Ronnie about that, she confirmed it.

"Alberto had been sleeping in the truck. There's a sleeping bag in the back, along with some extra blankets you can use for padding. Do you think you can get by with that?"

"Sure," Matt said without hesitation. "I'm liable to be more comfortable than the rest of you. I've never liked cots very much, and a sleeping bag on the hard ground can be pretty uncomfortable."

Ronnie yawned and said, "I know it's early, but I may go ahead and turn in anyway. It was a long day, driving all the way into town and back, and we're always up early in the morning to get started on the day's work."

"Good night, then," Matt told her.

She started to turn away from where he stood beside the truck, but she paused and looked back at him. "I'm convinced it really was a stroke of good luck when you came walking along that road, Matt. Good luck for us, I mean."

"And me, too," he said.

He pulled himself up onto the lowered tailgate and sat there for a few minutes, watching and listening to the night. The students had taken the lamps with them when they went to their tents. He could see some of them glowing through the canvas and around the entrances, but a couple of the tents were already dark.

Matt tilted his head back and looked up at the stars. To creatures with the short life spans of humans, they seemed unchanging. And they were merciless, he thought, shining down on good and evil alike. Maybe *merciless* wasn't exactly the right word.

The stars just didn't give a damn about what happened on this puny planet. Being out here like this made Matt uncomfortably aware of just how tiny the denizens of this world really were.

Tiny, maybe, but important enough for Mr. Dark to screw with their lives, for reasons of his own that Matt couldn't yet begin to fathom.

He was thinking about that when loud, angry words came from the other side of the camp and shattered the night's hush.

"Back off, dude, or I'll rip your fuckin' heart out!"

CHAPTER SIX

Matt dropped off the tailgate and hurried toward the sound of the disturbance. He heard a voice he recognized as belonging to Jerry Schultz saying, "Hey, take it easy, man. I just want to talk to April."

"She's got nothing to say to you, and she's not interested in anything you have to say."

"Well, I...I'd like to hear her tell me that herself."

Several other people had emerged from their tents in response to the commotion, including Ronnie, Varley, and Hammond, whose rotting visage was horrifying in the dim light, bad enough that it would have made a normal person run away screaming.

Matt, for good or ill, was no longer a normal person, of course. And even he flinched inside when he looked at Hammond.

Everyone gathered around a tent where Scott Conroy and Jerry stood facing each other in angry confrontation.

Actually, Jerry looked more scared than angry, Matt thought as he came up to the two young men. Enough light spilled through the tent's entrance for him to get a good look at them. The flap that normally covered the opening was thrown back. Matt saw April inside, sitting on a sleeping bag with her knees pulled up and her arms around them.

She had her head down, as if she didn't want to see what was happening just outside the tent.

"What's going on here?" Varley demanded. "I heard shouting."

"It's nothing important, Dr. Varley," Scott said. "Just somebody nosing around where he's not wanted anymore."

Jerry swallowed. He was a little bigger than Scott but a lot softer. But as Matt watched, he saw Jerry's determination overcome his fear.

"I still haven't heard that from April herself," Jerry said. "You don't speak for her, Scott. I just want to talk to her."

"You've talked to her enough."

Hammond said, "We have important work to do out here. Very important work. We didn't come all this way just for you people to play adolescent games!"

Even though Hammond looked like a walking corpse, he was still a stuffy, pompous windbag, Matt thought.

"Sorry, Dr. Hammond," Jerry muttered. "I just want to talk to April for a minute; that's all."

"Oh, for—" Hammond stopped and looked through the tent's open flap. "Milligan, if that's what it'll take to put an end to this idiocy, get out here and talk to this fat cocksucker!"

The others stared at him, including Matt. Most of them seemed shocked. After a couple of seconds, Ronnie said, "Andrew, I'm not sure that's really the best—"

"I'm sorry," Hammond broke in. "It's just been a long day, and I'm tired." He summoned up an insincere smile. "Sorry, Jerry. I didn't mean anything by it."

"That's...uh...that's all right, Dr. Hammond," Jerry said.

Still smiling, Hammond held out a hand toward the tent. "April, if you would..."

Slowly, she crawled out of the tent and stood up. As she put a hand on Conroy's arm, she said, "It'll be all right, Scott. I'm fine, really."

"I just didn't want him upsetting you even more," Scott said.

April looked around. "Please, everyone, just go on about your business. We all need our rest."

"That's right," Varley said. "We'll be digging early in the morning."

As the crowd began to scatter, April faced Jerry. "Say what you have to say," she told him.

Jerry looked around. "Can't we have some privacy?"

"Scott can hear anything you have to say to me."

"Then it's true? The two of you really...really are back together?"

"That's right. I'm sorry, Jerry, but you never really trusted me, and because of that, you kept pushing me away."

Matt started drifting back toward the truck. The way this was going, somebody was going to start saying "XOXO" any minute, and he didn't want to hear it.

One of the other grad students fell in beside him. "Almost had a good show back there, didn't we?" the guy said.

Matt glanced over at him, trying to recall his name. Rankin—that was it, he thought. Rick or Rich Rankin; Matt wasn't sure.

"Yeah, I guess," he said.

"Poor April's bound to lose either way."

"How do you mean?" Matt asked.

"Well, she's way out of Jerry's league. She'd be lowering herself to hook up with him. And Scott...well, Scott's just trying to convince himself that he's not gay. That's a losing battle. Believe me, *I* know."

"Okay," Matt said. He didn't care who coupled with whom among this bunch, but listening to Rankin was probably the easiest way to get him to go on his way.

"He'll figure it out sooner or later," Rankin said. "Good night, Mr. Cahill."

"Good night," Matt said. Rankin veered off toward one of the tents, and Matt headed for the truck.

When he got there, he looked back at the tent where Jerry and April still stood. Jerry was gesturing and talking earnestly. April just shook her head and turned toward the tent. Scott Conroy stood nearby, his arms crossed and smugness radiating from him. He said something to Jerry and then followed April into the tent.

The entrance flap fell closed, cutting off the light.

But Matt could still see well enough to see Jerry standing there, his shoulders slumped in defeat. Matt recalled the line from some poem about it being better to have loved and lost than never to have loved at all.

Sometimes, poets didn't know shit.

—

The rest of the night passed quietly enough, although Matt was restless, his dreams haunted by visions of Mr. Dark and all the evil he had witnessed in recent months. He woke up sweating a couple of times, even though the dry, high desert air grew rather chilly before morning.

Everyone would be responsible for cooking, cleaning up after meals, and all the other mundane chores that kept the camp functioning while the dig went on. This morning two of the young women, Maggie Flynn and Astrid Tompkins, were preparing breakfast. Matt accepted a cup of coffee from Astrid, a young black woman with a killer smile.

Thinking back to his high school days, Matt recalled that most of the really smart girls had also been pretty good-looking. He didn't know why that was, but obviously that was still the case. Jerry was right: all six of the female grad students were attractive.

After breakfast, which was over by the time the sun had risen much above the horizon, the members of the group scattered to three dig sites. Dr. Varley headed toward the spot where Matt had felt that eerie, unpleasant sensation the previous evening. As Matt trailed behind him with an armload of tools Varley had asked him to bring, he said, "Excuse me, Doctor, but are you sure this is a good place to dig?"

Varley stopped short and turned around to look at Matt with an irritated expression on his lined and weathered face. "And exactly how many books on archeology have you written, Mr. Cahill?"

"You know I haven't written any," Matt said.

And I've never even read any, but I know a bad place when I see it.

"Well, then, I think we'll leave those decisions up to me," Varley said.

Matt nodded. "Sure, Doctor." What else could he say?

April and Scott assisted Dr. Varley, along with Sierra Hernandez and Chuck Pham. Hammond's excavation was a couple of hundred yards away. He had Brad Kern, Rich Rankin, Noel McAlister, and Maggie Flynn working there with him. Still farther away, almost on the other side of the settlement, Ronnie was excavating one of the collapsed kivas with the help of Jerry, Ginger, Astrid, and Stephanie Porter. Matt circulated among all three locations, fetching equipment and tools for the scientists and helping to haul away chunks of rock that were too big for one person to handle.

Hammond was as ugly as ever with the rotting sores on his face, but they didn't seem to be getting any worse, which surprised Matt a little because he had expected some progression. He kept a close eye on the others as well, in case sores began to pop up on their faces, but so far that hadn't happened. He didn't really like some of them, but he knew it was possible for people to be assholes without being truly evil.

Matt kept drifting back to Varley's excavation, convinced that if anything happened, it would be there. Varley had used stakes and twine to lay out a rectangle with a large rock at each corner. As Matt studied it, he realized how symmetrically the rocks were placed. They appeared to be markers designating an area about eight feet by fifteen feet.

When Matt stood there next to the excavation, he still felt the definite sense of unease that had cropped up inside him when he was here the night before. He wished he could talk Varley out of digging here, but every time he even broached the subject during the day, the elderly professor cut him off short.

About the middle of the afternoon, Ronnie scrambled out of the kiva, looked around, and then waved her arms at Matt, who was over by the truck. He had already spotted her as she emerged from the hole in the ground and recognized a sense of urgency in her movements. He started trotting toward her even before she signaled to him.

She motioned for him to stop and called, "Round up everyone and bring them over here, Matt! We've found something they need to see!"

Matt couldn't tell from her attitude if the find was something good or bad, but Ronnie certainly seemed excited. He gave her a thumbs-up and headed for the other locations to spread the word.

"What's this all about?" Hammond asked irritably when Matt told him Ronnie wanted to see everybody at the kiva. "Did she tell you what she'd found?"

Matt shook his head. "Afraid not, Doctor. She just said everybody should go over there."

"All right, all right," Hammond muttered, adding to the students working with him, "Come on."

Everyone gathered around the kiva. The stone wall of the well-like structure was still partially intact, but it had collapsed in places and over the centuries allowed dirt to spill in and fill the hole. Ronnie and her helpers had dug down, exposing the broken top of the circular wall and emptying some of the dirt from the lower part of the kiva. Matt knew vaguely that the Indians had used these places in their religious ceremonies, but that was the extent of his knowledge.

Ronnie had gone back down the metal ladder that rested inside the hole. Ginger and Astrid were down there with her, but Jerry and Stephanie were on the ground outside the kiva with the others.

"What is it, Dr. Dupre?" Varley asked. "A significant find?"

"I think so," Ronnie said. She took something that Astrid handed her and came up the ladder to show it to the other members of the group. What looked like a dirty brown stick about a foot and a half long was really something else, Matt sensed as the unease grew inside him.

When Ronnie reached the top of the ladder, Hammond practically snatched the thing out of her hand.

"Good Lord," he said. "That's a human femur."

"Look at the markings on it," Ronnie said.

Everyone leaned in except Matt. He wouldn't have known what he was looking at.

He didn't have to wait long to find out, though. April made a face and asked, "Are those...teeth marks?"

"I think so," Ronnie said. "It looks like something has gnawed all the meat off that bone."

"Not some*thing*," Hammond said with excitement in his voice. "Some*one*. No wild animal did this. Those marks were made by human teeth." A grin stretched across his rotting face. "What you've found here, Dr. Dupre, is indisputable evidence of cannibalism!"

He didn't have to sound so damned happy about it, Matt thought.

Then again, considering that Hammond's face was rotting off his skull, maybe he did.

CHAPTER SEVEN

They were all excited by the discovery, even the ones like April, who were grossed out by it.

"We've uncovered several other bones with these markings," Ronnie said. "Also marks that look like they were made by flint knives or axes."

"Excellent, excellent," Varley said. "Continue with your excavation, Dr. Dupre. Do you need some extra help with cleaning, identifying, and tagging the specimens?"

Ronnie shook her head. "No, my team and I can handle it, at least for now. But I thought you'd all like to know."

"Of course," Hammond said as he handed the femur back to her. "This is very exciting."

They all stood around talking about it for a while; then Varley said, "We should get back to work."

The other teams returned to their digs, leaving Ronnie, Jerry, Ginger, Astrid, and Stephanie to work in and around the kiva. Jerry spread out a tarp on the ground and arranged all the bones they had found so far on it.

Matt watched him for a minute and then asked, "Are you going to try to reassemble the whole skeleton?"

"No, not here," Jerry said. "That's a job that'll have to be done back at the university. Anyway, there may be more than one skeleton down there. We're still pretty high up in the kiva."

Matt frowned. "You mean there could have been a whole bunch of bodies in there?"

"Sure." Jerry sound cheerful about the prospect, which Matt supposed meant that he was a true scientist. The evidence left behind was more important than all the people who had died to provide it.

"The Indians normally didn't use these kivas as burial pits, did they?"

"We don't really know everything they were used for," Jerry said. "The later Puebloan tribes used them primarily for ceremonial purposes, but the Anasazi and the other early peoples in this region had them, too, and we don't know why. I don't recall reading about anybody ever coming across evidence of them being used as burial pits...until now. And what happened here wasn't exactly a burial, you know."

Matt frowned. "What do you mean?"

"Well...you heard what Dr. Dupre said about all the meat being gnawed off the bone. When you finish with a chicken wing, what do you do with the bone?"

"Throw it in the garbage," Matt said as a hollow feeling crept into his gut. "This was a garbage dump for cannibals."

"Looks like it might've been," Jerry said.

"Jerry," Astrid called from down in the excavation. "We've got more bones here!"

"Coming," Jerry said.

Matt felt a little sick and just wanted to get away from there. Ancient cannibal Indians...just one more indication, as if he or anybody else needed it, that human evil wasn't a recent invention.

By the end of the day, the tarp Jerry had spread on the ground was covered with human bones, and another one had been filled as well. Matt stood looking at them as the sun went down and thought about the incredible amount of human suffering they represented.

Ronnie came up beside him. "Pretty impressive, isn't it?"

"In a gruesome sort of way, I suppose."

"Well, yes, there's that to consider, of course. I'm not an expert in forensic archeology, but even I can tell that these people were killed, hacked apart, and eaten, probably raw. The ends of the bones where they were dismembered don't show any signs of charring, as they would if they'd been cooked."

Matt started to take a deep breath, then stopped abruptly because of what he might smell. Then he realized that the stench of death was long gone from this place. It just smelled of dust.

"How many people are we talking about?" he asked.

"Again, I'm not an expert in that field, but I would guess somewhere between two and three dozen. And it's likely we'll find even more as we continue to dig. There's no sign of the pile ending anytime soon."

"Dozens and dozens of people," Matt murmured. "Murdered and eaten."

"I know, it's terrible. You're probably asking yourself what could cause such an atrocity."

He looked over at her.

"Actually, it ties in with something we've come to believe about the Anasazi and why they abandoned these pueblos. There's evidence to suggest that the region was hit with a whole string of disastrous droughts and crop failures. In an area that doesn't get much rain to start with, the margin for error in such things as growing corn is very small. And when there's a severe drought, the animal population is always affected, too, and becomes smaller. So if both hunting and raising crops didn't produce enough food to feed the people who lived here..."

"They started eating each other," Matt said.

"Yes, and then of course the ones who did survive probably wouldn't want to stay in those places that reminded them of what they'd done. So they moved away and the result is this."

Ronnie waved her hand to indicate the ruins around them.

Matt shook his head as he slipped his hands in the hip pockets of his jeans. "No offense, but I don't know if I completely buy that explanation," he said. "For this many people to have died so violently, it seems more like a bunch of them went crazy. Like an orgy of killing. It wouldn't have gone on and on like a gradual thing."

"Mass hysteria?" Ronnie asked with a frown. "That's more likely to manifest itself in group suicides, like in Jonestown or that comet cult in California. Not in mass murder. Anyway, if you don't mind my saying so, Matt...it sounds almost like you're speaking from personal experience."

He shook his head. "I just know what I've read in the papers and seen on TV," he lied. He had seen how evil could spread like wildfire through a group of people, though he wasn't sure he had encountered it yet on this scale.

"Well, we'll keep digging," Ronnie said. "Maybe we'll turn up some positive evidence of what happened."

He noticed that she was standing a little farther away from him than she had been a few minutes earlier. *Great,* he thought. *Now she thinks I'm a psycho killer.* He supposed he had sounded a little crazy.

But she didn't know the things he knew, couldn't see the things he could see. If she could, she would be a lot more worried.

———

The work continued at all three digs the next day. Hammond and his group hadn't found anything worth noting, but Dr. Varley's team had dug down far enough to reveal that the four "rocks" at the corners of the rectangle were actually the tops of four pillars. Matt paced around the excavation worriedly.

Varley wasn't doing any of the actual digging himself, due to his advanced age. Scott and Chuck did most of that while April and Sierra sifted through the dirt for artifacts.

"What does this look like to you, Doctor?" Matt asked Varley.

"Those pillars are supports for a roof," Varley said, pointing to them. "The irregularities on the tops indicate that they were broken off at some time, so it's safe to assume that originally they were taller. Not all kivas were underground, you know, nor were they all circular. Many of them were square or rectangular and built partially or completely aboveground. I believe what we have here are the ruins of a large, partially sunken kiva with stone walls and a roof."

"You haven't found any bones here, have you?"

Varley smiled and shook his head. "No, no bones. Those seem to be confined to Dr. Dupre's excavation."

If that was the case, Matt wondered why this place bothered him even more than the one that contained evidence of murder and cannibalism.

Late that afternoon, Scott and Chuck uncovered something else. Matt was hunkered on his heels near the edge of the excavation as the two young men leaned over and brushed dirt away from what took shape as a large, smooth, flat stone surface. This wasn't sandstone. It gleamed black, like obsidian.

"Dr. Varley, look at this!" Scott called.

Varley, April, and Sierra came up to the rim of the pit and gazed down into it, along with Matt.

"What is it?" April asked.

"Keep digging," Varley ordered. "We need to determine the object's dimensions."

Shovels bit into the dirt. Scott and Chuck scraped it away until the stone had been revealed down to a depth of several inches. Its edges were square cut. It was about three feet wide and maybe seven feet long.

"It's an altar," Varley said in a hushed voice.

"Like for religious ceremonies?" Scott asked.

"Or maybe for human sacrifices, like in the movies," Chuck said in his West Texas drawl.

Sierra took him seriously and said, "I didn't know the Anasazi sacrificed people."

"We didn't know they practiced cannibalism until now, either," a new voice said. Matt glanced up and saw Andrew Hammond standing near the excavation, a smile on his disfigured face. "This is exciting, Howard, very exciting."

Varley nodded. "Yes, it is."

Scott was feeling around at one end of the altar. He said, "Dr. Varley, something's carved into the stone down here. I can't tell what it is."

"Uncover it," Varley ordered as he leaned over and rested his hands on his knees so he could peer more closely into the pit. "Dig the dirt away from it before we lose our light."

Scott and Chuck wielded their shovels with even greater enthusiasm. Matt felt coldness growing inside him as they uncovered more and more of the altar at one end.

"What is that?" Varley muttered. "The stone is so dark it's difficult to see the markings."

He straightened and started for the ladder. Matt stood up, too, suddenly even more anxious than he had been.

Varley motioned to April and Sierra. "Girls, come with me. You've been part of this, too. You deserve to see what we've found."

Matt felt something wild growing inside him. He started to reach for the elderly professor's arm, not knowing what he would say but feeling a growing need to stop this.

Hammond got in his way. The man's rotting lips drew back from his teeth in an animal-like snarl as he said, "Leave them alone, Cahill."

Suddenly Matt wished he had gotten his ax out of his duffel bag and split Hammond's head open that first day, like he had thought about doing. He might have been hauled off and arrested for murder, but that would be better than what was about to happen here.

"Get the hell out of my way," he said.

Hammond laughed. "You're too late," he told Matt. "Too late."

It was true. Time was screwy somehow. Varley, April, and Sierra had climbed down into the excavation and were crowded around the altar with Scott and Chuck. Matt stepped around Hammond so he had a good view as Scott knelt and brushed the last of the dirt away from the lines carved into the stone.

In the garish red light of late afternoon, the lines formed an unmistakable image, one that Matt had seen all too many times in the past few months.

It was the face of Mr. Dark, and just above it was another striking, sinister image, a snake eating its own tail.

And as Dr. Howard Varley murmured, "Fascinating," a huge blister formed on his cheek, burst, and oozed bilious green pus that trickled down and dripped off his jaw.

CHAPTER EIGHT

"Get out of there!" Matt yelled. "Get out while you—"

But it was already too late. The four grad students reeled back from the altar, and as they did, sores appeared on their faces as well.

Something slammed down on the back of Matt's neck, driving his face against the ground. Blood spurted from his nose. He twisted to look over his shoulder and saw Hammond looming above him. The professor's hands were clubbed together and lifted to deliver another blow.

Matt shot an elbow back into Hammond's belly. The impact knocked Hammond to the side and gave Matt the chance to roll away from him. As he did so, he lifted a booted foot and caught Hammond under the chin with a kick that sent the man sprawling.

Matt scrambled to his hands and knees. He saw Varley climbing out of the pit. The elderly professor's face was covered with sores now, the red marks standing out in stark contrast to his snow-white hair.

"Doctor, get away from that thing!" Matt yelled as he came to his feet.

Varley roared, "Shut your motherfucking mouth!" He stepped off the ladder onto the ground at the edge of the pit and pointed at Matt. "Get him!"

Scott was right behind Varley on the ladder. With almost superhuman agility, he leapt out of the excavation. He had brought his shovel with him, and he gripped the handle and swung the blade at Matt's head with blinding speed.

Matt ducked under the swinging shovel and stepped in to slam a punch into Scott's midsection. The blow sent Scott staggering back a couple of steps, but he caught his balance quickly.

Chuck was out of the pit by now, also armed with the shovel he had used to help unearth the altar. He raised it high above his head, unleashed what sounded like a rebel yell from his throat, and brought the shovel down. Matt leapt aside from it. The shovel clanged loudly on the ground.

April reached the top of the ladder. Her wholesome beauty was gone now. Sores had erupted all over her face. Green corruption dripped from them, and strips of rotting flesh peeled off her nose and chin. She screeched curses as she ran at Matt with her hands extended in front of her, the fingers hooked like claws.

He grabbed her arms and flung her against Chuck. The two of them got tangled up together. Matt needed that respite because Scott was coming at him again. He caught the shovel before the blade could bash his brains out. His foot snapped out in a kick that caught Scott in the left knee and made the young man's leg buckle. Matt shoved him to the ground.

The yelling had gotten the attention of the others on top of the mesa. From the corner of his eye, Matt spotted several of them running toward him to find out what was wrong.

He waved his arms at them and yelled, "Get back, get back!" He didn't know how far-reaching the effect given off by the altar might be. Even though it hadn't changed him as it had the others, he could feel it, radiating from the carved face of Mr. Dark like ripples in a pond.

This was what had happened to the people who lived in this pueblo almost a thousand years earlier, he thought. Madness had spread from the altar and washed over the mesa, leading to a frenzy of slaughter and depravity.

Blood Mesa was a good name for the place, all right. It had been drenched in blood in those long-ago days...and soon might be again.

"Get in the truck and the pickups!" Matt shouted at the others. He didn't know if the vehicles would provide any safety, but they would be more secure than the tents. Maybe if he could get the rest of the group to flee, he could stay behind and deal with the ones who'd been changed by Mr. Dark.

That meant he'd probably have to kill all of them.

Or be killed by them. While some mystical force seemed to protect him from the touch of Mr. Dark, he could be harmed by those who had been prodded into evil by the creature.

Brad Kern and Noel McAlister were the closest of the grad students from the other groups. They had run ahead of Maggie and Rich. Suddenly both young men stumbled and clapped their hands to their heads as if they had been struck by migraines at the same instant.

Brad fell to his knees and clawed at his face. Chunks of flesh came away, shredded by his fingernails. Noel managed to stay on his feet, but sores were appearing on his face, too. Matt watched in horror, wondering if waves of evil had reached out from the altar and touched them, too. Was there any way to stop this, to reverse what was happening, to save these people?

Hell, was there any way for him to save himself?

Noel's unsteady gait strengthened. He lowered his hands, laughed, and charged at Matt. Behind him, Brad surged to his feet and joined in the attack.

Like a football lineman, Matt went low and threw himself at their knees. They crashed into him and tumbled out of control over him. Matt slapped his hands against the ground and pushed himself into a roll that carried him past the two fallen grad students.

Maggie and Rich had stopped and were staring at Brad and Noel, clearly confused about why they had attacked Matt. Matt hurried to his feet, grabbed their arms, and urged them toward the truck.

"Go! Go!"

Behind him, terrified screams filled the night. Matt and the students swung around and saw that Astrid had stumbled into the path of Hammond, Varley, Scott, Chuck, April, and Sierra as they gave chase. Varley had hold of her and clawed at her face as she screeched.

"Kill her!" Varley cried. "Kill the fucking cunt!"

Scott and Chuck shoved him aside and started flailing at Astrid with their shovels. Her screams were cut off short as the two young men battered her to the ground.

The horrific scene had distracted Brad and Noel. They ran to join in as everyone who had been affected by the altar swarmed around Astrid and began tearing her to pieces.

After seeing that, Maggie and Rich didn't need any more urging to make a run for it. They dashed toward the truck.

Matt ran behind them, glancing over his shoulder as he did so. He realized it wouldn't do any good to seek shelter in the pickups. Scott and Chuck could just shatter the windshields and windows with those shovels.

The truck might be a different story. It was taller, the windshield and windows not as easy to reach, and he had the keys to it in his pocket. If he could get in the truck and get it started, he might be able to use it as a weapon.

Ronnie and the students who had been with her ran up to Maggie and Rich. Matt was close behind them.

"Hide in the ruins!" he told them. "Grab some shovels or something to use as weapons! Go!"

Ronnie clutched his sleeve as the others scattered. "Matt, what...what's happened?"

"They killed Astrid!" Maggie said with a hysterical sob. "They tore her to pieces, Dr. Dupre! They're crazy!"

"You need to get out of here, Ronnie!" Matt said. "And don't go anywhere near Dr. Varley's excavation!"

The pursuit should have caught up to them by now. Matt looked over his shoulder and felt cold horror go through him. Hammond and the others hadn't resumed the chase. They were gathered around Varley, who was carrying Astrid's head, which had been hacked raggedly from her neck with the blade of a shovel.

"My God," Ronnie said in a voice hushed with awe and fear. "They're...they're insane."

She couldn't see the evil taking physical form on their faces the way Matt could, but she could see the results of it still dripping blood as the head swung back and forth in Varley's hand as he held it above his head and the others circled around him in some sort of macabre dance.

Matt took hold of her arm and began to back toward the truck. "Remember the bones in the kiva," he told her. "The people who lived here went mad and turned on each other. That's what's going on."

"I don't believe it!"

"You can see it for yourself, damn it! Look what they did to Astrid!"

"Something must have caused this. We have to help them—"

"We can't," Matt said. "All we can do is try to keep them from killing us."

Ronnie shook her head stubbornly as she backed away beside him. "That's not possible. It's some sort of disease. We need to get them to a hospital—"

Matt wouldn't have expected any other reaction from a rational, highly educated person. To people like Ronnie, there was always a scientific explanation for every problem, and there was always a way to fix it, too.

Matt knew better. "Rational" had nothing to do with it. He was looking at pure chaos in human form, and so he wasn't surprised when the circle suddenly broke apart and Chuck screamed and charged at him, waving his blood-smeared shovel.

"I'm gonna bash y'all's fuckin' heads in!" he yelled, spittle flying from his mouth.

The others followed his lead, dashing toward Matt and Ronnie as they screeched obscenities.

"Run!"

Matt sprinted toward the truck, keeping his hand clamped on Ronnie's arm so he dragged her along with him. Terror soon had her running just as fast as he was.

What she was seeing might baffle and offend the scientist part of her, but the human part was smart enough to be scared shitless.

Jerry, Rich, Ginger, Maggie, and Stephanie had disappeared into the ruins of the ancient pueblo. Matt didn't see any of them, and he was glad of that. Night was coming on, and they might be able to hide.

On the other hand, the darkness would make it more difficult to see the things that were stalking them.

And that was the way Matt thought of them—as things. The people they had been were gone. He wondered if Andrew Hammond had been human at all, the whole time they had been up here.

Their feet pounding on the hard-packed ground, Matt and Ronnie reached the truck. Matt yanked the driver's side door open and boosted Ronnie into the cab with one hand while digging in his jeans pocket for the keys with the other. As Ronnie slid across the seat, Matt vaulted into the cab after her. He pulled the door shut just in time for it to stop the shovel blade that Chuck swung at him. Metal clanged against metal. Matt used his left elbow to push down the lock button while he jammed the key into the ignition with his right hand.

"Lock your door!" he yelled.

"Got it!" Ronnie said. She flinched away from the window as Sierra climbed onto that side of the cab and started slapping at the glass while yelling frenziedly.

Chuck was trying to pull himself high enough on the side of the cab to get a good swing at the window with the shovel. Matt twisted the key and tromped the gas, hoping he wouldn't flood the engine. It caught with a rumbling growl as Hammond, Varley, Scott, and April threw themselves in front of the truck.

Matt slammed the truck into gear and sent it lurching forward. Ronnie screamed as the people caught in the vehicle's path scrambled to get out of the way. Hammond, Scott, and April made it, but Varley just wasn't fast enough.

The old man threw up his arms and shrieked as the truck ran him down. Matt felt the bump as the heavy wheels passed over Varley's body. Nothing could survive that.

"My God, my God!" Ronnie cried. "You killed him!"

"You saw what they did to Astrid," Matt said. "I wish I'd gotten a couple of the others, too."

"You're crazy! You're as crazy as they are!"

He kept his left hand on the wheel as the truck bumped around several partially collapsed walls. With his right hand, he grabbed her shoulder and shook it.

"Look at me!" he told her. "Look at me, damn it! You saw their eyes. You saw their faces. Look at mine!"

He turned his head to look over at her. Ronnie stared at him with wide, panic-stricken eyes for a moment, then drew in a deep, shuddery breath.

"All right, maybe you're not quite as crazy," she said. "But did you have to kill Dr. Varley?"

"Yes," Matt said. "I'm sorry. I know they're your friends, Ronnie. But there's no way we can help them. All we can do is try to save ourselves and the others who haven't gone mad."

"We can get the others and drive away! As long as we're in the truck and moving, Dr. Hammond and the others can't stop us."

Matt nodded as he clutched the wheel and tried to keep the truck under control. "That's what I'm hoping. We need to get off this mesa."

But at the back of his mind lurked another thought. That altar was uncovered now, and its evil had already begun to spread. How far would it go? And if Hammond and the others who were affected by it were left to venture out into the world, what damage would *they* do?

Matt didn't know the answers to those questions, but he was pretty sure they wouldn't be good. He wanted to save Ronnie and the unaffected students, but ultimately the most important thing he could do here was stop the others and somehow destroy that altar, which might, just might, reverse the effect and keep him from having to kill them.

Yeah, he thought. That was all he had to do.

CHAPTER NINE

Matt switched on the truck's headlights and leaned on the horn, sending a long, strident blare over the top of the mesa.

That would help the crazed ones track them, but it couldn't be helped. He wanted to draw the unaffected students to the truck. It would be better for all of them to be together.

He had to come up with a plan, and he thought it would be a good idea, too, to get Ronnie's brain working, to distract her from all the confusion and horror she had to be feeling. Besides, she was a highly intelligent woman. He could use her help.

"Listen to me," he said as he sent the truck bucking and bouncing through the ruins. "It's too long a story to tell you how I know this, but believe me, it's true. The reason this is happening is because Dr. Varley and his group uncovered a sacrificial altar in their excavation."

"A sacrificial— What are you talking about? The Anasazi didn't practice human sacrifice."

"April said the same thing...just before she started trying to kill me. They changed right before my eyes, Ronnie. I swear it."

He didn't tell her that Hammond had been evil all along. That detail would just complicate things unnecessarily. Let her think Hammond had been affected along with the others. In the end, it didn't matter.

"You're saying this is some sort of supernatural thing? That they've been...possessed, for want of a better word?"

"*Corrupted* might actually *be* a better word. They've been changed."

"And they can't be changed back?"

"If there's a way to do that, I don't know it," Matt said. "And I've tried."

She looked over at him sharply. "This isn't the first time you've seen something like this?"

"No. I know it sounds nuts, but it's true."

"You aren't here by accident, are you?"

Even under these circumstances, he couldn't hold back a laugh. "No. I'm not."

"You sound like one of those people who wear aluminum foil on their heads to keep the government or the aliens from controlling their thoughts."

"I know. But ask yourself this: how long have you known Dr. Varley?"

"Seven years," Ronnie replied, her voice catching a little.

"In all that time, he never tried to kill you or hurt anybody else, did he? He never danced around with a dead girl's head in his hand."

Ronnie gave a little moan and choked out, "Of course not."

"Then it's obvious *something* changed."

Silence from Ronnie for a moment, then, "You're right, Matt, something changed. But I can't believe that story about the altar. It's...it's a virus or some sort of toxin. It has to be."

If she wanted to believe that, fine, he told himself. It didn't change what they had to do.

Before Matt could say anything else, a shape darted toward them from the right. Matt took his foot off the gas as he recognized Ginger Li. She screamed, "Help! Help me!"

Matt hit the brake. The truck skidded and screeched to a halt. Ronnie started to open her door, then stopped and looked at Matt. He nodded to her. Ginger's face was still clear of sores.

Ronnie swung the door open and said, "Get in here." Ginger crowded in beside her as Ronnie slid closer to Matt. They might be able to get one of the other young women into the cab.

"Close the door," he told them. "We need to keep moving." Ginger slammed the door. "And lock it," Matt added unnecessarily. Ginger was already pushing the button down.

Once that was done, she collapsed in a shuddering heap against Ronnie, who put her arms around her. "I...I saw what they did to Astrid," Ginger said. "What's *wrong* with them?"

"Something bad has happened to some of the others," Ronnie told her, which seemed like the understatement of the year to Matt. "We don't know exactly what it is, but we have to stay away from them until we find everybody who's all right; then we're getting out of here."

"I want to go home!" Ginger wailed.

"Soon," Matt told her. "Soon, I hope."

Ronnie comforted Ginger while Matt continued searching for the other grad students who had scattered through the ruins. After a few minutes, Ronnie looked over at him and said, "I've been thinking. If you're right about that altar—and I'm not saying you are—would destroying it put a stop to this madness?"

"I don't know. Maybe."

Matt didn't hold out much hope that destroying the altar would save those who were already affected, but at least that might stop the evil it contained from spreading. Whether that evil was caused by Mr. Dark—or had *created* Mr. Dark—he didn't know. That image of the snake eating its tail, what was it called? *Ouroboros*. The name leapt into his head, recalled from some otherwise forgotten book.

It was a symbol of something endlessly dying and being reborn. In this case, something that had haunted the dreams and lives of humanity all the way back into antiquity.

"Then we should blow it up," Ronnie said.

"Blow it up? How do we do that?"

"With some of the dynamite we brought with us."

"Dynamite!" Matt repeated. "Nobody said anything to me about having dynamite around!"

"Just one small crate of it, in case we needed to do any blasting in the excavations. It's in Andrew's— Dr. Hammond's—tent. He's handled dynamite before, so he brought it with him."

Matt took a hand off the wheel and scrubbed it over his face. If he had known that Hammond, with the evil already in firm control of him, had brought dynamite along, he would have been even more worried. Of course, things had already gone pretty bad anyway, almost as bad as they could—

Dusk had started its rapid descent on the landscape, and from the corner of his eye Matt saw the sudden spurt of fire in the gray gloom. At the same time, he heard the roar of an explosion. He braked again and looked across the mesa toward the spot where a cloud of smoke and dust billowed into the air.

"Oh my God!" Ronnie said.

It was too much to hope that one of the other grad students had gotten hold of the dynamite and blasted the altar into a million pieces. The others didn't even know about it yet. Someone else had used the explosives.

And Ronnie had just said that Hammond had experience handling dynamite.

"Shit!" Matt said. He goosed the accelerator and cranked the wheel as he swung the truck toward the site of the explosion.

The headlight beams lanced across the mesa and lit up the cloud of dust as it drifted apart. Matt knew what he should be seeing now, but it wasn't there anymore.

"The Indian's Head," Ronnie said. "It's gone."

"The Indian's Head?" Matt repeated. "That big rock?"

She nodded. "The one that sat just above the trail up here. If it's not there anymore, that means Hammond used the dynamite to blast it apart. The pieces must have fallen on the trail and blocked it."

"If that's true, we can't get down. We're trapped up here," Matt said.

That made Ginger let out another frightened wail.

"Hammond may be crazy, but that doesn't mean he's not smart," Matt said. "Yeah, we're stuck."

Ronnie swallowed. "On top of a mesa with seven lunatics who want to kill us, and it's going to be dark in another few minutes. Is that what you're trying to tell me?"

Before Matt could answer, a shape hurtled from the top of a partially collapsed wall and smacked into the hood of the truck. Brad Kern grabbed hold of the truck and pressed his leering face against the glass of the windshield.

CHAPTER TEN

Ronnie and Ginger both screamed. Matt whipped the steering wheel back and forth, swerving the truck from side to side in an attempt to make Brad lose his grip and fall off.

But he hung on, and with his long arms and legs he resembled a giant insect attached to the windshield.

Matt wasn't sure what Brad intended to do. He didn't appear to be armed, and he couldn't get into the cab as long as Matt kept the truck moving.

A second later, Matt got his answer. Brad drew his head back on his neck as far as he could and then slammed his forehead against the glass.

The windshield was too thick for Brad to shatter it, but that didn't stop him from smashing his head against it again and again. Blood began to smear the glass. Matt sensed that Brad would continue to ram his head against the windshield until his skull fractured and he bashed his brains out. He was that desperate to get at them and kill them.

Ronnie and Ginger both screamed as Brad butted the glass again. Matt tried a different tack and stood on the brake. The truck jerked to a sudden stop.

That was enough to dislodge Brad. He flew off the hood and landed on his back. His face was already a bloody ruin, but whatever was in control of him now kept him from feeling any pain. He started to climb to his feet.

Brad appeared not to see the bulky figure that loomed up behind him. All his attention was focused on the truck and its occupants.

So it must have taken him by surprise when Jerry Schultz slammed the big chunk of rock against the back of his head. The impact drove Brad to his knees. Moving with frantic speed, Jerry hit him again. Brad fell on his face. Jerry dropped on top of him, digging both knees into Brad's back to pin him on the ground.

Then Jerry hit him again and again until Brad's head was just a gory lump of misshapen flesh and bone.

Jerry dropped the bloody rock and reeled to his feet. He stared at the truck, so Matt got a good look at his face in the headlights.

Not a single sore. Jerry had killed Brad to defend himself and the others, not because Mr. Dark had made him crazy.

Matt cranked down his window and called, "Jerry, get in here!"

With relief washing over his face, Jerry ran toward the truck. Ginger opened her door for him.

Jerry paused just outside the vehicle. "Are you guys all right?" he asked.

"We're not crazy, if that's what you mean," Ronnie said. "Get in, Jerry."

He shook his head. "No, it'd be too crowded in there. I'll ride in the back. We're getting out of here, right?"

"We can't," Matt told him. "That explosion a few minutes ago blocked the trail down from the mesa. We're just trying to stay away from the others."

"What's *wrong* with them? What happened to them?"

"Explanations later," Matt snapped. "Climb in the back and let me know when you're ready."

Jerry nodded. He hurried away from the cab, and a moment later Matt heard him call, "Okay, I'm in!"

"Hang on!"

Matt started driving again. He glanced at the gas gauge. The tank was a little more than half full, enough for him to keep driving for a while.

But where was he going to go? He needed to do something besides run. That wouldn't stop the evil emanating from the altar.

The interstate was only about three miles away. Was it possible the effect could reach that far? Would everyone driving by on the highway go insane? A nightmare scenario played out in Matt's head in which the altar's effect spread across the entire Southwest. And if that happened, where would it stop?

Would it stop?

He shook those thoughts away. *Concentrate on the here and now,* he told himself. *Deal with the danger close at hand.*

Stay alive.

"I see somebody!" Jerry yelled from the back of the truck. "It's Rich and Maggie!"

"Where are they?" Matt shouted.

"Behind us! Trying to catch up! Slow down and they—Shit!"

"What is it?"

"The others are after them! We gotta help 'em, Mr. Cahill!"

The smartest thing might be to speed up and let Rich Rankin and Maggie Flynn fend for themselves. Matt knew that.

But he couldn't do it. He braked again, bringing the truck to a shuddering halt.

Ronnie grabbed his right arm as he used his left to swing the door open.

"Where are you going?"

"To help them. Get behind the wheel."

"I can't drive a truck like this!"

He pointed to the clutch and the gear shift lever sticking up from the floorboard. "Push that down, push that over there like that, and hit the gas. You'll figure it out."

"Matt!"

But he pulled away from her and dropped to the ground. He ran to the back of the truck. The flaps of the canvas cover were tied back, and the tailgate was down.

"Jerry, toss me my duffel bag."

Jerry threw the bag onto the tailgate. Matt reached inside it. As he did so, his eyes cut toward the figures running toward the truck. Rich and Maggie were in the lead, but Scott and Chuck were close behind them, followed by April, Noel, and Hammond.

Matt pulled his ax from the duffel bag.

"Shit!" Jerry said. "What're you gonna—"

Matt strode out to meet them. He was damned sick and tired of the killing, tired of being forced to take lives in order to save lives. But once again, he was in a position where he had no choice. He lifted the ax and held it in both hands.

"Get in the back of the truck," he told Rich and Maggie as they sprinted past him.

Then he stepped forward and swung the ax.

Fixated on Rich and Maggie, Chuck didn't even try to avoid it. The keen edge of the blade caught him cleanly in the throat. Matt felt it shear easily through flesh. The blade caught a little on the bone, but only for a second before cleaving right on through it.

Chuck ran out from under his head as it popped in the air.

The body, geysering blood from the suddenly empty neck, ran several more steps before it collapsed. Chuck's head thudded to the ground at about the same time.

Matt was already pivoting, trying to continue the same swing and take Scott down with it. Scott's reflexes were too fast, though. He blocked the ax with the shovel he still carried. The collision almost knocked the weapon out of Matt's hands. He hung on, twisted away, and tried a backhanded slash. Scott avoided it.

That brought Scott's guard down enough for Matt to kick him in the stomach. As Scott doubled over, Noel charged past him. Matt clipped the young man on the side of the head with the ax handle. Noel lost his balance and went down.

Hammond and April, unable to run quite as fast as the athletic young men, had fallen behind. Hammond stopped and motioned for April to stay back. He wore a backpack now, and Matt wondered if it had more of the dynamite in it.

"Give it up, Cahill," Hammond said. More of the rotten flesh sloughed off his face as he grinned. "You can't get away. I took care of that. All you and the others have to do is join us, and you'll be fine."

Matt backed away as he gripped the ax. "I don't think so, Doctor," he said.

He didn't take his eyes off Hammond and the man's remaining allies. He couldn't look behind him, but he knew he was closer to the truck, which was still idling. The engine's growling rumble was the only small shred of comfort available to Matt right now.

"You're going to die screaming," Hammond promised. "Just the way she did."

Matt knew he shouldn't say it, but he couldn't stop himself.

"She?"

Hammond slipped the backpack off. It was already open, so all he had to do was plunge his hand into it and pull out Astrid Tompkins' battered head. It was barely recognizable.

No one would ever see the young woman's beautiful smile again.

It was all Matt could do not to launch himself forward like a berserker, to lay into them, hacking right and left with the ax. But they still outnumbered him four to one, and if he fell now, that would leave Ronnie and the others on their own. Matt knew that without him around to help them, Hammond's group would hunt them down, one by one if necessary, and slaughter them.

And probably eat them, he thought, remembering the "garbage dump" Ronnie had uncovered.

The truck's engine suddenly revved. Matt had to glance back. He saw it rumbling toward him in reverse.

"Stop him!" Hammond yelled.

Matt turned. The truck was close enough now that he was able to leap forward and land on the tailgate. Jerry was there to reach down and grab his shirt, making sure Matt didn't tumble out of the vehicle.

"Got him!" Jerry shouted.

With a grinding of gears, the truck lurched forward again, leaving Hammond, Scott, April, and Noel behind. Matt scooted deeper into the bed.

"Who's driving?" he asked.

"Rich thought he could handle it," Jerry explained.

The cab was pretty full by now, with Rich and Maggie added to Ronnie and Ginger. Rich seemed to be doing all right driving the truck.

"Was...was that Astrid's..." Jerry couldn't bring himself to say it. "Was that Astrid?"

"Yeah," Matt said. "I'm sorry."

"This is crazy."

"That's the word for it," Matt agreed. He couldn't see Hammond and the others behind them anymore. Night cloaked the mesa. The cones of light from the truck's headlights provided the only illumination other than the stars.

He went to the front of the truck bed and called, "Rich, stop!"

When Rich had brought the truck to a halt, Matt dropped off the tailgate and hurried up to the cab.

"I'm driving again," Matt said. "Rich, stay up here in case I need you to take the wheel. The rest of you, get in the back with Jerry."

"What are you going to do?" Ronnie asked.

"We'll head back to the camp," Matt explained. "There are picks and shovels there we can use as weapons, and I want to see if maybe Hammond left some dynamite in his tent. I'd like to see what blowing up that altar would do."

Ronnie must have explained to the others about the altar, because they seemed to know what Matt was talking about. She said, "So we're going on the attack?"

"That's right. We outnumber them now, six to five."

Ginger spoke up, saying, "Where's Stephanie?"

In a quivering voice, Maggie said, "The last time I saw her, she was with Astrid."

That wasn't good, Matt thought, but there was nothing they could do about it now. If Stephanie Porter was still alive, she needed to crawl into a hole and hide. That was the best chance she had of surviving this bloody night.

Ronnie said, "Maybe we should vote—"

"We're not voting," Matt broke in. "We're going to get whatever we can lay our hands on to fight with, and we're taking the battle to them."

For a second he thought Ronnie might argue with him. The tolerance and diversity of the academic world were all well and good, but tolerance didn't mean shit when you were faced with somebody whose only goal in life was to kill you, and possibly gnaw the flesh off your bones.

Ronnie must have realized that, because she jerked her head in a nod and said, "Fine. Let's go get the bastards."

CHAPTER ELEVEN

Matt circled around the ruins, heading back toward the camp. He wished he could drive without headlights, so Hammond and the others couldn't tell right where they were, but it was too dark for that. He couldn't risk driving into a hole and busting an axle.

Ronnie, Ginger, and Maggie had climbed in the back with Jerry. Rich rode in the cab with Matt, the ax lying on the seat between them. He glanced down at the weapon and asked, "You...ah...carry an ax around with you, Mr. Cahill?"

"I used to work in the timber business," Matt replied, as if that explained it. "My whole family did. That ax belonged to my father, and his father before him."

Rich didn't press the issue. Instead he said, "At first I didn't really think they were dangerous. They just looked sort of crazed, you know. But then they started chasing us, and I knew that if they caught us, bad things would happen."

"That's putting it mildly," Matt said.

"And then they caught Astrid..." Rich couldn't go on for a moment. "You think it's all because of some altar that Dr. Varley's group uncovered?"

"I'm pretty sure that's the case."

"That's what made the Anasazi go nuts and start eating each other?"

"Does it matter?"

The tents loomed in front of them, the canvas bright in the night as the headlights swept over them. As Matt slowed the truck, he called to Ronnie and the others in the back, "I think we've beaten them back here, but stay inside the truck until I've taken a quick look around."

"Be careful, Matt," Ronnie called back to him.

The truck had stopped. Matt left the engine running and picked up the ax. He said to Rich, "If anything happens to me, or if you and the others are in danger, don't wait for me. Just grab the wheel and get the hell out of here."

"And then what?"

"Keep moving, I guess. You'll be on your own."

"Mr. Cahill...what Dr. Dupre said. Be careful. Please."

"I intend to," Matt promised.

He swung down from the cab. The night was quiet except for the rumbling of the engine.

Then a wind blew across the top of the mesa, and he heard the wailing that Ronnie had described to him earlier. That was just the wind moving through the ruins, he told himself. It wasn't the wailing of lost souls.

He wished he could believe that a hundred percent.

Most of the expedition's supplies were piled near Dr. Varley's tent. Matt didn't remember exactly what was there, but as he looked over the supplies he had a feeling some of the picks were gone. That probably meant Hammond, Scott, April, Noel, and Sierra were armed now.

A couple of picks were left, though, and several shovels. After scanning the night intently for several moments as he stood there gripping the ax, Matt called to the people in the truck, "All right, come grab a shovel or a pick. Make it fast."

Jerry was the first one out of the truck. He picked up one of the long-handled shovels and heaved a sigh.

"I feel better now," he said as he brandished the shovel. "At least we can fight back."

Matt remembered how Jerry had smashed Brad's head with that rock. "I'd say you've already done that."

"Yeah." Jerry's face twisted. "I...I can't believe I did that. I was just too scared to stop hitting him."

Jerry had done the right thing, Matt thought. Maybe he would understand that one of these days. If he was lucky enough to survive the night.

The others armed themselves. Matt handed one of the picks to Ronnie and told her, "Give that to Rich. It's shorter than the shovels, so it'll be easier to carry in the cab."

"What are we going to do now?" Ginger asked.

"Stay together and keep your eyes open," Matt said. "I'm going to check Hammond's tent and see if there's any dynamite there. If you see or hear any of the others, let out a yell. Jerry, come with me."

Jerry swallowed hard. Clearly, he would have preferred to stay with the others, but he didn't argue. He hurried along behind Matt toward Hammond's tent.

Matt had the ax ready as he approached the tent. Nothing was moving around it, though. He used the ax to push aside the canvas flap over the entrance.

He halfway expected some horror to come exploding out of the tent at him, but nothing happened. He had matches in his shirt pocket—useful for lighting oil lamps, campfires, and such—so as he stepped inside he fished out one of them with his left hand and snapped it into life with his thumbnail.

The match's flickering glare revealed that the tent was empty. So was the small wooden crate that sat beside Hammond's cot. Matt didn't recall seeing it before. It was possible Hammond himself had unloaded the crate and stashed it in here the first day atop the mesa.

Hammond had already been touched by Mr. Dark at that point. Had he had the whole plan in mind from the beginning? Matt couldn't help but wonder.

He was about to turn away from the empty crate in disgust when he spotted something sticking out from under Hammond's cot. The match burned down to his fingers, and he had to drop it. The flame went out.

Matt knelt and felt around on the ground with his free hand. His fingers closed around some sort of cylinder. It had a slightly greasy feel to it. Matt's hand tightened around the thing.

He knew he was holding a stick of dynamite. It must have fallen on the ground and rolled under the cot while Hammond was scooping the rest of the explosives out of the crate to take with him.

Feeling a little nervous about holding the cylinder—he recalled hearing how unstable dynamite could be—Matt checked both ends of it. The dynamite didn't have a blasting cap attached to it, and no cap meant no fuse, assuming Hammond had even brought along any fuse. Most blasts were set off electronically these days.

So what good was it going to do him? He remembered seeing movies where the hero set off dynamite by shooting at it, but was such a thing even possible?

Anyway, he didn't have a gun. As far as he knew, there wasn't one anywhere on top of the mesa.

Maybe there was some other way. He tried to remember everything he'd ever read or heard about dynamite. The explosive in it was actually nitroglycerin, which was much easier to detonate. Sometimes some of the nitro would sweat out of a stick of dynamite and form a slick coating on it...

Sort of like the greasy surface of the stick he was holding.

Matt's heart pounded harder. If some of the nitro had sweated out of this stick, a hard blow might be enough to detonate it and set off the rest of the explosive soaked into the cylinder. Hitting it with a shovel or pick might do the job.

But in order to do that, a man would have to be close enough that the resulting blast would take him out, too. Using this stick of dynamite to blow up the altar would be a suicide mission.

It might come to that, he thought.

For now, he pulled the blanket off Hammond's cot and used the ax to cut off a piece of it. Then he carefully wrapped the dynamite inside the blanket, rolling the fabric around it several times before he slipped it inside his shirt. If he didn't jostle it around too much, and if nobody walloped him with a shovel in just the wrong place, carrying it that way ought to be reasonably safe.

He didn't think he would find anything else useful in here. He was about to step out of the tent when he heard Jerry exclaim, "Mr. Cahill! Somebody's coming!"

Matt pushed the flap aside again as Jerry went on, "Oh my God! It's Stephanie! She's all right!"

Matt stepped outside as Jerry hurried to meet the figure stumbling toward them. Starlight reflected off Stephanie's blonde ponytail.

Some instinct warned Matt. He called, "Jerry, wait—"

Too late. Jerry had almost reached Stephanie. Suddenly she sprang forward, her arm shooting out. Starlight winked on the blade of the knife just before she plunged it into Jerry's chest.

Stephanie let out a screech of demonic laughter.

Jerry dropped his shovel and stumbled back, pawing futilely at the handle of the knife buried in his body.

"I got him!" Stephanie screamed. She rushed after him, grabbed his arm, and sunk her teeth in it.

Footsteps rushed at Matt from the side. He twisted and brought up the ax with all his strength. The head caught Noel McAlister in the abdomen and ripped on up his torso, opening up his stomach. Noel screamed and ran into Matt, who pulled away as he felt the hot gush of blood and innards spilling out of Noel's body.

Matt wanted to try to get to Jerry, but Scott had appeared out of the darkness, and he and Stephanie were already between Matt and the luckless grad student.

All too aware of the stick of dynamite nestled between his belly and his shirt, Matt turned and ran instead. He had to get back to the truck and then to the excavation where the altar was located. The dynamite was his only real chance to end this.

And he was the only one who could do it. If any of the others got too close to the altar, they would be affected by the evil coming from it, too. He was the only one who seemed to be immune. He wondered why that was, but there was no time to figure it out now.

"Matt!" Ronnie screamed before he reached the truck. He spotted struggling figures around it. As he came closer he saw Ronnie, Ginger, and Maggie slashing wildly at April and Sierra in an attempt to hold them off.

Sierra didn't see Matt coming in time. He swept up the ax and brought it down in the back of her head, sinking the blade deep into her brain. He tried to jerk it loose as Sierra collapsed, but the ax stuck in her skull. He had to plant a foot in her back and wrench it free with a crunching, sucking sound.

April screamed, "You fucker!" and ran off into the darkness.

"Get in the truck!" Matt told Ronnie and the others. "Go!"

He ran to the cab and jerked the door open. Rich was already sliding out from behind the wheel.

"I told them to get in the truck so we could get out of here, like you said for me to do, Mr. Cahill. But Dr. Dupre wouldn't come. Not without you."

Matt nodded as he laid the ax between them. It was sticky with Noel's guts and Sierra's blood and brains.

Such a cost. Such a horrible, tragic cost, because none of the people he had killed tonight actually deserved to die. They hadn't done anything wrong except for being there. Because of that, their blood was on his hands, along with the blood of far too many other people. It would never wash away, either. Only his own death would wipe out the stain.

If things went as he planned, that death might not be too long in coming.

"Everybody in back there?" he yelled.

"We're in!" Ronnie called back. "Go!"

Matt put the truck in gear and tromped the gas. The big truck barreled ahead.

"Where are we going now?" Rich asked.

"To Dr. Varley's excavation," Matt said. "We're going to put an end to this."

CHAPTER TWELVE

Matt wasn't halfway across the mesa when the sudden blaze of lights up ahead made him hit the brake.

"What's that?" Rich asked.

Matt bit back a curse. "Hammond's been busy. He must have used one of the pickups to haul those portable lights and the generator over to Dr. Varley's excavation."

"Why would he do that?"

Matt shook his head. "I don't know."

"Matt, what's wrong?" Ronnie asked from the back of the truck. "Why did we stop?"

"Hammond's got the altar lit up."

"Do you think he's going to have a...a sacrifice?"

Matt closed his eyes for a second and tried not to groan. He hadn't thought about that, but it made sense. That's what sacrificial altars were for, after all.

And even more worrisome, if he succeeded, what effect would it have on the altar's power? Was it possible the evil and the madness could get even stronger?

Matt moved his foot from the brake to the gas. At this point, all they could do was plow ahead and hope for the best.

Before he had gone another fifty yards, though, something roared up on the right and smashed against the fender on that side of the truck. Matt caught a glimpse of one of the pickups, running without lights, just before the collision. Then the impact jolted him and made him let go of the steering wheel.

The truck slewed across the ground. It weighed a lot more than the pickup, but the attack had taken Matt by surprise, and striking the truck at an angle like that, the pickup had forced it to veer to the left. The headlights suddenly played across one of those deep crevices that extended in from the edge of the mesa.

Matt grabbed the wheel and hauled hard on it. The pickup had backed off a little, but now it rammed into the truck again, trying to force the truck to plunge into that crevice.

Matt was ready this time. He managed to hold the truck on course...which was still going to take it much too close to the brink. He twisted the wheel some more, going on the attack.

With a furious grinding and clash of metal, the truck struck the pickup on the driver's side. In the backwash of lights, Matt saw Scott Conroy behind the wheel, his face contorted by insane hate. Scott struggled to control the pickup, but Matt sent the truck slamming against it again.

The pickup went over, flipping and rolling across the rugged, rocky ground.

Matt hoped it would catch fire and explode, but he didn't have time to see if that happened. He spun the wheel some more, turning away from the crevice just in time. The truck's left wheels missed the rim by less than a yard.

Flipping on the dome light, Matt glanced over at Rich and studied the young man's face. No sign of sores yet, but he knew he couldn't get much closer. If he did, he ran the risk of exposing the people with him to the altar's effect. If they were corrupted, too, the odds against him would be that much higher...not to mention the fact that even more innocent blood might wind up on his hands.

He braked. Rich asked, "Why are you stopping?"

"Everybody out!" Matt called by way of answer. He threw the door open as the truck shuddered to a halt.

Taking the ax with him, he climbed out and joined the others at the rear of the truck. He looked at them as closely as he could in the starlight. Everyone seemed to be all right.

"This is as close as you get," he told them. "Rich, the wheel is yours. Everybody else, stay ready for trouble."

"Matt, I don't like the sound of this," Ronnie said. "What are you going to do?"

He smiled and touched his shirt where the cylinder of explosive rested. "I've got a stick of Hammond's dynamite here. I'm going to use it to blow up the altar and see if that will put an end to this."

"You mean you're going to throw away your own life?"

"Not if I can help it," Matt lied. "I'll set the fuse and get the hell away from it before it blows."

What he said wasn't a complete lie. There was no fuse, but he didn't consider giving up his life for this cause to be throwing it away.

"Andrew will try to stop you," Ronnie argued. "We need to go along to give you a chance to set off the explosion."

Matt shook his head. "You can't do that. If you get any closer to the altar, you'll be changed, too."

"And you won't?"

"I was there when the damned thing was uncovered, remember?" he said. "For some reason, it doesn't affect me.

This is the way it has to be, and we can't afford to waste any more time. I'm going. Take care of yourselves."

He turned to walk toward the lights.

Ronnie caught up with him, took hold of his sleeve to stop him. As Matt turned toward her, she leaned in and kissed him, the sort of urgent, passionate kiss that would have shaken him all the way down to his toes under other circumstances.

He was a little too scared for that right now...but the kiss helped. No doubt about that.

"I'll say a prayer for you," she whispered.

"Can't hurt," he said.

Then he strode forward again, the ax clutched in his right hand.

CHAPTER THIRTEEN

The generator coughed and chattered as Matt approached, providing the power for the lights that threw their stark, brilliant glare down into the pit. He dropped to a knee before he reached that glowing circle and wished he could see what was going on down there without having to crawl right up to the edge.

That was the only way, though. He started forward on hands and knees. The rocky ground was hard on his palms, although his jeans protected his knees to a certain extent.

So far he hadn't been able to hear anything over the racket of the generator, but he began picking up voices now. Were they chanting something?

Matt edged closer, so he could see over the rim of the pit. He knew that what he saw shouldn't have shocked him—he should have been prepared for almost anything—but even so his guts clenched.

Jerry Schultz's body lay on the black altar. A crimson flower of blood stained the front of his shirt. Scott hadn't been killed when the pickup flipped, because he was back in the pit now, standing at Jerry's right while April was on the left. Andrew Hammond was at the foot of the altar, where the face of Mr. Dark was carved. He was facing away from Matt and had taken off his shirt, exposing his pale and somewhat chunky torso.

Hammond's hands were in the air above his head. He was chanting something that was gibberish as far as Matt was concerned, although he supposed it was probably the ancient Anasazi language. Scott and April looked like they were about to have orgasms from listening to Hammond. He held out a knife. "Spread his steaming guts around him and let the blood flow freely," he intoned in English this time.

Scott started to reach for the knife, but April leaned forward and snatched it from Hammond's hand.

"Let me," she said with a huge smile on her face that chilled Matt almost as much as those tons of snow and ice had. The New Mexico heat seemed far away now.

April tore Jerry's shirt open, baring his chest and belly. Matt stared down into the pit, his eyes narrowing suddenly as he saw a tiny red sore on Jerry's cheek. A few more were scattered here and there on the young man's face.

Of course Jerry was still alive, Matt realized, no matter how dead he looked. If you were going to have a sacrifice, you had to have a living victim.

Matt had planned to wait until the three of them were busy with their grisly work, then leap into the pit and flail around with the ax until he had cut them down. But if Jerry was still alive, he couldn't wait. Maybe, just maybe, he could get Jerry away from here, away from the effect of the altar, before he blew it up.

But as he tensed his muscles, ready to spring into action, Hammond called, "Now, Stephanie!"

Shit! He had forgotten Stephanie Porter.

Matt rolled to the side just as the pick wielded by Stephanie dug into the ground where he had been lying a shaved heartbeat of time earlier. He kicked up, burying his boot heel in her belly. With a heave of his leg he sent her flying over his head, into the excavation.

As Matt rolled over and scrambled to his feet, he saw Stephanie land on the edge of the altar at the far end. Her back hit its sharp edge first, and even over the generator he heard the crack of bone as her spine snapped. She fell to the ground beside the altar, her upper half writhing frenziedly while her lower half lay limp.

Before Matt could move, Scott came up the ladder with superhuman speed and tackled him. They rolled across the ground and slid over the edge into the pit. The sudden drop took Matt's breath away. He crashed down with Scott on top of him. The ax flew out of his hand. Scott's fist slammed into his jaw, stunning him.

Matt fully expected Scott to beat him to death, but Hammond's voice rang out, ordering, "Don't kill him yet! We'll sacrifice him, too."

Scott dragged Matt to his feet and held him from behind with one arm looped around Matt's throat. At the far end of the altar, Stephanie had stopped twisting around and lay there with her breath rasping in her throat. April still had the knife, and at Hammond's gestured command, she raised it again over Jerry's stomach.

With a weak flutter of the lids, Jerry's eyes opened.

"A...April...what are you...April, I...I loved you—"

"And I loved you, Jerry, or at least I tried to," April said as she smiled down at him. Then her lips drew back from her teeth in a hideous grimace. "You were just too fucking weak!"

She plunged the knife into Jerry's belly.

188

He screamed. April yanked down on the knife, slicing him open. The knife clattered on the black stone of the altar as she pulled it out of his body and dropped it. Her hands plunged into the gaping wound she had created in his midsection and brought out shiny, blood-smeared coils of intestines. Jerry kept screaming.

Matt's mind was racing. Jerry still had the tiny sores on his face, but for some reason the power of the altar wasn't affecting him as strongly as it had the others. Since Jerry still clung to a shred of his humanity, maybe he could put that to use.

"Fight back, Jerry!" Matt yelled. "Fight!"

He thought Jerry might be too close to death to muster any strength, but somehow Jerry's arms lifted and his hands shot out, taking April by surprise. He grabbed her wrists and threw her toward Hammond.

At the same time, Matt leaned back against Scott, lifted his feet, and planted both of them on the side of the altar. He could feel its heat even through the soles of his boots. Straightening his legs and kicking as hard as he could, he propelled Scott back against the wall of the excavation.

That impact was enough to jar Scott's grip loose. Matt twisted free, scooped up the ax he had dropped a few minutes earlier, and swung. The blade caught Scott in the forehead and split his skull, cleaving bone and brain almost all the way to his shoulders.

Matt pulled the ax loose as April, screaming obscenities, came at him. He poked the ax in her stomach and caused her to double over. Turning the blade, he came up with it and caught her under the chin.

There was enough force behind the blow that it sliced her whole face off.

April collapsed, probably trying to scream through a mouth she didn't have anymore. Matt turned toward Hammond, but the professor was already practically on top of him. Hammond caught Matt around the body, pinning his arms to his sides so he couldn't use the ax, and forced him back against the altar.

The black stone's searing heat stabbed into Matt's back and made him yell in pain. He head butted Hammond. Rotten flesh split. Hammond reeled back. Matt butted him again. Maybe it was real, maybe it just looked that way to Matt's eyes, but the flesh was peeling away from Hammond's face now, revealing the skull beneath. Matt broke the man's grip and shoved him back against the side of the pit. Hammond had time to scream, "No!" before the ax began to rise and fall, rise and fall.

Matt didn't stop until there was nothing left but quivering chunks of something that had once been human...but not anytime recently.

Breathing hard, Matt swung around toward the altar. He saw Jerry lying there, trying feebly to stuff his guts back inside his belly. Matt went to him, got an arm around his shoulders, and said, "We'll get you out of here."

"No..." Jerry's voice was a weak whisper. "I can't."

"You've got to. I have a stick of dynamite. I'm going to blow this damned pit to hell, and everything in it."

"Can't..."

"Dr. Dupre and some of the others are still alive and all right," Matt said. "They can take care of you, Jerry."

Jerry shook his head.

"There's no choice. I have to be here to set off the dynamite."

Jerry looked up at him. "You'll...blow yourself up."

"That's the way it's got to be."

One of Jerry's hands clutched at him. "No! I'm...as good as dead...anyway. Let me...set it off."

"I don't think you're strong enough. You'd have to hit it pretty hard with a pick or a shovel."

Somehow, Jerry managed to smile. "Gimme...a chance. If I can't...you can always...come back and do it."

He had a point, Matt realized. By all rights, Jerry should have been dead already. He couldn't have more than a few moments of life left. But maybe that would be enough.

"Let me help you sit up," Matt said.

Jerry groaned as Matt pulled him to the far end of the altar and helped him into a sitting position. Some of the loops of intestine still rested on Jerry's thighs.

As Matt started to get one of the picks lying in the excavation, Stephanie reached out and clutched weakly at his leg with one hand. Matt looked down at her and said, "I'm sorry." He meant it, too.

That didn't stop him from splitting her skull with the pick.

Then he handed the tool to Jerry. He reached into his shirt and pulled out the blanket-wrapped stick of dynamite as he went to the lower end of the altar, the end where the face of Mr. Dark was carved.

"You won't be laughing much longer, you son of a bitch," Matt said as he unrolled the fabric from the greasy red cylinder.

He placed the dynamite on that end of the altar, where the blast would totally obliterate the carving when it went off. "Can you reach that with the pick?" he asked Jerry.

"Yeah...I can do it...Mr. Cahill." Jerry took a deep breath. The movement caused the guts that had spilled out of him to squirm a little. "You better...get out of here."

"Give me a minute or so to put some distance behind us," Matt said. "But only if you can. If you feel yourself slipping away...go ahead and hit that sucker as hard as you can."

"I will," Jerry promised. He summoned up a faint smile. "Blood Mesa. Good name...for the place."

Matt was in awe of the strength that filled the mild-looking young man. The strength not only to fight off the effect of the altar but also to cling to life for this long when he was so badly hurt.

"So long, Jerry."

"So...long. Tell Dr. Dupre...I expect...a good grade."

"Top marks, Jerry."

Matt went up the ladder, taking the ax with him, and sprinted toward the place where he had left the others with the truck.

He had run several hundred yards when he slowed, stopped, and turned to look back. Nothing had happened. He drew in a deep breath. It seemed like he might have to go back and set off the dynamite himself after all. Maybe Jerry had died before he could strike the blow, or maybe Mr. Dark had finally taken complete control of him...

The blast was so powerful it jolted Matt off his feet and threw a ball of fire into the air above the pit. Matt rolled onto his belly and covered his head with his arms to protect it as chunks of rock began to rain from the night sky.

Several of them thudded into him. They would leave bruises but no permanent injury.

Finally the last of the gravel that had been flung into the air by the blast stopped pattering down around him. He climbed to his feet. The explosion had destroyed the generator and the portable lights, too, so again only starlight washed down over the mesa.

Then the truck's headlights clicked on. Matt turned and walked toward them, gripped by a huge weariness that made him stumble and almost fall.

Then Ronnie was beside him, running to meet him and put an arm around him and help him. "You did it, Matt!" she said. "You did it! It's over."

"This time," Matt said, so quietly he didn't know if she heard him or not. He didn't say it again.

———

Sheer terror was utterly exhausting. The other four survivors slept the rest of the night while Matt stood guard. When dawn had grayed the sky enough for him to see, he took the ax and went back to the excavation.

The blast had caused the pit to collapse on itself, burying not only the altar but also the bodies of Jerry, Hammond, Scott, April, and Stephanie. The toll was high, but it would have been higher if he hadn't been here, and if Jerry hadn't destroyed the altar. Maybe as high as the whole world.

He walked back to the trail that led down from the mesa. As he expected, he found that the broken remains of the Indian's Head blocked the path. It would take heavy equipment to clear the trail.

But a person could slide through some of the narrow gaps and climb over the other obstacles. The interstate was only three miles away. Ronnie and the other three survivors could walk it, especially if they got an early start before the day got too hot. They would be footsore when they got there, but they would be alive.

He went back to the truck and got his duffel bag. The others were still asleep. He changed out of his blood-drenched clothes, put the ax in the bag, and closed it, slung it over his shoulder. It would be better for all concerned if he was well away from here before they woke up.

His luck ran out as he was about to walk away. Ronnie pushed herself up on an elbow and whispered, "Matt?"

He motioned for her to be quiet. She got to her feet, and they walked out of earshot of the others before she said, "What do you think you're doing? You're going to abandon us here, after everything we've been through? You can't just walk away."

"I have to. The sort of thing we've just been through... that's my life now, and it's better if I face it alone."

"What are we supposed to do?"

"Walk back to the interstate and call for help. If I was you, though, I wouldn't tell the authorities exactly what happened up here. Just tell them it was, I don't know, a drunken brawl that got out of hand."

"With eleven people dead, do you really think anybody will believe that?"

"They're more likely to believe that than the truth," Matt said.

Ronnie wasn't able to argue with that. She just stared at him for a long moment and then said, "Damn it, Matt, it's not fair. You save our lives, you stop God knows what sort of even worse thing from happening, and then you just walk away and don't tell anybody?"

"That's the way it needs to be. The way it has to be."

"It's just not fair," Ronnie said again.

Matt thought about everything that had happened to him in the past year and said, "Not much in life is."

—

An hour later, an elderly rancher in a pickup stopped to give him a lift as he trudged along the two-lane blacktop.

"Where you headed, son?" the old-timer asked.

Matt nodded toward the windshield. "Thataway."

THE END

THE DEAD MAN:
KILL THEM ALL

By Harry Shannon

CHAPTER ONE

Near Dry Wells, Nevada
Friday, 8:12 a.m.

"Help! Over here!"

Matt Cahill shaded his eyes. Even this early in the morning the fierce Nevada sunshine slammed down like a giant metal press. The desert was flat and freckled with flat rocks. Clumps of blue sage sprouted here and there, tiny flowers open and gasping with thirst. Matt had jumped off a flatbed truck when the driver turned east, figuring he'd easily catch another ride, but no one had passed this way in more than an hour. He'd started walking and was completely lost. Now he wondered if he was also hearing things.

"Help!"

A male voice? Then Matt spotted the boy, who was jumping up and down, waving frantically. He also saw a shirtless, sunburned man in overalls nearby, walking in circles. He took in the two racing bicycles resting against the side of what appeared to be an old, boarded-up mine located on some scruffy ranch property. Matt dropped his backpack, his grandfather's ax, and his worn bedroll and sprinted in that direction.

He jogged past a sign that read "Kearns Property Leave Shit Here," and as he got closer to the boy, the situation clarified itself. The redneck man was shouting and cursing, delusional or completely drugged out. He had some mining tools and bottles of water, ropes and a few sample sacks. Perhaps he'd been prospecting in the mine when something collapsed. The two bikes were top-of-the-line, the kind used for long distances.

One of the riders was missing.

Panting, Matt arrived at the spot. The boy, a thin kid with freckles, wasn't as young as Matt had first thought, maybe late teens. He had been crying. "She's down there, my kid sister is down there. Do you have a cell phone, mister? I called our dad for help, but mine just up and died. I'm not even sure he heard me."

Matt shook his head. "Sorry, I don't. What happened?"

The boy said, "We were daring each other, just screwing around. My kid sister went down in there as a joke and something collapsed. Now I can hear her calling for help, but there's no way down."

"No way down?" Matt looked at the miner, a wreck of a human with missing teeth. "How do you get down in there, friend?"

The man screamed and batted at his own clothing. Speed freak, maybe. He looked useless. Spit flew from his mouth.

The kid said, "I tried to crawl in, but it's straight down— something fell apart. This old bastard won't tell me what to do."

Matt stepped closer and looked into the mine shaft. The kid was right: behind the ring of rocks, everything just dropped away, but he heard the girl calling for help. Matt stepped back, evaluating. The miner had a lot of equipment, much of it modern. He'd clearly been down below many times. There were small cutting tools, extra-strength ropes, and a pair of night-vision goggles. The guy was just too stoned to help. Matt walked closer, but the miner grabbed a claw hammer and threatened him.

"Easy, old-timer. Are you Mr. Kearns? Look, I just need to borrow some of your gear," Matt said.

"The fuck back!" Kearns bellowed as he swung the hammer at Matt's head. Matt stepped inside the blow, knocked it up and away with his left hand, and punched twice, once over the heart and once in the side of the neck. Kearns sank to his knees, red faced and retching.

"Stand back. What's your name?" Matt said to the freckle-faced kid.

"Jeb Pickens."

"Jeb, you keep an eye on that crazy son of a bitch. If you have to, hit him in the balls with something."

Matt Cahill grabbed some rope and a bottle of water from the miner's stash. He examined the night-vision goggles, which seemed easy enough to work, so he took them, too. He moved quickly to the mine entrance. *Here goes...*

Matt secured the rope to a boulder near the entrance, then lowered himself into the cool, dark mine. The air thickened...small things scuttled away...a rattler stirred and expressed annoyance. Matt tried to move slowly and deliberately. The movements weren't that foreign to him and his strong arms supported him—he'd climbed up and down hundreds of trees as a lumberjack. Working with one rope wasn't all that different. As he descended into the shaft, the sunlight shrank above him and his eyesight gradually failed.

"I'm coming down," Matt called. "Try to step back out of the way."

"Okay." A female voice. Below him, close now.

Matt paused for a moment, slipping the goggles on and experimenting. After a few seconds he found the right switches and the gear clicked on. The world turned green and black, images distorted and weirdly flowing, but he could see. As Matt continued to lower himself, hand over hand, he looked down.

She stood at the bottom of the trench and to one side, a teenage girl in denim shorts and a loose men's T-shirt. She carried herself well, seeming more scared than injured. That was good, because Matt had to help her climb back out. He dropped down next to her, assessing her expression. Her eyes glowed strangely in the infrared light. He'd almost forgotten that she couldn't see a thing. He touched her arm and she jumped.

"Are you thirsty?"

She nodded, so he opened the water bottle and fed her a few sips, then drank some himself. It was warm but delicious.

"My name is Matt Cahill," he said. "What's yours?"

"Suzie."

"Well, Suzie, I'm going to lead you to a rope. Can you climb?"

She nodded in the dark. "Just get me out of here. I've never been so scared in my entire life."

"Take my gloves," Matt said. "They'll help you get back up." He took Suzie's hands gently, helped her tug on the work gloves. Then he led her to the rope, almost banging her head with the long nose of the NV goggles. Strange contraption, but remarkably effective. Matt thought, *No wonder our soldiers have such an advantage in combat.*

The girl found the rope, and Matt guided her feet to the first footholds. Looking up, he described the climb as best he could, put his hands on her waist and gave her a good start up the wall, then stepped back.

"Just keep going, Suzie. You'll see the sunlight soon. If you have to stop and rest, take your time. I've got some gear on. I can see okay down here."

Matt decided not to tell her he wasn't fond of creepy crawlies.

Eventually the girl reached the top—Matt could hear the boy screaming for joy. After testing the rope, Matt began to climb back up. Without the gloves, the rope cut deeply into his hands, but they were calloused from years of physical labor. He kept his eyes on the rock face, just to make sure nothing slimy or furry was planning a sudden assault. Boards and rock groaned and moaned around him, and suddenly the walls began closing in—Matt felt claustrophobic. He wanted to get the hell out of there before something else collapsed. He was born for the mountains, not for a dark cave in the desert.

As he reached the top, the world went white. Suddenly Matt couldn't see.

He cursed, almost let go of the rope. He'd forgotten to turn off the goggles, and the sudden appearance of sunlight as he reached ground level momentarily blinded him. Matt found foot purchase in the rock, let the NV goggles dangle around his neck, and blinked feverishly, then kept his eyes closed for a while, his muscles trembling. White spots gradually turned dark again, and Matt opened his eyes. His vision had returned to normal. Satisfied, he climbed the rest of the way out and rolled into the hot sand, relieved and panting.

"Mister, we are so damned grateful, I can't tell you!" Jeb exclaimed.

Matt sat up. The miner had crawled away and was sitting near a cactus, cradling his claw hammer. Matt waved, "Sorry about that, mister."

"It wasn't my fault," the man said. A crafty look crossed his pocked features. "That Dark Man done it. He pushed her down there. He does all kinds of bad shit."

Matt Cahill felt a chill in his bones. *Mr. Dark is here?*

Before he could ask any questions, the two teens started screaming and waving. Someone was coming from the highway. Their father at long last, driving a battered white police cruiser.

It said "Dry Wells Sheriff" on the side.

CHAPTER TWO

Dry Wells, Nevada
Friday, 9:06 a.m.

Matt Cahill walked down the sidewalk and through the ghost town with Sheriff Pickens by his side. Word of the rescue had spread quickly. Folks came out onto the old wooden sidewalks to stare, and a few older people even cheered him. It seemed there were very few residents left in this town. Most of the young citizens had moved away in search of better schools and jobs. Those who stayed behind had a deep love for local traditions and the state's rich history. Clearly the teen he had saved was a precious commodity, and Dry Wells was understandably grateful for Matt's good deed.

Their sheriff was a big man, wide and tall, with white hair bound in a ponytail and a large, arrogant beard. He looked to be in his early sixties, and Matt had taken him for an ex-hippie who'd originally come out to a commune to smoke pot and get laid. Pickens was the kind of man who grew up and sobered up but had never returned home. His tan uniform was stretched tight across his ample belly and thick arms, and his chest hair was like a scrap of white shag carpet. His wife had died some time ago.

"Thanks, mister!" a gray-haired woman called. She was dressed as a nineteenth-century prostitute, frilly dress and all. She probably ran the tourist shop beneath the old brothel. Feeling a bit silly, Matt waved hello. He felt like a politician on parade.

"You're welcome."

Matt Cahill had stuffed his battered hat in his pocket and slung the bedroll, long ax, and backpack over his right shoulder. Although he certainly looked the part of a cowboy, Matt came from timber country. The nearby Ruby Mountains looked a lot more like home than this ghost town did. Matt didn't belong down with these flatlanders, on the edge of an eternal desert. He tried to smile and get past this experience, but he felt distracted.

His mind was on what the miner Kearns had said— something that made it sound like his nemesis, the Dark Man, had been here recently. Matt figured he would put in just enough time with the sheriff to be polite, and then go back and check out that possibility. He felt better on his own and out in the open anyway. On top of that, he'd already attracted way too much attention.

Knowing he was trapped for the time being, Matt tried to relax and let his momentary celebrity roll off him. He smiled and waved and let people shake his hand.

"Buy you a beer?" Sheriff Pickens said. "Least I can do."

Matt said, "I'm sure you have more important things to do. I think I'll just relax for a while and then be on my way, if that's okay."

"It's your town for as long as you want it," Sheriff Pickens said. "We're beyond grateful for what you've done."

Matt paused on the sidewalk and took in his surroundings. Though there were homes and small ranches surrounding it, historic Dry Wells itself looked like the abandoned set of a classic cowboy movie. The narrow wooden-plank sidewalks were bordered by split-rail horse hitches and fronted small buildings faded by weather and the relentless Nevada sun. The overall shape of the tourist town was loosely oval, with the main opening facing east. The sheriff's office and small jail cells sat at the west end, with a small alley on either side. In the center of the street sat a small gazebo littered with beer bottles and trash.

To the north and south there were empty storefronts, a grocery, Wally's Saloon, a closed tourist shop, a two-story hotel with a handful of empty rooms, and an abandoned movie theater. On the other side of the street sat an office and stables. A hand-lettered sign read "Vet." Next to that building squatted an old whorehouse left fully decorated just for show.

All in all, it was kind of fun.

Pickens laughed. "You trying to memorize the place?"

"I like it," Matt said. "I come from a small town."

The sheriff grinned. "Folks say we should put a mirror at one end, just to make it look bigger. Come on, let's get us some shade."

The two men walked briskly west past the old hotel toward the alley, boots thumping over the splintering wooden boards. The Nevada sun sat in the pale sky like a huge white blister, and the heat remained oppressive, the air dry and still. Back to the east, where the town opened up, a pair of black vultures swam a lazy oblong over roadkill. Nothing moved on the black ribbon of highway. Many of the town's storefronts were empty, a lot of the windows broken. Matt licked his lips. It would be high noon soon. Most living things wouldn't want to be outside. *Damn, it gets hot...*

As if reading his mind, Sheriff Pickens said, "You want to wait an hour or two before you go back out there."

"I'm starting to agree with you."

The radio on the sheriff's belt crackled and he answered it. "What's going on, Barbara?"

A woman spoke hurriedly, something about an accident. Pickens sighed. "I got me something to take care of, Mr. Cahill. How about you go on inside and relax for a bit. Maybe we can talk again before you leave."

"Sure."

"Look," the sheriff said, "please reconsider letting us put you up for the night. I'd at least like to buy you a big steak dinner."

When Matt didn't respond, Pickens sighed. "You'll think on it?"

"I'll think about it," Matt said, just to get away. "We'll see."

CHAPTER THREE

Dry Wells, Nevada
Friday, 10:59 a.m.

As the wickedly hot desert wind moaned and strained at the dusty bathroom window, Sally Morgan stared into the cracked mirror above the sink and ran a brush through her long blonde hair. Sally was still on the right side of thirty, but her blue eyes were losing their twinkle, some fine lines had broken through, and her body was softening. She sighed. Life had taken a pretty girl born to conquer the world and stuffed her into a tight waitress outfit. It was like a bad practical joke. She sniffed her armpits, sprayed on a little more perfume, and returned to work.

The tiny saloon called Wally's was dimly lit, festooned with neon beer signs and old cowboy memorabilia. A large antique wagon wheel hung over the polished wooden bar, and George Jones whined from an antique jukebox. The street entrance was a dented metal door, but the inner entry was all atmosphere—old style batwings with slats. Sawdust covered the floor. Sally often wondered what had prompted the owner to invest in a tourist saloon in old-town Dry Wells, much less name it after himself.

Wally's was a dump.

The joint was never crowded, barely turned a profit. Then again, what the hell prompted *her* to continue to stay here? At least Wally got to live in the saloon and stay drunk all day, which he was right now, passed out facedown on the bar. All Sally got was spare change, smart-assed remarks about hooking, and tiny bruises on her ass cheeks from all the pinching.

Kyle Brody was still in his corner, nursing a beer. Sally knew he had a thing for her. Whenever he could get away from the garage, he'd hang around like some kind of body-guard, trying to act charming, but Kyle was a big, clumsy boy with red hair and blotchy freckles. Still, maybe he was the best she'd be able to do. Sally hadn't had sex since that charming traveling salesman had turned out to be a Mormon from Utah with three wives and thirteen kids. Kyle smiled. Sally smiled back.

Someone grabbed at her ass. Zeke and Hog were shit-faced again, and it wasn't even lunchtime. Sally wondered what their boss paid them for. The rancher was known to be a penny-pincher, so why did he allow his two hands to hang out in old town plastered all day? They were a real pair, chubby Hog with his huge biceps and skinny Zeke with his knives and his rattlesnake mean. They went back and forth between Molly's Pussy Parlor and Wally's Saloon like a pair of trained monkeys. Molly's for sex, Wally's for a break and couple of more drinks.

Another grab at her butt. Sally dodged the groping hand and forced a thin smile. "Want me to refill that pitcher, Hog?"

"I'd like to fill your pitcher, babe," Zeke said. "You need to put some time in over to the Pussy Parlor. Hell, I'd pay double."

Hog snorted, which was the second source of his unsubtle nickname.

"Maybe it's time you boys switched to coffee."

"Fuck that, babe. I'd pay *triple!*"

Sally slipped by their clutching fingers and walked sideways toward the stranger at the other corner table. Matt Cahill. The guy everyone was calling a hero. Up close, he was a big man, dark haired and muscular. His work shirt and jeans were dusty, and he carried a backpack with a lumberjack's ax strapped to it along with a small sleeping bag. The stranger had a battered cowboy hat pulled down low over his eyes. It looked like he was catching a nap before hitting the road.

"Can I get you anything else?"

Matt looked up. Sally was struck by how handsome he was, in a rough-hewn way. He had careful, intelligent eyes that didn't undress her. He really focused on her face, as if searching for something. It made her skin ripple and her legs part just a tiny bit. *Easy, girl, you're not in high school anymore.*

Cahill didn't speak, just smiled and shook his head.

Sally turned, then jumped back. Now Hog and Zeke were bracing her, blocking her way.

Uh-oh.

Over at the bar, Wally raised his head drunkenly. He fumbled to support himself, bleary-eyed, but wasn't sober enough to intervene.

"We're making you an offer," Zeke said pleasantly. His breath reeked. "A three-way for triple. You can't refuse."

Out of the corner of her eye Sally saw Kyle slowly get to his feet. She silently willed him to stay put. He was a good boy, one of the only decent males left in Dry Wells, and she didn't want to see him get hurt. Kyle had tried to stand up to Zeke and Hog before. It hadn't gone so well. Zeke carried a couple of small knives and moved like a cat. Hog had guns like other men's thighs and could poleax a steer with one of those fists. They liked to hurt people.

"Easy, boys," she said. "This may be Friday, and we've got cause to celebrate, but it's way too early for me to have to be calling Sheriff Pickens on you. Hell, you still got the whole weekend ahead. The whorehouse is across the street. This here is just a bar."

"For now," Hog said.

"That old fart can't do nothing and you know it, gal," Zeke said. He moved a step closer, the better to stare down her top at her breasts. He seemed to like it that Sally was now breathing rapidly from fear. "You ever have two big men at once? Might like it."

"Let her be," Kyle said.

Zeke smiled at the sound of Kyle's wavering tenor. Sally realized that this was what Zeke had really been after all along. The fight. He and Hog exchanged grins. Zeke nodded, and Hog turned, lumbered over to deal with young Kyle. He picked up a chair, raising it over his head, ready to smash it over the young man's head. Kyle tried to duck but lost his balance and ended up on his ass on the sawdust floor. Meanwhile, skinny Zeke reached out for Sally with his right hand, intending to grope her breast. Sally took a deep breath to scream, knowing that there was likely nobody around outside, that it probably wouldn't do her any good.

The handsome stranger came out of nowhere and grabbed Zeke by the wrist. In a voice low and urgent, he said, "Hey, pal. Take it easy, okay?"

Hog turned and saw that the stranger was now interfering. Pleased, Hog waddled back their way like a rhino crossing a mud paddy. His fat face was clenched into a huge red fist of excitement.

Meanwhile, the stranger let Zeke go. "Guys, I don't want any trouble."

Zeke laughed. "Mister, your 'tude just wrote a check your body can't cash."

Sally gasped with alarm. Zeke produced a switchblade with his free hand, popped the wicked blade out, and stabbed at the stranger's thigh. But the man wasn't there anymore. He had moved out of the way, back toward his pack and sleeping bag. Hog changed direction to cut him off but moved too slowly. Cahill grabbed his ax and used the handle to pop Zeke low in the groin.

Zeke gasped and dropped the knife. He sank to his knees, gripping his balls with both hands.

Pissed off, Hog charged.

Sally couldn't believe her eyes. The handsome stranger stayed put. Hog was bigger, outweighed him by forty pounds, but Cahill didn't move. His assailant launched a haymaker at his chin, but the stranger stood fast. At the very last second, when Hog was slightly off balance, Cahill knocked his arm up and out of the way. He punched Hog twice with the end of the ax handle, rapid-fire, right in the soft spot above the belly and between the ribs. Hog went white, sank to his knees gasping for air. He rolled over onto his side and drew up his knees like a baby trying to let loose a huge fart. The stranger tossed his ax onto his sleeping bag.

"Just breathe, man. The pain will go away." Cahill went down on one knee. He lowered his voice, said something to

Hog and then repeated it to Zeke. He was whispering, but Sally caught the gist of it. He actually apologized again for hurting them and told them both to go sober up. He said to lay off the girl from now on.

Like a pair of whipped puppies, Zeke and Hog helped each other limp out the batwing doors. They didn't look back.

What amazed Sally was that Cahill didn't seem to be an expert at martial arts. Maybe he was just a man used to fighting in bars. He looked a bit shaken but wasn't even breathing hard.

The man looked over at Kyle, who had struggled back to his feet and was holding a candle as if wishing it would magically turn into a weapon.

"You okay, kid?"

Kyle's cheeks went pink. He'd just lost a substantive dick-measuring contest. Sally stared at the stranger. She shook her head. "Mr. Cahill, you move like you've had a few fights in your day."

The man shrugged. "A few."

"We thank you."

"No sweat."

Sally watched as he turned to get his dusty pack, bed-roll, and hat. He dug into his jeans to find a few dollar bills. He handed them to her, finished his beer, and turned to go. The harsh sunlight surrounded him, turning his features shadowy and mystical. Sally tucked the money into her bra and held out her hand.

"Sally Morgan, Mr. Cahill."

"Mr. Cahill was my father." The handsome stranger hesitated as if he'd grown tired of meeting people. He shook her hand. "Matt. Call me Matt."

CHAPTER FOUR

Friday, 11:14 a.m.

Matt Cahill walked back through the ghost town, this time with the pretty young waitress. Despite the sunshine, he had his battered hat stuffed in his pocket. He kept the bedroll, long ax, and backpack over his right shoulder.

"You're pretty much as advertised," Sally said.

"Excuse me?"

"You pulled Suzie Pickens out of a mine shaft. And then you come into my bar and straighten out two of the local bullies like it was nothing much. Whole town is buzzing about you. You must have some kind of powerful cereal for breakfast."

Matt sighed. "Can we talk about something else?"

She grinned. "Sure is hot, ain't it?"

"Okay, how about telling me where we're going?"

The girl gestured, pointed. "To my car."

"How far?"

"Right down that alley. Now, where is it you need to go, cowboy?"

Matt paused to wipe sweat from his brow. "What is the fastest way to get back to the Kearns ranch? I'd appreciate a lift, but no need to take me all the way."

Sally stopped, and her boots thumped on the wooden slats. A trickle of sweat ran down the sweet crevice between her full breasts. Matt tried not to follow it with his eyes, looking up, busying himself with adjusting the ax and pack. A dust devil twirled by behind her sunburned shoulder.

"Sure," Sally said. "But answer me this: Why the hell would you want to go back out there?"

Matt shrugged. "Why not?"

"You really want to know? Because Zeke and Hog work on the spread right next to Kearns."

"Oh."

"Look, those two are bad enough, but there are also some new strangers out that way. Four guys that showed up crack of dawn this morning."

"So?"

"So they are damned spooky. They came in for breakfast and they were armed to the teeth. Looking for someone, I'd expect. They're so mean, they make Zeke and Hog nervous."

Matt frowned. She had his attention. "What did they look like?"

"Desperados, with buzz-cut hair and a shitload of muscles. Their leader, Scotty, was cute, but he has Zeke's kind of eyes, like a predator who gets off on the suffering of others. Know what I mean?"

"I think so." Matt felt his pulse twitch. He had no reason to believe this had anything to do with him, but still...He shifted his pack, ax, and bedroll to the opposite shoulder. "These men—did they actually hurt anybody?"

She shook her head. "Not yet. No, nothing bad happened, but they made sure we all got the feeling something might if we don't behave. I think they wanted us to know that, to feel spooked. They are up to something."

"Do folks spook easily around here?"

"They are my friends and like family," she said, "but they all live in fear. They'd back down from a dog with a hard-on. That sort of mind-set tends to encourage bad guys, if you know what I mean."

"Yes, Sally," Matt Cahill said with a laugh. "I know what you mean." He wiped his forehead. "Did anyone try to stand up to them?"

"Sheriff Pickens walked up and had a talk with the one called Scotty, but as you know, our sheriff's getting on in years. Those teenage kids keep him young since his wife died, but hell, his chest dropped into his gut when Bill Clinton was president. Put it this way—these guys were professionals. They didn't seem too intimidated."

They passed the closed movie theater and Matt peeked inside. The furniture was covered with blankets and drop cloths, and the John Wayne posters on the wall were decades old. *What an interesting old town.*

"Sally, I still don't see why that has anything to do with me just revisiting the Kearns place."

"And I still don't see why you'd want to go back there."

He couldn't tell her about the Dark Man. Kearns had likely just been raving from drugs. Still, Matt had to follow anything that looked like a valid lead. Maybe it would come to nothing. Perhaps the man was just another crazed redneck cooking speed in a shack who'd imagined the whole thing. Still, just in case, Matt needed to get this thing over with. He had to find and stop the Dark Man. And hopefully return to the life he once had.

But he didn't tell her that. What he said was: "I want to talk with him about living alone in the desert."

"You writing a book or something?"

"Or something," he said. "Look, thanks for the concern, but I can take care of myself."

Sally sighed. "I figured that part out."

A bald head appeared in the window of a storefront. They both jumped. "Jesus, Bert. You scared me half to death."

Matt saw that the bald man was wearing a white apron stained with blood and juices of some kind. The sign outside said he was a grocer. Bert had a large, red-veined nose and a twitch under one eye.

"Howdy, mister," Bert said. "Thanks for what you did for Suzie Pickens. Whole town is buzzing about it." His curious eyes gave him away as desperate for human contact and maybe a bit of gossip.

"Sally! Wait up."

Matt turned. The young redheaded man from the saloon jogged to catch them, then slowed to a walk. Like so many other men in this part of the country, Kyle had the rawboned look and worn hands of someone who kept his own cars running. Meanwhile, Bert the grocer seemed to remember something and popped his head back inside the darkened store. Kyle came closer, stopped a few feet away. Matt could sense how possessive he felt, but the ego-driven part was well tempered by a genuine concern for Sally.

"I'm Kyle. I just wanted to say thank you, mister. Those two are mean as a pair of badgers."

Matt lowered his pack and bedroll, extended his hand. "You're welcome."

The two men shook. Matt could see that Kyle wanted to stay, to keep a sharp eye on Sally. Matt couldn't blame him. She had to be the best-looking female for a couple of hundred miles in any direction. Instead, Kyle said, "You've made quite an impression on Dry Wells in one morning."

As if he weren't there, Sally said, "Like I said, I'll drive you about halfway back. After that you'll have to hitch a ride from the highway. Best take a big bottle of water with you. The roads aren't exactly jammed up around here. I've got some in the car. See you later on, Kyle."

Knowing he was beaten, Kyle stuffed his hands into the pockets of his jeans and backed away with a forced smile. He turned his back and walked off. Matt cocked his head at the girl.

"Wow. Now, that was subtle."

"Come on," Sally said. "My car is around the corner past the jail."

As if on cue, the sheriff appeared in the doorway of his office.

Sally greeted him warmly. "Sheriff Pickens."

"You on your way already, son?"

"Yeah, need to get moving."

"Matt, I owe you big," the sheriff said. "Whole town does. You ever need anything, anything at all..." Behind him in the gloom, Matt could just make out the antique bars of a jail cell and a desk cluttered with papers. He saw a couple of hunting rifles anchored by a long rack on the wall. Matt nodded.

"Tell the kids I said good-bye."

"I will."

They shook hands and Matt resumed walking.

As if sensing something out of place, Sheriff Pickens called out after them. "Hey, you all right there, son?"

Matt just waved his right hand without looking back. His mind was on the strangers Sally had mentioned. Matt knew he didn't particularly want to meet them. Still, he had to investigate what the miner Kearns had said about a dark man in the desert. Matt was worried, as the sheriff had sensed, but Sally didn't seem to notice anything. She led him down an alley that ran behind the one active street in this part of the ghost town. Two feral cats watched Matt go by, one black and one white. Their eyes seemed to be glowing, as if they were spying for the Dark Man.

Although the air cooled as the shadows took over, the smell of feces and dead animals was still oppressive in the stifling heat. At the end of the alley, they entered a small area with cracked pavement, where Matt saw a beat-up old white Toyota with a black replacement hood. The backseat was littered with junk-food bags and piled-up clothes ready for the washing machine. The car was facing another opening, out to the highway. Wind caressed them and the air became fresh and clean.

"My chariot."

The Toyota was unlocked and the windows were down. Matt tossed his pack, ax, and bedroll into the backseat and got into the passenger side. The car smelled like Sally stole a cigarette now and again. She started the car and rolled slowly down the alley, over gravel and the desiccated remains of small animals. He liked her profile, the full cheeks and thin nose. The way she concentrated on driving, looked both ways before heading out onto the highway. He was paying so much attention to Sally that he missed the black van parked near the edge of the ghost town, the two motorcycles on top, and the very odd look of the men inside.

One tracked his movements with a video camera.

CHAPTER FIVE

Friday, 12:49 p.m.

Once they were out on the open road, Sally put on sunglasses, popped in an old Emmylou Harris music cassette, and floored it. The engine roared like someone—perhaps the kid called Kyle—had souped it up. This girl was a rush. The wind whipped her hair back and flushed her cheeks. They soaked up the sunshine but didn't say much, didn't really have to talk. They were clearly attracted to each other, but he was a drifter, just passing through.

Matt enjoyed his brief time with her. She had no idea who he was, and he liked that. He wished he could stay longer, but he suspected he was nearer to locating the Dark Man than he'd been in weeks. The prospect of another face-to-face meeting both thrilled and frightened him. His torment, the curse of recognizing evil in others, would never end unless he stopped the Dark Man. *Somehow, someway, someday...*

Sally drove, and Emmylou Harris sang "Too Far Gone" with a clear soprano voice that broke Matt's heart. The wind howled as if struggling to slow them down. When Matt looked over his shoulder, the Ruby Mountains behind them were retreating into low clouds and the green foothills were shimmering like a mirage. In front of them the Nevada landscape went flat, high-desert bleak, just bleached fists of tumbleweed and the grinning skulls of long-dead cattle. They tore up the road to the 41 cutoff, and then Sally slowed down and whipped off the highway with a spray of sand and rocks. A hot and dusty silence descended.

Sally licked her lips. "Don't do anything stupid out here all by yourself." She lowered her sunglasses and took him in one last time. "Cowboy, I owe you. I really mean that. You ever want to collect, you know where to find me."

"Wally's Saloon in historic Dry Wells, Nevada. Yes, ma'am."

She kissed him on the cheek. It had been a long time, and Matt felt himself stir. She kissed him on the mouth, and he kissed her back, but then Sally pulled away.

"You'd best go," she said in a husky voice. "Stay clear of those bastards you beat up, avoid the strangers, find out whatever you need to know from Kearns, and get the hell out of Elko County. You'll be safer that way. Sure you don't want me to come with you?"

Matt shook his head. "No, thanks. I'll be fine, so long as somebody comes along in the next couple of hours."

She laughed. "There are cars out here, Matt. Just not a lot of them." She tossed him a large plastic bottle of water from below her front seat. "You take care."

He slid out of the car, grabbed his backpack, ax, and bedroll, and put on his beat-up cowboy hat. "You, too, Sally."

She sped away without looking back. Matt Cahill knew a part of her heart had stayed with him. She'd made him think of his dead wife, Janey, and sadness thickened his breathing. He shouldered his things and walked over to the fork in the road, where he set his gear down, slammed the ax head down into the earth, and propped his hat on it for a bit of shade. He had a seat, closed his eyes, and waited for the drone of the next car headed south and west.

The sun beat down, frying his bare skin, drying his body out like a strip of old leather. Matt wondered how he'd come to be so alone in the world. Not for the first time, he thought, *Shit, why me?*

Of course, the only possible answer was *Why not you?*

Time passed, and then a shimmering little silver bug appeared on the horizon. A car was coming his way. *About fucking time.*

Matt swallowed several gulps of water and got to his feet. Apprehension tickled his stomach. This might all be for nothing, but it felt good to be close to finding out. When the car seemed close enough, he stuck out his thumb. He willed the driver to throw caution to the pathetic lack of wind, take pity on a slowly roasting hitchhiker, and take a risk.

As the car got closer, Matt noticed it was drifting from side to side. The observation gave him an uneasy feeling. He shaded his eyes. The road looked empty all the way back to the horizon. All things considered, Matt figured he'd have to take whatever he could get.

The vehicle was a flatbed Ford truck, with a piss-poor paint job somewhere between silver and blue. The windshield had a long crack across it. The front fender hung low, like a penis at half-mast, and the right front headlight was missing. The driver pulled up and parked with the engine still running. The engine sounded like the car looked. Matt walked closer and saw that the driver was a man around fifty, compact and wiry, with big bottle glasses and a dyed comb-over. He wore a checkered red-and-white cowboy shirt with a string tie, and he seemed exhausted.

"Well, shit. You gonna stand out there all day looking at me?" The driver had a tenor voice, scratchy and annoying. Fortunately he drove the next several miles without saying another word.

The driver dropped Matt near where he'd been standing when he'd first heard the call for help. Matt could see the old mine shaft, and beyond it some buildings. He walked past the "Kearns Property Leave Shit Here" sign. After about a quarter mile, an old house came into view. It was low to the ground, slanted to one side, painted white to deflect some of the smothering heat. There was a splintering wooden porch and a rocking chair. Behind the place was a shambles of a garage, car parts everywhere, old farming equipment, rusty wrecked cars half covered with thirsty weeds.

Matt dropped his backpack, ax, and bedroll in the sand. He studied the shack for a while, looking for any movement. Kearns had already seemed out to lunch. A man who lived alone out here might just as soon shoot a stranger as ask questions.

And then he saw it, a faint shimmering in the air near the back of the garage. Matt felt his stomach clench with disappointment. He gave the buildings a wide berth and walked around to the south. There was a small stovepipe chimney at the back of the garage, and it was releasing heat and a trace of smoke. Matt sniffed the air, smelled something sharp and chemical. His shoulders slumped. The guy was cooking meth. Matt turned to go.

"Don't you fucking move. I'll blow you out of those boots, motherfucker."

Matt froze. His scrotum tried to shrink into a slipknot.

An eerie specter rose out of some trash and a bit of cactus. He was covered with dust and powder. Kearns again. This time the man cradled a sawed-off shotgun in his arms, business end pointed Matt's way. The twin barrels seemed to sneer. The guy still wore those ripped overalls, no shirt, and had blistering, sunburned skin. He was one butt-ugly sight, balding and toothless and sallow. Matt, as accustomed to horrific apparitions as he'd become, almost cringed at his appearance. Now it was clear that the rot wasn't from evil. It was from the crystal methamphetamine the dumb peckerwood was cooking and shooting.

"Mr. Kearns, I just came to apologize for striking you. I'll just be on my way."

"Who the fuck asked for an apology?" No front teeth, a slavering lisp. "You from the gummint?"

"I'm not from the government, no, Mr. Kearns."

"Bullshit." Kearns spat. "You get off my land."

"Sure..."

Suddenly Kearns shrieked. A crow and two vultures took flight in alarm as the sound echoed. Startled and afraid of the shotgun, Matt flinched.

"What is it?" he asked.

Kearns fired the shotgun, aiming toward his own house. Out here in the middle of nowhere, the noise was like the bark of a giant dog. "Stay away from me, you bastard! Stay back!"

Spooked, Matt looked. The house. The rocker. *There was nobody there.*

Kearns squinted, carefully studying his porch for the movement of a creature that didn't exist. Matt took advantage of the distraction and edged toward his belongings. Kearns clearly had a bad case of amphetamine psychosis— full-on auditory and visual hallucinations. If he had really seen the Dark Man, the experience had run together in his mind with dozens of other delusions. He'd be useless in terms of acquiring new information. The trip had been a waste of time—and could still be a fatal mistake.

The gun discharged again. An echo barked back a few seconds later, and then one more. The crow cawed as if amused. Kearns screamed in a voice high and shrill. He fired at it the bird, and blood and feathers exploded in all directions.

"Take that, you skinny, black-winged motherfucker!"

Matt trotted over to his stuff but didn't take his eyes off of Kearns. He gathered up the backpack and sleeping bag and reached for the ax. Matt thought he heard some kind of low throbbing sound, wasn't sure from where. Could have been the panicked blood thundering through the veins in his own ears. Facing down an enemy was one thing. A psychotic with a shotgun was quite another.

Kearns hunkered down like a man taking a dump in his pants, which was actually quite possible, all things considered. He gripped the shotgun in his trembling right hand and with his left he dug into his filthy pocket for another shell. He seemed to have forgotten Matt's presence or written it off as a hallucination. Kearns reloaded and stalked toward his own home.

But Kearns stalked nothing and fired at nothing. Matt backed away, the ax in his right hand and the pack and bedroll over his left shoulder. He was almost out of range of the shotgun when he noticed the humming sound again and pegged it for an engine.

A vehicle this far from the highway?

A large one, a truck or a van, and it sounded closer. Perhaps he could hitch a ride away from this madhouse.

"Ugh!"

Kearns threw his hands up as if upset by something, and the shotgun went sailing. Matt blinked. Part of the redneck's head disappeared, to be replaced by a strange pink cloud that floated away. Kearns dropped to his knees and fell over dead.

He'd been shot, and Matt hadn't heard a thing.

Someone was using a silencer.

Matt ducked and tried to run, but something slammed into the side of his head, and he dropped his gear. The world went white with pain, spun in a circle, and turned pitch-black.

CHAPTER SIX

Friday, 4:32 p.m.

Matt came to but kept his eyes closed. He was inside and could feel cool air-conditioning on his exposed skin. His arm ached—like an IV needle had been badly inserted and then clumsily taped down. The back of his head was pounding. No one could have gotten close enough to hit him without Matt sensing it, so he'd been shot with something, perhaps a beanbag. *Cops or military? But why?*

"Sleeping Beauty is awake." A man's jocular baritone. "Bro, we have been trying to catch up to your ass for a week. This morning we got here ahead of you. At last we meet!"

Matt forced his eyes open and squinted. He was on a gurney but not in a hospital. This was some kind of gigantic van—he could tell by the shape of the walls. Everything around and below him vibrated a bit. The speaker was dressed in black with a web belt and a sidearm. *Mercenary all the way.* He had a friendly, boyish face and a good-natured grin.

"My name is Scotty, Cahill," the man said. "And of course we already know who you are."

The scary stranger Sally had mentioned. Scotty instantly reminded Matt of someone. Someone he knew. His head hurt too much to focus. He rolled his head to the right. There *was* a needle in his arm. And some kind of a transfusion bottle there, but something didn't look right. What was it? Matt struggled to make sense of his situation. He felt weak and dizzy. And then it finally hit him. They weren't giving him fluids or medication.

They were drawing his blood.

Lots of it.

"You hungry?"

"What?"

Scotty repeated, "You hungry? Our medic says you'll last longer if we give you some fruit and orange juice once in a while."

Matt felt the world slide sideways and tilt. He was growing weaker by the second. Matt knew he wasn't like other people—not anymore, not since he'd come back from the dead. No one was guaranteed immortality. How many pints of blood in a human body? Something like ten? How much had he lost already?

They were bleeding him.

"Two things I get off on," Scotty said. "Football and old movies. You ever watch Laurel and Hardy? Those two old comics from the silent movie days? One tall and skinny, one short and fat. Loved those guys. You know, it turns out the dumb one was the brains."

"Huh?"

Scotty grinned again. The boyish smile prompted Matt's memory. "Andy," he said. His voice was already becoming a desperate croak.

"Andy?"

"You remind me of my friend Andy." A lifelong friend Matt had to kill after the Dark Man and the rot of evil took him over. And now that same rot was spreading across

Scotty's face, eating away the flesh on his chin. A thin stream of pus dribbled from his right nostril.

"That so?" Scotty seemed pleased. "Cool. Hey, thing is, under other circumstances, we probably could have been friends. Hope you realize this isn't personal, Cahill. If it was up to me, I'd keep you around. Orders are orders."

Matt shivered. The air was cold and he felt weak. "*Whose* orders?"

"Boss man says to take your blood, so we take your blood. Ours is not to reason why." Scotty yawned. Something ugly and black writhed like a worm of smoke in the back of his throat as if fighting to get out.

"Don't do this," Matt said. "It's murder."

"War is hell," Scotty said. And he flashed that Andy grin again. Matt felt fear and a deep sadness, both for himself and for Scotty, who might have been a decent person once but was past saving now. Matt didn't want to die like this, but he was too weak for much of anything else—and growing weaker by the minute. He closed his eyes.

Scotty slapped his face lightly. "Stay awake, dude. We want you around for as long as possible."

"Screw you."

"That's it! Come on, you don't want this to be too easy, do you?"

"I don't want this at all."

Matt rolled his head the other way. A couple of mercenaries sat nearby. One was sucking on what smelled like a joint. The other was snoozing. The sliding side door to the van was open a crack. Another mercenary stood guard outside, but without much panache or enthusiasm. These men were well trained, but evil was on board, eroding their focus. Individual discipline was sliding. Appetites running amuck. They all reeked of sin. If Mr. Dark wasn't actually running the show, he was most certainly involved. Had to be in some way.

Matt studied his foe. Tried to speak. "Why?"

Scotty blinked. "Why take your blood? Dude, you're fucking famous. Matt Cahill, the man who was frozen solid for three months and brought back to life. The word went out among the very, very, very rich that you are Ponce de Fucking León himself, the owner of the secret of eternal youth. It was only a matter of time until someone hired a guy like me to come and find you."

"Who?"

Scotty smiled. "Guess it doesn't matter if I tell you. The checks come from some very smart men with money. Old men who contribute heavily to the university where you were first studied."

"The university?"

"Alumni, shall we say."

"They think it's in my blood?"

"They say it *has* to be, dude. Somewhere in your blood or your DNA. So they figure it's something money can locate and copy, or at least secure the rights to." Scotty leaned closer. His breath stank of the rot eating him from inside. "Oh, I know what you're thinking. Why not just steal a sample and go to work on that? Why bleed you dry? So I asked the same question. Seems to me we could take some, let you eat and rest, then take some more, and even go on and on for months or years that way."

"Uh-huh."

Just let me stay alive long enough to figure a way out of here...

"But no, we're supposed to get as much as we can over a few days, then punch your ticket and dispose of the body. In case you're curious, it will be a state-of-the-art cremation. That is, we plan to burn your ass up with a frag and split."

"Why kill me? Just to leave no evidence?"

"Monopoly, dude. Once we have enough healthy samples, taking your ass out leaves no way for anyone else to compete. Business is murder these days."

Matt licked his lips. "Water. Please."

Scotty snapped his fingers. The mercenary with the marijuana sighed, pinched out his joint, and got a small bottle of water. He tossed it to Scotty, who opened it and poured a taste into Matt's mouth. "Go easy, partner. Wouldn't want you to get sick. We'll turn off the drip now, let you get some strength back."

Matt managed to make his left hand crawl up to grab the bottle. He wanted to handle it himself. He took another sip. "You must feel really proud of yourself."

Scotty blinked once, then looked away.

A hit, a palpable hit.

The mercenary got up, walked around the gurney, and stopped the blood flow. He put some grapes and orange slices on a paper plate and set it down on Matt's legs. Something in Scotty's weakened mind wandered, though, and instead of feeding Matt he began to absently snack on the grapes himself. He looked normal again, and then horrific. These dangerous men were rapidly being taken over by their own mindless appetites.

Matt swallowed some more water, choking a bit but keeping it down. He looked to his right, where the needle protruded, and his mind raced for some kind of answer. He was alone in a huge trailer parked out in the desert, guarded by mercenary soldiers recruited in the cause of evil. Everyone thought he'd left town. The rancher he'd visited was dead, and perhaps Matt would be blamed for the murder. As for any chance of rescue, no one even knew he was here. Only one thing was certain.

Matt was in deep, deep shit.

CHAPTER SEVEN

Sunday, 11:34 a.m.

He lost track of the number of times they woke him up to give him water, fruit and juice or to change the trickle of urine in the bedpan. As soon as he'd regained some of his strength, they'd start collecting blood again. Matt was light-headed all the time now, and his vision was blurring. The mercenaries looked horrific, their souls pocked with the unspoken evil of what they were doing. One with a shaved head never looked at him. One with thick red hair never stopped. The stoner never quit smoking. Their lack of sympathy and interest betrayed souls too far gone for any kind of recovery.

These were trained mercenaries, in great condition and still quite lethal, but the Dark Man had found a way to touch them. They ate Matt's food on a whim, smoked dope, drank booze, and napped. When Matt was able to concentrate, he wondered if these men would even remember what they had done here. They seemed beyond caring.

And Matt didn't have much longer to live.

The mercenaries rotated positions. Scotty was the only one with a smidgen of bedside manner. The others rarely spoke, except to grunt a request or use a four-letter word. One had the habit of constantly scratching his balls. They argued violently, exercised, cleaned their weapons endlessly, burped and farted, slept and snored. Sometimes they fought like animals over a scrap of meat. Killers without a purpose.

Matt was pretty certain it was just the next day, not two days later. The sun was up again, and the light and shade he could see through the small opening suggested it was approaching noon. He'd finally realized why they kept the door open, despite the constant air-conditioning. The pot smell bothered Scotty.

As Matt slowly died, Scotty talked about Charlie Chaplin and Fatty Arbuckle. Finally he switched to professional football. He had an obsession with the classic teams of the sixties and early seventies, especially Miami. He droned on and on about the Dolphins' perfect season with Larry Csonka and Jim Kiick and Mercury Morris at halfback. The backup quarterback Earl Morrall. He described plays against the Redskins and a big playoff game against the Chiefs that went into overtime.

Matt came to appreciate those talks because listening to Scotty gave him something to hold on to, something to think about other than gathering darkness and the fear of bleeding to death. He wondered if he'd see Janey after he died and hold her again. That thought was a comfort.

"Boss?" one of the mercenaries asked. He was standing guard in the doorway, with an AK pointed down at the floor.

Scotty stopped in the middle of describing Larry Csonka plowing through three defenders and knocking himself silly running into the goalpost. He seemed annoyed by the interruption.

"What?"

"Somebody is outside," the guard said. "Women."

"The fuck?"

The other bored mercenaries rushed the door like frat boys, their weapons at half-mast.

Scotty sighed and stared down at the bed for a few seconds. When he looked up, his face was just raw meat and writhing worms. Matt cringed as Scotty shook his head and a couple of gray worms fell off and dropped writhing on the bedsheet.

"I don't care if it's the chicks from *Black Swan* licking each other," Scotty said. "Stay sharp or I'll shoot you myself."

The stoner went to the window, opened it, and jammed himself into the corner with his weapon pointed outside. To Matt, the man's eyes were black holes. His nose had fallen off. The other two went to their assigned posts as well. Scotty patted Matt's leg in an absurd parody of politeness.

"Excuse me for a second."

Scotty gripped his weapon and went to the door. He kept the weapon behind his back and filled the doorway. Matt gathered himself to call for help but then realized he'd just get whoever was outside killed.

The breathless voice of an unfamiliar female. "Sorry to bother you, honey."

"Hold it right there, honey," Scotty said. Matt watched as Scotty's fingers tensed on the Glock. Matt hoped whoever it was wouldn't be killed right there in front of him.

"We're coming back from a party in Elko," another woman said. Her voice sounded slurred. "We got a flat tire."

The stoner said, "I'll change it."

Scotty shot him a dirty look. He peered out the door again. Seemingly satisfied, he relaxed. "Just stay where you are, okay? Someone will be out in a second."

He closed the door, looked at the stoner. "Get them out of here."

"Kill them?"

"Not unless you have to. Someone might come looking before we're done with Cahill. Go change the tire and get the fuck back inside. Red, you cover him from the window. Don't let any of them see your weapons. Anything goes wrong, take all three of them out."

Three?

The mercenary called Red went to the window. Whatever he saw there made him whistle with appreciation.

Matt tried to raise his head, but the effort made him dizzy. He considered calling for help but didn't want to put the women in danger. Exhausted and queasy, he closed his eyes again and passed out.

When he came to again, the trailer was silent except for the humming air-conditioning. He felt shaky but not as bad as he had. He rolled his head to his right. They had once again stopped draining his blood. Two brownish slices of apple and a half-empty bottle of water sat beside him on the white sheet, placed there almost as an afterthought.

Some time had passed. Matt tried to sit up but failed. He tried again, got up on his elbows. The van was quiet. *Why?* Matt looked around.

No one else was moving. The mercenaries were passed out cold. Scotty was on the floor in the fetal position, nearly sucking his thumb, his pus-filled face and blank eyes twitching. The other three were in poses around the trailer. Empty bottles of beer and whiskey lay on the floor. Some of the furniture was tipped over. There was no sign of the strangers. Matt started to pass out again, but he fought the impulse.

He had to get the hell out of here—now. And then he heard footsteps.

Someone was coming.

Matt struggled to free his hands. He got his left arm loose and pulled on the tape holding his right arm to the board, tape that covered the needle that had been draining his life pint by pint. The door creaked open. Panicked, Matt managed to tear at the tape. Then a shadow fell across the bed.

Matt Cahill look up and saw the most beautiful sight he'd ever seen. Sally, her face framed by sunlight. She had come to rescue him. Sheriff Pickens, Wally, and Kyle had come with her. The two other women waited outside.

CHAPTER EIGHT

Monday, 8:53 a.m.

"That ought to get it," Doc said. The silver-haired cowboy sat back and closed his black bag. Matt had resisted yet another needle, but Doc argued that he needed a transfusion, nutrients and B_{12} with a bit of a stimulant. Just moments later, Matt did feel quite a bit better. He was seated upright in a chair in Sheriff Pickens' office. He'd refused to lie down again. He'd had enough of feeling helpless.

"Whatever you just did, it worked pretty well," Matt said.

"Ought to. I've practiced on quite a few wounded horses," Doc said without the slightest trace of a smile.

A jealous Kyle had discreetly followed Sally and Matt out of town. He'd wanted to make sure his rival was gone for good. Kyle explained the truth sheepishly but also seemed proud because of how it had all worked out. He'd seen the huge van drive up and kidnap Matt, but knowing he couldn't possibly take on mercenaries with weapons, Kyle had hung back and followed the van until it parked out in the desert. Then he'd raced back to town, and the people of Dry Wells couldn't stand by and let him be kidnapped. They owed Matt Cahill. Something had to be done.

Sheriff Pickens had come up with the plan. Sally and Suzie Pickens had dressed as hookers. They'd taken another volunteer from the whorehouse, a girl named Maggie. The women had approached the trailer while Sheriff Pickens and some of the men watched from a distance. Wally covered them with a hunting rifle.

The girls had gotten the mercenaries to drink a bit of drugged booze, then slipped away before anyone could get hurt. Then they'd all waited half an hour, returned when it was safe, and brought Matt and his bedroll, backpack, and ax back to Dry Wells. Sheriff Pickens hadn't wanted to risk trying to take the men into custody without more backup.

"But now," Sheriff Pickens said, "our problem is that the bastards are going to wake up again soon. And it won't take long for them to figure out what happened. We helped you get away. They'll want to get even. And that means they'll be coming for you. For us."

"Get help now," Matt said. "Those men are trained professionals."

"Sure, that's what I'd figured on doing as soon as we got back, son. Just turns out that I can't."

"Can't you call the state police? The National Guard? Somebody?"

"No, because we got us some more shit luck in Dry Wells," Sheriff Pickens said. "There's a badass forest fire going on down the 41, and everything is closed tighter than a gnat's ass. The Guard is all tied up fighting the fire, and everyone else is either evacuating or blocking the highways. They got to keep away every swinging dick with a six-pack of beer and a digital camera. And the phone lines went dead a few minutes ago. Can't raise a signal. The long and short of it is, we're on our own, at least through tomorrow."

Matt didn't think it was a coincidence that the phone lines were down and the signals were jammed. It was intentional. The university had paid a lot of money for this team and their support staff. They seemed to think Matt was worth a fortune.

Surprised, Matt saw that Zeke and Hog, the two bullies from the bar, were here with the rest of the residents. Stone sober now, they seemed both tense and oddly deflated. Neither man seemed eager to meet his eyes, but Matt just nodded his appreciation and the two seemed to relax.

"I appreciate what you all have done for me," Matt said. "But saving me is bound to bring suffering. I should go."

"If they do come for us," Doc said, "we're going to need every man we can get. Including you."

"Let him leave!" a woman called. Other people shushed her up.

Kyle shrugged. "Let's just man up and do something for once."

Bert the grocer said, "Easy for you to say. You're young, you got no kids and nothing to lose."

More people crowded into the room. Uncomfortable, Matt found himself the center of attention again. Yet this wasn't about him anymore. It had grown much bigger than that.

"Far as I'm concerned, Kyle is right," Sheriff Pickens said. "I owe my daughter's life to this man. He's been here a day and in my opinion he's already changed us for the better. I for one ain't going to let those bastards murder him. I won't just look the other way. This is our town, damn it."

Many of the townsfolk agreed. Several others remained silent.

"And I'll repeat that," Doc said. "Matt here has proved he's got brains and balls. We're going to need his help to protect ourselves tonight."

Sally, still wearing tight clothing and smeared hooker makeup, as was Suzie Pickens, spoke up. "We're going to have to figure out how to do that pretty damned quickly."

Bert the grocer looked at Matt. "Or we could just give you back to them and say we were sorry."

Matt nodded. "I'd understand if you did. But think about it. The problem is, now you know they murdered Kearns in cold blood and you know about what they tried to do to me."

"Which was what, exactly?" Doc asked.

"Something illegal as hell. They were after my blood and organs." The townspeople wouldn't believe the truth if Matt told them. He barely believed it himself. "Guess maybe somebody needed a kidney."

"Well, okay, maybe it ain't so bad. All we have to do is hold them off until help arrives," Wally ventured.

The sheriff shook his head. "Matt is right. They're gonna come for Cahill, and they're gonna also want anybody else they think might know more than he or she should. Which means all of us. Are we going to sit by and let that happen?"

By now the remaining townspeople had edged into the room. Matt knew he didn't have time to make friends with the fifteen or twenty permanent residents of old-town Dry Wells, but he had to win them over immediately. Because the clock was ticking. He scanned their faces, but the townspeople just waited for something to happen. A black crow cawed outside the window like an angel of death.

"It's your town, your decision." Matt got to his feet. "You want me to go, I'll go."

"If I thought that would work, I'd probably show you the way out of town," Zeke said. Everyone seemed surprised that he was speaking out. "But it likely won't. These desperadoes broke the law. They look badass to us. They aren't going to take any chances folks will talk about what happened out there. Hog and me, we say make a stand."

Silence.

Hog said, "Mr. Cahill, you beat us fair and square, and you weren't mean about it. We remember things like that."

"We ain't fighting men like you three," someone called. "We're just farmers and ranchers."

"I know it's not fair that you're in this position. But here we are." Matt looked down. Suzie Pickens and her brother were each on one knee. Sally was seated cross-legged on the floor, staring up at him, wide-eyed and smitten. Doc, Wally, and all the others watched him as silence took hold. They were waiting, obviously expecting him to take charge, even though he didn't know the first thing about combat. And then it hit him. Matt had been wondering why he'd come back to life, why he'd been spared. This was another one of those times when it felt like destiny. His arrival had caused the situation, but it had also saved lives and brought the whole town together. Perhaps this was all supposed to happen.

Matt said, "Kyle, can you draw me a detailed map of the town? Every building, hiding place, electrical panel, water source, whatever you can think of that might help us out?"

Kyle nodded, then exploded into motion. People began whispering as the young man dug in a desk drawer for paper and pencils. Sally joined him and they both got to work. Seeing that, the other residents gained a bit of confidence. They were standing taller, even though Matt didn't have a plan—he just sounded like he did. Apparently, that was enough for the time being.

Oh man...

"Okay, I'm no expert," he said, "but I'll try to figure out how to buy us the time we need until the National Guard can get here."

The sheriff said, "Listen up. One thing I do know about is firearms. This is crucial, okay? Once we figure out the best defensive positions, you're all going to have to think about finding cover, not concealment. Concealment is a rosebush. Cover is a brick wall. Get it? These men shoot, and bullets go through just about anything."

Matt rolled his shoulders. He felt a lot stronger now, almost normal. "Give some thought to some booby traps we can rig to at least slow these bastards down." He looked around the room. "Does anyone have a working telescope, or at least a great pair of binoculars?"

A teen in the back raised his hand.

"What's your name, son?"

"Timmy, sir."

"Timmy," Matt said, "you need to grab some bottled water and climb the tallest building. Get as high up as possible, son. Start looking around and don't stop. These guys are well trained. They may come from any direction, or more than one. You're our listening post, our eyes and ears. Someone else needs to go with him and wait down below to carry the word. Pick him or her now. And remember what the sheriff said. Stay down, behind bricks, not brush, okay? Get your stuff and go."

Matt continued to bark all the instructions he could think of until everyone had some initial function. He figured it was better to have them all staying busy, and in the meantime he could focus on setting up some specific defenses.

And on how the hell he'd manage to bluff his way through something he knew so little about.

"Doc? How long before those drugs wear off?"

Doc looked at his watch. He seemed less terrified, a bit resigned. "Pickens was right, basically. If he drove back out there now, there's a good chance that one of them would already be awake enough to shoot his ass dead. I'd say most of them won't be coming out of the fog for at least a couple of hours, though. Maybe three or four, tops."

They didn't have much time.

CHAPTER NINE

Monday, 1:04 p.m.

Matt sat in the sheriff's office, clumsily cleaning an old Taurus .357 the way the lawman had told him. Sally sat across from him, taking stock of the other weapons, laying the guns and ammo on a table.

Matt sighed, feeling overwhelmed. He was a fraud, but these people were desperate for a leader. The smart thing to do would be to run—and hope he could get the mercenaries to follow him and leave the town alone. But what if they wouldn't follow? Worse, what if he got away and the town paid the price?

"I'm sorry I ever came here," Matt said aloud.

"I'm not," she said. "You saved a life, and then saved my bacon in the bar. In some strange way, you've inspired us to come together as a town." She paused. "Are we all going to make it through this?"

"I certainly hope so." He resumed cleaning the gun. "I guess it depends on who steps up when the time comes."

"What do you mean?"

Matt fumbled with the three speed loaders and set them aside with the newly cleaned .357. "I don't know most of the people in Dry Wells. Bert is okay. Hog and Zeke may come through, they seem to have had a real change of heart. Wally—he's an alcoholic, but in some ways seems like the most genuine man in town other than Kyle. And that boy, Kyle? Well, he just loves you to death—you know that, right?"

Sally shrugged. "I'm all there is around here."

"You're underestimating him—and yourself."

"What about Doc?"

"He's scared, but he'll do okay, too."

"You spend a lot of time reading people, don't you?"

Matt didn't answer. He didn't want to have to explain how or why. He collected the handguns and put them into cardboard boxes. "Sally, get a couple of the women to help you distribute these, okay?"

"That's it, right?"

"I guess. We're down to firing up the kerosene lanterns, shouting at each other, hand signals, and anything else we can think of."

"Like it's 1875 or something."

"Pretty much. We're as ready as we're likely to be without any outside help. Remember, all we have to do is make it through the night."

She kissed his cheek. The kiss drifted to the side, and for a long moment their passions leaked out. Her hands grabbed at his back, but Matt broke away and kissed her forehead instead.

"You'd best get moving."

Sally sighed and hurried out.

When Sally was gone, Matt sat in his chair. He wondered whether there might still be some way to leave the citizens of Dry Wells out of the confrontation. The mercenaries needed his blood, not his corpse, so they'd have to be careful. As for Matt, he wasn't willing to be taken alive again, because there would be no guarantee Sally and the others would be safe. If Mr. Dark was around, perhaps there was some other solution, a different deal to be struck...a way to save the others, if not himself.

If Scotty gave him a chance, they'd have to talk.

CHAPTER TEN

Monday, 4:51 p.m.
Why are they taking so long? They should do something.

Sunset was coming soon. Matt Cahill walked down the middle of Main Street in old town, heading west toward Sheriff Pickens and the jail, making the rounds yet another time. He hoped to hell he looked inspirational. He waved at the men stationed on the roof of the hotel. Matt cupped his hands and called out.

"Got water?"

Timmy gave a thumbs-up.

"Remember what Sheriff Pickens said—stay the hell down behind the bricks. Cover, not concealment, right?"

Matt stopped in the shade of the old gazebo. He spun in a lazy circle, his boots kicking up dust. The sun was getting lower and the sky was beginning to color as evening approached, but the heat still lay on Dry Wells like a thick blanket. Matt let his eyes roam to check the windows and rooftops, making sure everyone was in place for the battle to come. Doors and windows had been nailed shut. Pits had been dug, streets blocked to slow the intruders down.

Matt licked his lips and his stomach rumbled. He was out of ideas and tired of waiting.

Suzie and Jeb Pickens were in the top windows of the old whorehouse, armed with hunting rifles. Each had a makeshift Molotov cocktail of kerosene and a rag stuffed in an empty jelly jar. They knew to be careful, since most of Dry Wells was made of wood and highly flammable.

Matt carried his ax over one shoulder. For security, he also had a Smith & Wesson snub-nosed .38 in his belt. He held a bottle of water in his right hand.

Had he covered these people as well as humanly possible?

Would they be ready and willing to fight, perhaps to the death?

Would he?

Kyle had managed to recover wicks for the old-style lanterns hanging outside all along the western street. He and Timmy had climbed ladders to put kerosene in them and test every one. Light would be their only defense. That and knowing the landscape far better than did their enemy.

Why are they taking so long? They should do something.

The mercenaries hadn't made any attempt to contact them or attack, even to explore their defenses. Perhaps it had taken them longer to recover from the animal tranquilizers than Doc had originally thought. Hell, those mercenaries were already drinking and badly infected by evil. If Matt was lucky, maybe one or two had even died by accident from a lethal combination of drugs.

Though right then Matt didn't feel very lucky.

Not since that damned avalanche.

Unfortunately, an attack in the darkness, using some kind of night-vision equipment, seemed to Matt to be the most likely scenario. He'd worn the goggles while rescuing Suzie Pickens, so he had some idea of how they worked, how they made everything crisp and clear in a greenish way. As long as the ambient light was low and constant, the users—

the mercenaries—would have the complete advantage over any normal human being.

But bright light hurt—and could buy Matt and the townspeople a few precious moments.

It was going to be four heavily armed men against sixteen defenders who had no real equipment and far less expertise. Their only advantage was that Scotty likely wanted to take Matt alive to draw more blood. The mercenaries would need to be careful with their fire and couldn't just come in and blow shit up. They knew the forest fire would keep law enforcement reinforcements from arriving for a while, though, so Scotty had probably figured a night assault to be the safest, smoothest plan of attack. At least that's what Matt told himself, though the truth was, he didn't know much about any of this. Not really.

Everyone seemed to be in place. If they could just last through the night, some kind of reinforcements should arrive via the National Guard or the police. Of course, the mercenaries knew that, too. And that every minute would count.

Why are they taking so long? They should...

"Mr. Cahill! Mr. Cahill!"

Matt looked up. The boy called Timmy, on the hotel roof, was calling him. He gestured toward the mouth of the town. Another teenage boy named Clete stood on the roof of Wally's bar, binoculars in his right hand. He pointed east.

"Someone's coming!"

At last.

Matt felt like throwing up.

"Hold your positions!" Matt called. He hefted the ax, kept one hand on the .38, and jogged east.

Sheriff Pickens and Wally had blocked the alleys to the west and the entrance to the east with old cars, wheelbarrows, junked bicycles, and trash cans. One defender held each position, with two at the open area.

With the approaching sunset at his back, Matt went to the car and motioned for Sheriff Pickens and Wally to duck. Wally looked half in the bag, as usual. His jaw was set and his eyes were grim. His soul seemed at peace. Thank God, he'd do.

Sheriff Pickens lowered his own binoculars. "We got us two men in a van, two on motorcycles. Looks like one of them is holding a white flag."

Matt took the binoculars and focused on the rapidly approaching clouds of dust. He immediately recognized the mercenaries in the van. The one who scratched his balls and the one with the red hair who smoked too much dope. He was easy to spot because of the smoke pouring out the passenger window. The one to the south on a motorcycle was the one who had always stared at him. Matt continued to scan the nearby desert. He finally located the man with the white flag. He almost jumped at how close the man seemed.

Scotty.

Through the binoculars he seemed confident and healthy, rather than twisted and evil. He wore shades and was smiling, chugging along, slowly waving the flag. Matt went up and down what he could see of the man's body. Body armor for certain. Two sidearms, one long like a cop's 9 mm, the other oddly shaped. He had a pair of goggles that looked like the NV stuff Matt had seen in movies. There was something else there on his chest, perhaps some kind of grenade. Matt was worried about grenades. The townspeople were scared enough already. Hell, so was he. It didn't seem likely that the mercenaries would use anything that random, though, for fear of killing Matt.

"That's them," Matt said. He handed the binoculars back to the sheriff, who raised one hand and waved it.

"Looks like they want to parlay."

"That it does." Matt thought for a moment. "Sheriff, can you loan me that flashlight for a bit?"

Sheriff Pickens cocked his head, shrugged, and handed it over. Matt put his ax down in the sand, stuck the flashlight in his belt—behind his back, next to the .38—and then grabbed his ax again.

"Thanks. Get them ready."

Pickens called out, "Nobody jumps the gun. Everybody just hold your fire until one of us gives the signal."

Matt Cahill scratched his neck. His pulse raced with anger and steadily increasing fear. The mercenaries could have and should have come after dark, when they'd have had even more of a natural advantage. Why hadn't they? Something seemed out of place. He didn't like surprises. He fingered the .38 beneath the back of his jeans next to the flashlight and cracked his knuckles. He was going to have to trust his instincts. Matt came to a decision.

"Okay, I'm going to go out and talk to him."

"You serious?"

"Believe me, I wish I weren't. Looks like I have to, though."

"You're out of your fucking mind, but better you than me." Sheriff Pickens picked up a hunting rifle and sighted on Scotty. "I'll aim for a head shot if this goes bad. Can't hardly miss from here. Wally and Bert will cover the others.

Don't worry, Bert may be a chickenshit at heart, but he's a damned fine shot."

Matt nodded and squeezed through the narrow space between the car blocking the entrance to Main Street and the front of Wally's Saloon. Three long strides later he was out in the open. He felt naked. Four guns were trained on his chest. Behind him, Matt heard Sally crying. It sounded like Kyle was trying to comfort her. Matt did not look back. He just started walking.

CHAPTER ELEVEN

Monday, 5:14 p.m.

It was nearly dark. The sunset flowed rapidly across the desert floor like spilled paint, dragging long shadows in its wake. The night approached quickly, eagerly, like a predator cornering prey. The rider to the south turned and shut off his motorcycle. The van stopped as well. Scotty rolled to a halt, got off his hog, and left it standing. Dusk swallowed them and the air began to chill.

I am out of my fucking mind for doing this...

As the evening glowered, Matt Cahill walked, ax on his shoulder, his eyes fixed on the lone man on the motorcycle. Scotty smiled brightly, as if delighted to see him. They stopped, by instinct, perhaps five yards apart. Up close, Scotty's eyes were bright and feverish. His nose was rotting away, writhing with worms. The flesh on his exposed arms was blackened and splitting and oozing yellow slime. He had two firearms on his belt, one unfamiliar and bulky, and that pair of NV goggles. He was also carrying one large grenade.

"Well, damned if you aren't causing us a bit of trouble after all," Scotty said. Something rattled, deep in his chest, as if parts of him were beginning to break loose. "Guess I underestimated you."

"The jury is still out."

"It seems like we got ourselves a bit of a conundrum. Love that word. The way I see it is, we need to take you back with us. You don't want to go. We got firepower and experience. You got innocent bystanders. You need this to take a few hours. We need it over and done. It's fourth down and forty and you can't punt. That about sum it up?"

Matt kept the ax pointed at the sand. He casually put his trembling right hand on his hip, moving it closer to the items in his belt. "You going to talk all night, or did you have a proposal of some kind?"

"Oh, I had me an idea," Scotty said. He drooled pus from a drooping lower lip. "Figured I'd ask you to do the right thing."

The shadows swept over them. They were only a few yards apart now.

"Shit," Scotty said. "Wanted to get here sooner, but Mack was too fucking stoned. Now it looks like we timed this all wrong. I can't hardly see you."

"Can't see your face anymore either," Matt said agreeably. "I don't mind, though. You really are turning butt ugly."

Scotty laughed. "There's something going on for sure. I can feel it. Sometimes when I look in the mirror, I catch something strange out of the corner of my eye, like that old *Candyman* piece of shit movie we saw when we were kids. Like there's someone else over my shoulder. Something freaky."

"There is," Matt said.

Black squatted on the desert floor with them. The town had no power. The volunteers had no night-vision equipment. The darkness had arrived. Matt realized that Scotty hadn't timed it wrong at all. In fact, he'd timed it perfectly. But then, so had Matt.

"So are you going to do the right thing, Cahill? Let us take you back, so that we don't have to kill all these innocent redneck men, women, and children?"

Matt squatted in the sand. He bought time, wanted his eyes to adjust a bit. "Well, I've thought about that all day. That's the big question. Does the Dark Man want me enough to let them go?"

"Who?"

He doesn't know who sent him. He thinks it's just the scientists from the university. But someone along the way is pure evil. They are all infected. I'll need to find out who sent them one of these days...

Scotty slowly rose, scratched the seat of his trousers. He moved a few steps closer.

"Look, Scotty," Matt said, as if he hadn't noticed, "we both know you're planning to kill the townsfolk anyway. The way I figure it, the only reason you're here now, instead of just attacking us later under cover of darkness, is someone got word to you. Help is closer than any of us expected a while ago. What happened? Did they put that wildfire out already?"

"You figured all that out on your own?" Scotty squatted, letting Matt know that he was still able to see reasonably well. "Okay, here's the thing, straight up. There is a busload of weekend warriors on the way down from Salt Fucking Lake or somewhere. ETA about an hour and twenty minutes."

"And that changes things."

"Indeed it does." Scotty scooted closer, voice lowering as if imparting secrets.

"Oh, Scotty? I also know I'm in somebody's sights and you can take me out anytime you want. I'm not stupid."

"Didn't think you were." He casually edged even closer.

Matt said, "But the thing is, you don't want me dead. You want me alive. And if you kill me out here, all that precious blood runs out into the sand and it's useless. Your boss will have to make do with whatever you've already got out there in the van. And if that's not enough, the university will be royally pissed off. You might not even get paid."

"True enough."

The pocked moon was rising. The starlight was dazzling. Matt had his own night vision now. He was no longer helpless. He tried to summon the courage to act. His limbs shook. In the darkness, under the full moon, Scotty's wicked eyes seemed to glow.

"So we just give you a badass flesh wound," Scotty said. He moved a bit closer. "Then we patch you up and take you with us. Game over."

"Nice plan. But you know what John Lennon said, right?"

Scotty grinned like the corpse he was rapidly becoming. "You wondering the same thing I'm wondering, Cahill?" He moved a bit closer, now only ten feet away.

"Yeah. Each of us wonders why the other one agreed to meet out here after dark. Why we're talking for so long. Thing is, for me it was stalling for time and one other thing. When it comes to you, I already know that answer."

Finally close enough for accuracy, Scotty made his move. His right hand darted for the tranquilizer gun on his belt, but Matt was expecting the move. He reached for his flashlight and rolled away, hearing a chuffing sound as the first dart went harmlessly into a clump of dead sage. At the same time, Matt flicked the flashlight on, temporarily blinding the men who had been focusing intently through their night-vision goggles. He rolled again and felt a tranquilizer dart thwack into his boot heel. He shined the light directly into Scotty's hideous face.

Scotty was a gory zombie now, flesh hanging from his body, organs and excrement sagging and bulging from his bloody fatigues, a literal sack of shit. His pupils contracted in blackened sockets. Matt clumsily located the .38 and fired twice, knowing the flash would further damage the vision of the other mercenaries if they still wore the NV gear. One bullet struck Scotty in the Kevlar and stunned him. Gunfire came from Dry Wells as a few of the townspeople fired in response to the shot. Scotty was hit again, this time in the shoulder. He spun around, the dart gun dropping from his fingers, and fell flat on his back in the sand, probably just stunned.

Matt crawled over to the downed mercenary on knees and elbows. He ripped the coveted NV goggles from Scotty's webbing, grabbed the grenade from Scotty's chest. He'd wanted the goggles for Timmy, the town's lookout. Matt kept moving, rolling away as fast as he could.

Scotty whispered, "Motherfucker!"

Half as a mercy, Matt brought up the .38 to blow Scotty's head off, but he felt the sand near his own head puff up. The report followed a half second later. Someone had him zeroed in. Panicked, Matt rolled behind Scotty's body and fired twice toward the van parked in the darkness. He flashed the light again, got to his knees, flashed it the other way.

Scotty moved, then sat up. Matt rose to his feet, decided not to waste his last two rounds so far from town. He kicked

Scotty in the head and flashed the light both ways again. Then Matt Cahill raced back toward town.

Townsfolk fired past him at muzzle flashes and where they thought the enemy was parked. At the same time, the mercenaries did their best to wound Matt and bring him down. Three times bullets tugged his clothing as he pounded through the sand, but somehow Matt made it to the parked cars. He threw himself in the air, slammed onto the roof of the old Toyota, rolled over it, and landed back inside his own lines with the night-vision goggles in his hand. He was wheezing and shaking like a willow in a windstorm. The townsfolk cheered.

Soon, though, they all sat uneasily, whispering back and forth. Now there was nothing else to do but wait.

CHAPTER TWELVE

Monday, 6:22 p.m.

Dry Wells was brighter now. They'd fired up the old-style streetlights. Kyle and Wally had them all working, plus most of the fighters had their own kerosene lanterns and flashlights. The town was lit up like a modern art piece, yellow and stripes of black shadow. The defenders could now see most of what would take place. They'd created some ambient light to work with, enough to slow down the effectiveness of any night-vision equipment. Still, the mercenaries had training and superior firepower.

Zeke and Hog had parked like Siamese twins up near the sheriff's office, holding both hunting rifles and handguns at the ready. They seemed brave enough in each other's company. Matt hoped that would hold when the firing started.

"You two ready?"

"Shit yeah," Zeke said. His voice cracked on the second word, but he managed a grin. Hog managed a giggle.

Matt jogged low across the middle of the street and took cover by the gazebo, kneeling down in the trash and dried sage. Doing his best to sound official, he called up to his lookout.

"Timmy? Stay down, but answer me. Do you or Clete see anything?"

"Nothing."

The teenager was still on the roof of the hotel keeping watch. The desert floor was a gigantic ink pad in every direction. At least he now had the night-vision goggles as an edge. The mercenaries no longer had the element of surprise. They would have to be careful every step of the way.

"All clear?"

And then, ignoring the order, Timmy raised his head to answer.

"Nothing, sir."

Chuff!

In the flickering light and shadow, the top of his head vanished, a mist of blood and bone. The kid dropped flat onto the roof like a bag of flour. He'd been shot from afar with a night-vision sniper scope. Seeing this, the prostitute called Maggie wailed and kicked at the outside wall of the whorehouse.

Matt grimaced and took a deep breath. His anger boiled over. "Here they come!"

Sheriff Pickens called out, "Stay down, damn it! Cover, not concealment!"

Scotty and company began their attack.

In the end, the mercenaries weren't cute about it. They just surrounded the ghost town, loaded up their weapons, and approached on foot, firing at will. They had body armor and darkness on their side, plus the ability to communicate via a group radio untouched by the jamming systems. They walked out of the shadows calmly, shooting to keep everyone down. Their fire was sparse but merciless, small dots of flame like pinpricks in a black balloon. Four tall bogeymen were striding arrogantly out of the eternal bedroom closet, shooting to kill.

They had no fear of death. They were already at its doorstep.

Matt pulled himself together. He gripped his ax handle.

The assault continued. While the townspeople handled the return fire, Matt studied the mercenaries' approach and worked out a plan. The stoner came from the west, toward the sheriff's office. Scotty crawled and hobbled in from the east, where he'd originally been wounded with a lucky shot. The redhead ran in from the dunes to the south, and the buzz-cut professional warrior jogged into Dry Wells from the north. From the direction and lay of the land, it seemed likely that this was the bastard who had shot Timmy. Matt hadn't seen anything of Clete, the other teen, since his friend had died. Matt couldn't blame him for staying hidden.

Zeke and Hog had moved and now crouched together near the old drugstore, grimly firing into the night. Hog had a small plastic tub full of extra ammunition by his massive thigh. They were surprisingly efficient, trading shots left and right in a manner that suggested they'd worked it out in advance. Still, all they could hope to do was slow things down. They had a lot of weapons, but they were still outgunned.

And so the mercenaries closed. Gunfire blazed. At first the enemies' silenced weapons sounded like corn popping, but the noise steadily grew louder as they approached. Matt ran from the gazebo to the whorehouse and checked upstairs. Suzie and Jeb Pickens were holding their own, firing carefully. Jeb had a small flesh wound on one hand, wrapped with a strip of torn cloth. Matt ran back down the stairs, passing one man he didn't know who had been injured by flying debris and a whore who had sprained her wrist while diving for cover.

He left for the old barn and loft, playing a hunch since it was poorly guarded. The defenders had thus far avoided using their Molotov cocktails. Someone else had set a fire in the straw, but when Matt arrived, the barn was empty. The fire was in a pile of straw in a small area surrounded by open dirt. Had someone, possibly Kyle, been smart enough to start a controlled blaze to light up the area? Perhaps it hadn't been set by the enemy after all. Matt turned to go.

The red-haired mercenary dropped down from the rafters, stunning Matt and forcing the ax to fly from his hand into the straw. Red punched Matt twice in the head and rolled him over to bind his wrists with plastic cuffs, clearly intending to drag him back into the darkness and the waiting van.

Matt rolled his eyes up and went limp, and the red-haired mercenary loosened his grip just slightly. Matt head butted him, rolled back over, and kneed the man in the face—a face that was already shattered by sin, dented and weeping blood and brains. Still the man fought on. They rolled together through the fire, and Matt's exposed flesh felt pain as it burned, but the mercenary didn't even flinch. Matt could smell singed hair as the two men struggled and grunted. Matt got his right hand free and drove it up under the mercenary's chin, forcing the man to bite his tongue half off. As blood spurted from the wound, he let go of Matt.

Matt spotted his grandfather's ax lying near a pile of cow dung and crawled toward it, but the red-haired mercenary recovered enough to climb up Matt's body, slowing him down. They both saw the .38 in the straw, and the mercenary lunged for the gun. Matt grabbed the pile of cow shit and smeared it into the man's bloody eyes, then got his fingers around the handle of the ax.

Matt swung hard and decapitated the killer, whose head rolled away and bowled a strike in the feed bags. The mercenary's trunk fell over and spurted blood, splattering the wooden slats of the stall. Matt threw up in the dirt but quickly gathered himself again. The battle raged on. The enemy was still out there.

Shouting and firing from outside. The smell of gunpowder and burning straw. Shaken, Matt got to his feet and ran to the front of the barn. He looked both ways. Across the street Sheriff Pickens shouted to him.

"Shit, he's gone, Cahill!"

He had lost track of Scotty.

One down, three to go...

CHAPTER THIRTEEN

Monday, 8:37 p.m.

Matt turned to run back toward the gazebo but saw movement across the way, a shadowy confrontation in the distance. Bert the grocer had been assaulted. A hunter who expected to be able to use his skills with a rifle, Bert was clearly unprepared for close fighting. So when the mercenary with the buzz cut appeared from the alley with a sawtooth knife and charged him, Bert tried to run. With a savage laugh, the killer ran him to ground, yanked his hair back, and reached across to slit the grocer's throat. Time slowed to a crawl.

Matt raced toward the spot, his bloody ax in one hand and the .38 in the other, hoping for a clean shot. Out of the corner of his eye he saw Hog pause and turn. The big man spotted Bert and the mercenary and sent two rounds their way. One took the soldier in the Kevlar vest and knocked him backward, stunned but still alive. Satisfied, Hog turned back to his assigned duties. Still running, Matt closed the distance. Suddenly the mercenary rolled, raised his knife to stab down at the exhausted Bert. Matt dropped to one knee and tried to get a shot, but Bert was in the way. The knife was coming down.

The missing teenager—Clete—exploded from the dark alley. He did not hesitate but attacked at once, climbing on the mercenary's broad back. He was thrown off immediately, but he'd bought a few precious seconds. Bert's wife came out of the alley next. Her enormous weight momentarily flattened the soldier, shoving his grinning face down into the bloody sand. He quickly threw her off, though, and lunged to gut her. Approaching fast, Matt fired twice but missed. He stopped a second time, trying for better aim. Fortunately, he didn't fire right away. Just then another body filled his vision.

Kyle emerged from the hotel with a pitchfork. He bellowed with rage and ran the mercenary through. Then, before Matt could close the distance, Kyle pulled his own pistol and shot the man in the neck, just to make sure. Blood sprayed his face. The exhausted citizens ran back to their assigned posts, exhausted but still determined to fight back.

Not bad, Kyle, Matt thought. "Kyle," he said, "remind me not to piss you off."

Kyle didn't see it, but as the mercenary died, his horribly contorted features, dripping pus and writhing with worms, relaxed into a human face. Evil had departed, but so had the soul of the human the force had inhabited. Not for the first time, Matt wondered what awaited these men and women who had been possessed by the Dark Man, once they got to the other side. It surely wouldn't be pleasant.

"Give me a hand, kid," Matt said.

They dragged Bert back to the saloon, where Sally worked with the women who were acting as medics. Bert was going to make it. Outside, the fire was lower, becoming sporadic, but the screaming was nonstop. Where Sally tended to them, those who were cut or shot cried out and kept bellowing. They didn't just lie down, like in the movies.

Two down, two to go.

Matt forced himself to stalk the sidewalk amongst the writhing shadows and the puffs of smoke, the reloaded .38 gripped in his right hand, the ax handy. Right now it felt like his best friend.

"Hog? Zeke? You guys okay?"

"We're good," Zeke called back.

Matt looked east. Sheriff Pickens and Wally were still by the parked cars, their rifles at port arms. Pickens shook his head, as if to say he'd been unable to locate his man. Zeke and Hog exchanged glances, then stood up, Hog facing into the center of town and Zeke still looking out at the city limits. A few seconds passed. Flames crackled through dry wood and a horse nickered in the barn.

A mercenary in black rolled across a parked car and took aim at the sheriff just as Pickens ducked. *Pop-pop.* The body was squat and compact, so it wasn't Scotty. It had to be the one who never looked up. Matt started toward the sheriff, but instinct told him he wouldn't make it in time. Hopefully, Pickens could handle himself. Hog fired cougar quick and nicked the mercenary's leg. Wally fired, too, but the mercenary drove him back under cover. The street puffed dust—Jeb and Suzie were also firing down from the whorehouse, but their angle was bad, and the mercenary rolled away.

Bravely, Wally stepped out of cover and took a shot, hitting the mercenary in the other leg. The man bellowed in rage and fired back. Wally tried to duck but was shot in the face. He fell backward into the street, twitched a few times, and lay still.

Matt charged, waving his arms, and the mercenary turned to face him. Before Matt could reach them, though, Pickens ducked and produced a wickedly short shotgun he'd had stashed beneath Sally's car. He did not hesitate, but placed the weapon in the crotch of his enemy and discharged both barrels. The mercenary split nearly in two and splattered in the dirt like chunks of steaming meat.

Three down.

Scotty to go.

Matt swallowed more bile. All around him, the firing gradually died out again as the townsfolk realized it was nearly over. Matt whistled sharply. One enemy remained, so they were all still in danger.

"Hey, Scotty? It's just you and me now."

Matt walked out into the center of the street, dust spraying up around his boots. He kept walking, and then he stopped, licked his lips. He called out, "Scotty? Let these people be. Let's finish this."

Shit, my voice is shaking. I sound like a poodle standing up to a Great Dane...

A kind of eerie silence fell, except for the low snapping of the steady fire in the barn. Matt could smell the wood smoke blended with the stench of death. Could faintly hear people murmuring, some crying out in pain. Dark reflections flickered up and down the empty street. Everyone held their breath. Matt Cahill waited, knowing there was only one way it could end.

"Matt?"

Scotty came out of the alley, holding a 9 mm down by his right leg, pointed at the earth. He had placed his body perfectly, between the empty movie house and the tourist shop, so none of the people defending Dry Wells had an easy shot. He was lost, looked like something dragged up from a grave a week after he'd been buried. His skin was filthy, with wounds oozing fluid and broken bones poking from torn clothing. His face was a frozen mask of shrieking horror, the countenance of a man buried alive. Matt Cahill stood out in the open, the .38 down at his own side, the ax in his other hand. The two men faced each other on the dusty, dark street. Shadows danced all around them.

"So here we are."

"Yeah."

"The 1972 Dolphins, dude. A perfect season. Look it up."

"I will."

Scotty grinned horribly, chuckling wetly from deep in his broken chest. To Matt, the laugh sounded disturbingly familiar, so much like his long-dead friend. The two enemies waited there in the street, all eyes on them. The fire made the town flicker like an old black-and-white photograph under a strobe lamp.

"I'm kind of screwed, aren't I?" Scotty asked. He coughed. "I don't know what's happening to me, but it ain't anything good, is it?"

Matt shook his head. "No. It's not."

Scotty looked down. "You remember that old movie comic, W. C. Fields? Talked through his nose?"

"Kind of."

Hog and Zeke approached from Matt's right, their weapons trained on Scotty, who pretended not to see them. Matt heard footsteps on the roof as the snipers moved forward, too. Sheriff Pickens stepped out of the shadows. Every gun in town was trained on Scotty now. Matt was the only one who saw the grotesque writhing of the wickedness under his putrid skin.

"W. C. Fields—he had liver disease from all the boozing," Scotty said finally. "The man was dying in some rest home when a drinking buddy came to see him. This guy caught Fields reading the Bible."

Matt kept his eyes on Scotty's hands, just to be on the safe side. He wondered where the mercenary was going with all this.

"The friend says, 'What the hell are you doing reading *that*, Bill?'" Scotty said. "And W. C. Fields just smiles and says, "Hey, I'm looking for loopholes, friend. Just looking for loopholes.'"

Scotty raised his eyes. His shoulders sagged a bit. "Man, I really need to get this over with."

Matt swallowed. "I know."

Scotty jerked his weapon up, though perhaps a bit more slowly than he could have. Matt wasn't sure. In any event, Matt was a split second faster as he threw the ax with all his might. It spun end over end, slammed into Scotty's Kevlar vest, and stuck there, throwing his aim off, turning him to the side. His one round whizzed by Matt's left ear. And then everyone in town opened fire at once. Scotty danced an obscene jig in the dust for a long moment, his body shredded and torn. Then he dropped to his knees and fell sideways into the dust. Matt watched his face become handsome again as the tortured soul departed.

It was finished.

EPILOGUE

Monday, 9:46 p.m.

The fires were almost out. The air had turned harsh, as sharp as a blade and filled with dark smoke and ash. Matt Cahill had already made the rounds congratulating and thanking the townspeople. He knew the military and police would be here soon. He had to leave—time was running out. A horse was saddled and ready a few yards away.

"You'd best get going," Kyle said. "I promise we'll all keep your presence here a secret."

"Good," Matt said quietly. "It's really better that way."

"Matt?" Sally said, her voice trembling. Kyle pulled her close. "Thank you."

Matt smiled in the darkness. Sally and Kyle stood together, which was as it should be. Kyle was a good kid, with plenty of guts. He'd take care of Sally, no doubt about it. Matt walked down the sidewalk. Sheriff Pickens and his teenage children waved from across the street. Suzie was crying. Matt searched for something to say. He knew there were no words. Finally he just tipped his hat.

"Take care."

"You too," Sally said.

And with that, Matt Cahill checked to be sure he'd properly fastened his ax, pack, and bedroll to the horse. He mounted up and rode away like someone from another century. Behind him, the weary citizens waved as they watched him leave for good.

Out in the darkness Matt paused. The evening had cleared as if relieved of an evil burden. Bright stars hung like tiny diamonds in the night sky. A chill passed over his body. He turned in the saddle, took one last look at the town of Dry Wells, sparkling there in the shadows like a forlorn jewel. Leather creaked and the horse nickered. In the distance, Matt could see the highway and another long string of flickering lights closing the distance. The approaching emergency vehicles and the National Guard. The town would be safe now.

Once again, Matt wondered if perhaps it had all been meant to happen. He had come back to life for a reason—or many reasons. Perhaps this was one of them.

It was time to move on. Like an old-time cowboy, Matt kneed the horse and turned away toward the safety of the Ruby Mountains. He rode away looking forward to entering the far more familiar tree line and the comfort of the mountains. He felt satisfied in some ways, but also deeply concerned. For Matt Cahill now had a new enemy to worry about.

The university.

THE END

ABOUT THE AUTHORS

Lee Goldberg is a two-time Edgar Award-nominated author and TV producer. His many books include *The Walk*, *Watch Me Die* and the bestselling Monk series of original mystery novels. His TV writing and producing credits include *SeaQuest*, *Diagnosis Murder*, *Monk* and *The Glades*. He's also worked as a consultant for networks and studios throughout Europe, Canada, and Sweden and has served on the Board of the Mystery Writers of America.

William Rabkin is a two-time Edgar Award nominee who writes the Psych series of novels and is the author of *Writing the Pilot*. He has consulted for studios in Canada, Germany, and Spain on television series production and teaches screenwriting at UCLA Extension. He is also an adjunct professor at the UC Riverside's low-residency master's program.

Harry Shannon has been an actor, Emmy-nominated songwriter, recording artist, music publisher, music supervisor, and vice president at Carolco Pictures. His novels include *Night of the Beast, CLAN, Daemon, Dead and Gone, The Hungry,* and *The Pressure of Darkness.* He also wrote the Mick Callahan suspense novels *Memorial Day, Eye of the Burning Man, One of the Wicked,* and *Running Cold.* His collection *A Host of Shadows* was nominated for the 2010 Stoker Award by the Horror Writer's Association.

James Reasoner has been a professional writer for more than thirty years. In that time, he has authored several hundred novels and short stories in numerous genres. Best known for his Westerns, historical novels, and war novels, he is also the author of two mystery novels that have achieved cult classic status: *Texas Wind* and *Dust Devils.*

David McAfee published his first novel, *33 A.D.,* in 2010. Today he has five novels and two short story collections with more to come.